PRAISE FOR HILARY DARTT

The Dating Intervention

"It was very hilarious, had loads of funny accidents and still had a way of being sincere and romantic … I also liked how much it was based around friendship, which added a nice, fresh take on a romance story. This is easily a five-star read."

NATURAL BRI BLOG

The Marriage Intervention

"This was a great sequel. I tend to like the first book the best of any trilogy but this second book was even better than the first! A feel-good read that actually had me crying at the end!"

KATY MESSARE

The Motherhood Intervention

"This book was a heart breaker but full of spirit. I loved it. I loved how the relationships evolved, fell apart, and came back stronger than ever. Pass me a vodka cranberry, please, and a box of tissue."

AMANDA THOMAS

THE MOTHERHOOD INTERVENTION

BOOK THREE IN THE INTERVENTION SERIES

HILARY DARTT

ISBN: 978-1-950335-04-6

CHAPTER ONE

SUMMER CARSON'S MOTHER LEFT HER IN THE GROCERY STORE WHEN SHE was ten years old, standing in the produce section next to a perfect pyramid of cantaloupes. As they approached the fresh herbs, Willow stopped and flung a hand into the air, dramatic, Scarlett O'Hara style.

"I forgot my coupons," she said, a touch too loudly and with a fake Southern lilt. "Left them in the car. I'll just run back and get them."

Summer thought to herself, *this is normal, right?* But her memory replayed scenes from earlier that morning, each one of them featuring a glass of honey-colored bourbon.

"You just wait right here, honey," Willow said, patting Summer's hand where it rested on the grocery cart handle. "I'll be right back. Pick out a cantaloupe, would you?"

Because she was an obedient child, Summer lifted melons to her face, one at a time, choosing one that smelled so much like it had already been cut open that her mouth watered. She set it carefully in the basket. Then she waited. And waited. After quite some time had passed, the produce man approached and asked if she was all right.

"Just waiting for my mom," she said.

She applauded herself for sounding calm, when inside, doubt had begun to creep its way into the spotlight. Yes, her mother should be back by now. No, it shouldn't take more than a minute to run out to the car and come back in. Maybe she should just check and make sure the car was still there. It wasn't. A quick glance outside revealed their beat up little hatchback was gone. Maybe Willow got out to the parking lot and realized she left the coupons at home. She just ran home to get them. *Or to get another glass of bourbon,* a little voice whispered.

Rather than subjecting herself to further questioning, Summer decided, she would get the shopping done. She walked slowly through the store, adding the usual items to the basket: orange juice, organic eggs, whole wheat bread.

She completed a full circle and then walked back to the produce section. Still, Willow wasn't there. Distant alarm bells began to sound in Summer's brain, and she forced herself to swallow, loosening the feeling of panic that lodged in her throat. Music played on the speakers, and Summer mouthed the words to "Sixteen Candles," which she knew by heart. She and her mother used to sing it over and over while washing dishes, mopping the floor or folding laundry.

The grocery store doors whooshed open and a police officer walked in. He scanned the produce department in half a second, and his eyes landed on Summer. He walked towards her.

A million thoughts ran through her mind. An unpleasant swirling sensation took over her stomach.

Was her mother dead?

Had she driven drunk, again, and finally crashed?

Had she killed someone? Someone else's mother?

Was the policeman here to arrest her, Summer, for letting her mom leave the store parking lot after taking a few slugs from her flask?

Was he here to take Summer to the hospital to say her final good-byes?

"Hi, there," the police officer said.

Summer took a deep breath.

"Hi."

TWENTY-FOUR YEARS HAD PASSED since the day Willow Carson drove off and left her daughter standing next to the cantaloupe, and Summer—now Summer Gray, thirty-four and married with her fifth child on the way—remembered it as crisply as if it were yesterday. Fifteen years had passed since Summer had even spoken to her mother. So why did the grocery store memory still cause her heart to race with panic?

She stood in the cluttered kitchen of her adult life, putting away groceries. The clandestine cantaloupe that had triggered the flashback rolled toward the edge of the counter. She caught it and set it behind the knife block in the corner.

"Don't forget about that melon until it's moldy and smelling up the kitchen," Summer said.

"Talking to yourself again, Mom?"

She laughed. "Yes, Sarah. And I've heard you doing the same. At eleven."

"I got it from you."

"You did. And my good looks, too, you lucky girl."

Summer's sons, Luke and Nate, barreled through the kitchen door as Sarah began putting groceries in the pantry. "You left Hannah in the car, Mom," Nate said.

"I did it on purpose," Summer lied. "So she wouldn't run into the street while we were unloading groceries."

Actually, she'd forgotten Hannah, whose little face would be crimson with rage when Summer eventually released her from her car seat.

She saw Sarah give her a skeptical look out of the corner of her eye, her eleven-year-old expression a bit too adult (and perceptive) for Summer's taste.

"What?" Summer said. "I did."

"Well, we've got all the groceries inside now, Mom," Luke said. "I used my super-secret ninja powers to carry them in. Didn't even touch 'em with my hands."

Someone made what Summer assumed was a super-secret ninja powers sound, and Summer laughed. "Can you guys please use those ninja powers to put the rest of the groceries away while I get Hannah out of the car?"

The boys threw their arms out at the pile of bags on the kitchen floor, shrugged when nothing happened, and disappeared into some distant galaxy. For a moment, Summer felt a prickle of guilt at having forgotten Hannah, but she quickly brushed it away. She wasn't her own mother, after all. Mistakes happened. And as long as those mistakes didn't happen on a ninety-degree day, everyone turned out fine.

She was just distracted, exhausted and eight months' pregnant. And so what if she secretly longed to get into a semi-major car accident or experience a semi-major illness so she could get a few days' vacation in a hospital bed? The thought gave her a strange sense of being pampered: nurses checking on her every couple of hours, someone delivering her food and taking the empty dishes away, no one expecting her to clean or drive or remember any appointments, field trip forms, lunch money or special projects. So what if she imagined driving the van right into the light pole in the middle of the grocery store parking lot so she could be whisked away in an ambulance? Not as sleek as a limo, but still. A hospital holiday. It could be a new thing. But she'd never really do it.

No, she wasn't her mother. When it had come time for Summer to create her own family, she had followed one rule: Whatever Willow had done, Summer would do the complete opposite.

So instead of having just one child, she was intent on having five.

Instead of the numerous flighty romances Willow ignited and squelched in rapid succession, Summer chose a husband who was dependable, reliable, and a good provider.

Instead of leaving her children at the grocery store, she left them in the car on a hot July day.

"Ugh," she found herself saying out loud as she pulled the van door open to Hannah's chants of "Out! Out! Out!"

Hannah had learned to walk earlier than all the other kids had, so now, at fifteen months old, Summer could simply set her down on the driveway and herd her into the house.

She smiled as Hannah toddled through the doorway, her pigtails sticking up on either side of her head. The moment was fleeting, though. Summer heard her phone ring just as Hannah walked directly into the doorjamb and started screaming.

An emotion she couldn't quite pinpoint began to rise up in her stomach as she scooped up the baby and carried her into the kitchen. Was it stress? Urgency? Frustration? The phone kept ringing, and although she knew it wasn't possible, Summer thought it sounded increasingly insistent.

While she could have sworn she put her phone on the counter, she couldn't find it among the bills, school papers, grocery bags and groceries. Hannah continued to scream and only then did Summer notice she had a huge goose egg just above her right eyebrow. Pushing a pile of papers out of the way, Summer set Hannah on the counter. The movement unearthed the phone. Summer answered it, grabbed a bag of peas out of the freezer and pressed it to Hannah's face, which, naturally, produced a fresh round of shrieks.

"Hold on, please," Summer said into the phone.

She moved Hannah into her high chair, tore open the bag of peas and dumped some on the tray. Then she locked herself in the bathroom.

"Hi, Summer, it's Amy from Dr. Thibedeau's office."

Dr. Thibedeau, the kids' pediatrician, let the kids call him Dr. Tippy Toes. They loved it.

"Hey. Did I miss an appointment or something?"

Normally, Amy would laugh, but when she didn't, Summer felt that feeling intensify. Stress. Anxiety. She wasn't sure.

"No," Amy said. "It's Luke's results from the scan. Dr. Thibedau wants you to meet with the heart specialist. I've already put the referral through, and they should be contacting you, um, pretty much right away to make an appointment."

They hung up and Summer sat down on the edge of the bathtub. An appointment with the heart specialist meant Luke's scan hadn't come back normal. From everything Dr. Thibedeau had said, an abnormal result meant surgery.

THE POLICE OFFICER must have noticed ten-year-old Summer's panic, because he put a hand on her shoulder, knelt down so they were eye to eye, and said, "Don't worry. You're not in trouble."

"Is my mom okay?"

"That's why I'm here. The store employees called us because they noticed you've been in the store by yourself for a pretty long time. Do you know where your mom is?"

That tight feeling in her throat again. She tried not to cry, but her voice shook when she answered. Her eyes stung and she blinked, hard. "She said she had to go back to the car to get her coupons. But she was taking so long that I went to look for her and the car was gone. I was thinking maybe she realized she left the coupons at home, and went to get them. So I did the shopping. But she hasn't come back."

The policeman nodded. Summer noticed his dark eyes taking in everything about her, from the messy ponytail and the too-tight jeans to the too-short shirt and the white Reeboks with the hole in one toe.

"We'll find her. Why don't you come with me?"

When she hesitated, he stuck out his hand for a handshake and said, "I'm sorry. I haven't introduced myself. I'm officer Andy Telluride with the Juniper Police Department."

He bought her a box of Cheez-Its and a soda, which would have sent her mom into a tizzy. He let Summer sit in the passenger seat of his patrol car while he used the radio to give someone else her address. While they waited (for what, Summer wasn't sure), he asked her lots of questions about her life. Which school did she go to? What was her favorite subject? What was her favorite book? He had a daughter about Summer's age, he told her, and she was reading "The Chronicles of Narnia."

A while later, the radio squawked and Summer heard another man's voice: "We found the subject. She's passed out on the couch at home. Says she came home to get coupons and fell asleep. Drunk as a skunk, this one."

Officer Telluride jumped, startled, and tried to turn the radio down, but Summer had heard enough. The drinking had gotten progressively worse during the past several months and people they encountered often whispered things like, "Wow, she's plastered," or, "Three sheets to the wind."

It almost *had* to come to this, didn't it?

Officer Telluride drove Summer home and asked her to wait in the car while he talked to her mother. She nodded, but when he went inside, she crept up to the front door and pressed her ear hard against its hot pink surface. Willow had insisted they paint it a gaudy coral to symbolize love and beauty. "We'll have both here, won't we, Summer?" she said at the time.

Not at the moment. Officer Telluride spoke calmly, but even through the front door Summer could hear the anger in his voice. He told Willow how scared Summer was, how hungry she was and how she had wandered the store for hours, alone. He explained that there are very bad people in the world, and one of them could have come along and snatched Summer right up.

While Summer felt a tiny bit defensive, she also felt more than a little angry at her mother. Because everything the policeman said was true. And because Willow didn't seem to register any of it. Summer could hear her saying over and over like a mantra, "I thought it was just for a minute."

When Officer Telluride came out the door, the energy radiating off his body in waves, he nearly stumbled over Summer.

"Sorry," she said.

Again, he knelt down so he could look straight at her. "I'm going to give you my card," he said. "If anything like this ever happens again, I mean *ever*, you call me. Do you understand?"

She nodded, grasped the card in her hand, and hugged Officer Telluride around the waist. He put one arm around her shoulders and squeezed back.

That was the first time Willow Carson disappointed her daughter, but it wasn't the last.

CHAPTER TWO

Most Thursdays, Summer looked forward to her Happy Hour meetings with her two best friends. In her ongoing quest to be reliable, unlike her mother, Summer had become the sounding board and the steadfast support for Delaney Collins (who was now Delaney Rhoades) and Josie Garcia. Not that they didn't support her, too, Summer thought as she approached the swinging doors of Rowdy's Saloon.

But over the course of the past twenty years, Summer had become the proverbial lighthouse. Her role was to provide guidance, find the silver lining, say the right thing. She could meditate her way through anything. Until recently. Life had become increasingly complicated.

Several months ago, her husband, Derek, had lost his job. Her freelance graphic design income wasn't quite enough to support a family of six. Then the Grays turned into a *growing* family, with Gray Baby Number Five on the way. Derek got a new job, but the hours were long, which meant Summer was home with the kids and their puppy, Chuck (the littermate of Josie's Marriage-Intervention-era puppy, Delilah), pretty much around the clock.

And now Luke. Her perfect little boy. He'd always had a heart murmur, and his pediatrician had recently become "concerned" about it. He'd ordered a million tests and then referred them to a heart specialist. The heart specialist hadn't called to make an appointment yet, and not knowing what was wrong or how the doctors planned to fix it set Summer's nerves on a razor-thin edge.

Happy Hour always provided some solace, because it gave her the chance to focus on Delaney and Josie and their lives. She looked forward to the weekly meetings like one of her children looked forward to a birthday party. Not that she'd had many birthday parties when she was a child, but she understood the excitement.

Summer could hear the twang of country music before she pushed the doors open. As she entered the saloon, Delaney waved in greeting. Summer took a deep breath, squared her shoulders and smiled.

"Your drink's on the way," Josie said with a smug, teasing smile.

Summer rolled her eyes. "Thanks. I love lemon water."

They giggled, and Summer slid onto her stool and pointed at Delaney. "You love lemon water too, don't you?"

Benjamin, Rowdy's long-time bartender, sauntered over with a tray. He set glasses of water in front of Summer and Delaney, and a vodka cranberry in front of Josie. Then, with a flourish, he set a bowl of green olives between Summer and Delaney.

"She just smirked," Delaney said, gesturing at Josie with her water glass.

"I did not!"

"You did, too! You smirked because you get a vodka cran and we get waters."

"Now, now, ladies," Benjamin said. "Don't argue. It's not good for the babies."

He tipped his black cowboy hat and walked away, and a beat of silence ensued.

"Actually, Delaney," Josie said, "I smirked because I was thinking about the first time you ate a green olive during Happy Hour. Your eyes rolled back in your head and you were like, 'This is so good.' That's how we knew you were pregnant."

Summer nodded. "Yep. You'd been making fun of my green olive obsession for months. And now you have one, too."

Delaney laughed. "Too true."

"So how are you feeling, Dee?" Josie asked. "You're officially into the second trimester."

"I mean, being pregnant is miraculous and everything," Delaney said, "but it's so uncomfortable. Why didn't you warn me, Summer?"

"You've seen me through four pregnancies. And eight-ninths of another." She gestured at the bulge that was her stomach. "I thought you knew."

"You're always so stoic, though," Josie said.

Isn't that the truth?

"How are you feeling?" she asked Summer.

"I'm okay," Summer said. "I mean, we're down to the last few weeks. So I'm uncomfortable. And big. And exhausted. But other than that…"

She saw Delaney and Josie exchange a look, but didn't call them on it. She was allowed to complain once in a while, wasn't she?

All of a sudden, Summer was back in the trailer she and Willow called home during Summer's sophomore year of high school. It was spring break. Josie had signed up for a professional-track teaching course at Juniper City College and Delaney was off on some exotic vacation with her parents. Temperatures skyrocketed, which was awesome when you lived by the beach, but not so much when you lived in the desert in a crappy single-wide trailer with no air conditioning.

To combat the dry, windy heat, Willow took to drinking more than usual. She spent most of her time on the couch, in front of an electric fan, pressing her sweating glass of bourbon against the side of her face between sips. Summer was hot and bored and cranky. One morning, she came out of her bedroom and sat next to Willow on the couch. If she had known her mother was inebriated, she never would have talked to her, much less said anything about the heat. But it was seven a.m.—way too early for a person to be drunk.

"It's hot this morning," Summer said, her tone conversational.

Willow's head turned slowly, her eyes half-closed. She looked at Summer from under heavy lids. Summer thought her mother was being silly, pretending to suffer from heat exhaustion. So she did what any teenager would do: she laughed.

"Don't you laugh, young lady," Willow barked. "I work hard to put a roof over our heads. Don't you complain about the heat, do you hear me? With the amount you eat, we can't afford air conditioning. If I hear you bellyache again, I'll take a wooden spoon to your backside."

Of course she rarely actually hit Summer, but she seemed to get some kind of wicked satisfaction out of threatening her. Willow muttered under her breath about what an ungrateful slug her daughter was, and for the next few days, she challenged Summer to complain every time they interacted.

"Have anything to say about this dinner?" she sneered when she plunked a bowl of chili on the table. "Want to share your opinion on your shoes?"

Spring break of her sophomore year was the worst week of Summer's life. She vowed never to complain again, and she always kept her promises. Especially the ones she made to herself.

"Earth to Summer," Josie was saying as Summer brought herself back to Happy Hour at Rowdy's. At the bar, the Thursday night college crowd talked and laughed over colorful drinks and cheap beers.

Summer forced a smile.

"Sorry. Reminiscing," she said.

"Liar. You were on a whole different planet," Delaney said.

"I was," Summer said. "But I'm back."

"Oh, good," Delaney said. "Where were you?"

With my lunatic mother in a flamingo-pink trailer with no air conditioning.

"Just thinking about my mom."

Summer felt like crying. She blamed the pregnancy hormones. The multi-colored lights strung around Rowdy's blurred and she blinked rapidly a few times to bring the whole scene back into focus.

"What's going on?" Josie said. "You've been acting weird since you got here."

"I have not," Summer said.

"Yes, you have," Delaney said.

"I haven't even had a chance to act weird," Summer said. She could hear the defensive tone in her voice, and took a deep breath. "I just got here."

"You haven't eaten a single olive," Josie pointed out. "You weren't even listening when Delaney said she's having twins."

Summer's attention snapped over to Delaney. "What? Really?"

"No," Delaney said, laughing. Josie laughed too, and said, "But you practically just admitted you're distracted."

Summer sighed.

"Plus," Delaney said, her expression becoming serious, "you never talk about your mom. I mean, like, ever. So it's weird that you were thinking about her."

Well, that just slipped out.

"I know. I think it's because I'm about to give birth."

"Lies," Josie said. "You've never mentioned her before when you're about to give birth. What's really going on?"

"It's nothing."

"Lies!" Josie said again.

"Stop sounding so gleeful," Summer said. "I'm just stressed, okay?"

Tears threatened again, rising pressure against a closed door.

Delaney gripped Josie's arm. "She's upset. She's going to cry," she whispered.

It was as if someone had turned the doorknob and flung that door open. Summer couldn't contain the tears, and she found herself wailing, her forehead on the table.

"It'll be okay," Delaney said, over and over, while Josie rubbed Summer's back.

Even though she was steeped in emotion, Summer didn't miss the silent conversation going on between her friends. They were worried—understandably so. She knew they meant well, but neither of them had the mental space to take care of her right now. She had to take care of herself, just as she had always done.

Summer cried all the way home after Happy Hour, purging herself before the kids attacked her as she walked through the door. She would walk in, and Derek would be there, dueling with the boys, swords slashing through the air and Hannah strapped to Derek's back like a little Yoda. Sarah would be sitting on the couch with a book, undoubtedly rolling her eyes at the shenanigans, acting as the formal timekeeper as bath time approached.

Derek had become Summer's buoy during junior year of high school, when they were seventeen. As Willow's alcohol threatened to drown Summer, Summer clung to Derek, the nerdy leader of the chess club, with the kind of desperation (disguised as devotion) that would have made even Josie blush.

Not that he minded.

They met on the second Monday of that school year. Summer, seeking an excuse to stay at school rather than going home to Willow, decided to join the chess club. She didn't know how to play, but she could learn. Eyes downcast and feet shuffling, she made her way into the activities room and sat at the table closest to the door.

Derek approached her cautiously, like a person would approach a rattlesnake. He introduced himself.

"I don't know how to play chess," she blurted out, and he laughed.

"No offense, but I didn't peg you for a chess player. Why are you here, then?"

"Just wanted something to do," she said, but what she was really thinking was that she wanted to stay away from home for as long as possible.

"Okay," he said slowly, and then he smiled. "I'll—I mean, we'll—teach you."

His grin, toothy and spontaneous, had her smiling back. Just like that, they became friends.

The memory of their first encounter bolstered Summer's mood as she arrived home after Happy Hour. When she opened the front door, the scene was pretty close to how she'd imagined it, only Hannah was running around from one brother to the other with a makeshift sword (was that a broken stick, or a piece of PVC pipe?), shouting, "Take that!" on repeat.

Derek was on the couch next to Sarah, engrossed in his own book. He looked up at her and smiled.

"How was it?"

She wanted to say so many things to him, in that moment. She wanted to say that Happy Hour was okay, but she'd really wanted to be home with him. She wanted to say that he was the one person she loved more than anything, and together they could get through Luke's illness. She wanted to say that she was scared, scared to lose her perfect little boy.

But instead of saying any of those things, she just smiled back.

"It was good," she said. "I'm glad to be home."

Sometimes she felt like he could read her mind. He didn't question her, but he stood up, took her hand, and pulled her close so they were standing side by side. He kissed the side of her head.

"I'm glad you're home, too," he said.

She leaned against him, feeling his stubble against the side of her forehead, inhaling his aftershave, absorbing his warmth. Sarah broke the spell when she said to her brothers, "It's bath time, you inferior beings."

To a chorus of groans, Summer herded the kids around for their nightly clean-up. Nate didn't make it more than a few seconds before putting a pair of underwear on his head. Luke, of course, stopped to play with a remote control car someone had left out.

Sarah directed Hannah in cleaning up her blocks, and Derek sang some cleaning song he'd made up. Summer secretly wished he'd stop singing, but bit her lip to keep from saying so. The doorbell rang, and with all the other noise, Summer almost didn't register the sound.

"Expecting someone?" Derek said. When she shook her head, he said, "Probably a salesman. Let's have the kids answer the door."

Chuckling, the two of them walked to the door together. Summer pulled it open, and the world tilted when she saw who stood on the other side.

"Hello, Summer. You look exhausted."

Her mother. Willow. Standing on her doorstep after more than a decade and a half of silence. No warning bells, no tingly sixth sense, nothing. Summer felt completely caught off guard, totally unprepared for this interruption in her life. How did the woman even fathom she'd be welcome here?

By now, the kids had stopped what they were doing, and, happily distracted from their clean-up, they crowded around in the hallway behind her.

So the first reaction that came to mind—slamming the door in Willow's face—probably was not the best choice.

"Hello, Willow. What a surprise."

Willow managed to force a hurt expression onto her face. "You're not going to call me Mom?"

Derek looked back and forth between the two women, his expression so quizzical Summer almost wanted to laugh. Instead, she inhaled loudly. He grabbed her upper arm. Having kept quiet for their maximum of one minute, the kids began pelting their parents with questions.

"Who is it?" Nate wanted to know.

"Is it a Bible thumper?" Luke yelled.

"Thumper, thumper, thumper," Hannah sang.

Sarah had come up behind them. "From the looks of it," she said, "I'd say this is—"

"Kids, this is Willow," Summer said.

Willow arched a painted-on eyebrow at her, and added: "Your grandmother."

CHAPTER THREE

SUMMER NOTICED WITH AN UNPLEASANT START THAT WILLOW'S FACE looked remarkably like her own. The parentheses around her mouth were a little deeper, but the shape of her chin (slightly too pointy) and the color of her eyes (cornflower blue) were exactly the same. There was no mistaking their genetic connection. It was the only one they had, Summer thought.

As the seven of them stood frozen in the doorway, Summer recalled that day fifteen years before, when she walked out of their house for good, vowing never to speak to her mother again.

Summer was nineteen, a skilled chess player and a high school graduate. After three years of working at the local ice cream shop and babysitting on the side, she had saved up enough money to get her own apartment.

It wasn't anything fancy, just a one-bedroom near downtown Juniper. Still, she felt beyond excited at the prospect of living on her own. She'd pored over home decorating magazines at the library, and had stopped into a few secondhand shops during the past couple of months to buy furnishings. These she had stacked in Derek's family's garage.

She thought later that her fear of telling Willow probably made the situation worse, but she couldn't do it over.

Summer had just finished a shift at the ice cream shop, and came home to Willow laying on the couch, smoke curling upward from a lit cigarette in one hand and a glass of bourbon on the table next to her. It was nearly impossible to tell whether Willow was awake. Her eyes were closed, but because of the way she'd propped her elbow on the cushion next to her, she managed to hold the cigarette straight up in the air.

Condensation on the bourbon glass had left a decent-sized ring on the table, which made Summer think it had sat in once place for a while. As Summer stood there, just inside the front door, studying her mother's face, her lithe body, and her perfectly painted toenails, she felt equal parts pity, satisfaction, and anger.

She pitied her mom, wished she hadn't fallen victim to alcoholism and ruined a perfectly good life. She felt satisfied that she'd be moving on, that Willow wouldn't ruin her own life. And she felt anger that she wanted nothing more than to get away from her own mother.

Derek had proposed just that morning, and of course, Summer had accepted.

They planned to marry in a year, which gave Summer time to live on her own, to get her feet under her. But she wasn't ready to tell Willow that, just yet. She'd undoubtedly make marriage seem like the worst possible scenario in the world. But Summer had seen it work in Derek's family. She knew what a good marriage could be. She knew what a good family could be. Willow wouldn't believe it.

So for now, Summer would just tell her about the apartment.

"Mom?"

Nothing.

"Mom."

Willow's eyelids fluttered.

"Mom!"

Willow startled and if Summer hadn't been so nervous, she would have laughed.

"Jesus Christ, Summer, you scared the shit out of me!"

"Sorry, Mom."

"What the hell do you want?"

Well, this wasn't going nearly as smoothly as Summer had hoped. She took a deep breath.

"I got my own apartment," she said.

A long silence ensued, during which nerves blurred Summer's vision.

"Well, isn't that nice." Willow lifted the bourbon off the coffee table and downed its contents, then hauled herself to her feet. "How are you gonna pay for that?"

"I've got money saved. I have two jobs. I'll manage."

Willow nodded, and for a moment, Summer thought she'd congratulate her. But she should have known by the way Willow stared out the window towards the street, her eyes unfocused and her lips pressed into a thin line, that congratulations were not forthcoming.

"You think it's easy?" Her voice was low and gravelly. With her cigarette hand, she gestured to their surroundings—the trailer with its threadbare pea green carpet and peeling linoleum floors—and said, "You think keeping your own place is easy?"

Unsure of what to say, Summer didn't answer.

"It's not," Willow said. "It's hard. And you're soft. You're not cut out for hard, honey. But best of luck to you."

Summer felt her mouth drop open, and she snapped it closed before doing an about face and walking out the door, promising herself she'd never let Willow hurt her again.

It took Willow fifteen years to come after Summer. For a split second, Summer wondered if her mother had changed. Then she spoke, and confirmed she was exactly the same person she'd always been.

"Holy shit, Summer. Are these all yours? And another one on the way? Jesus Christ."

Summer heard Derek's sharp inhale and had the insane urge to laugh.

Now Willow addressed Derek: "You've been busy, mister. Are they all yours?"

"Kids. Bed. Now," Summer said.

Sarah, her eyes as round as coins, pried Hannah off Derek's leg, picked her up and shepherded the boys to the back of the house. For once, they didn't protest.

"What are you doing here, Willow?" Summer said when they were gone.

"I'm your mother. I've come to see you. I presume this is your husband?"

The front door swung closed. Summer couldn't escape a suffocating sense of doom. Why hadn't they chosen a house with a larger entryway?

Derek put one arm around Summer and extended his free hand. "I'm Derek. Summer's husband and father to these four—five, if you count this one" (he pointed at Summer's belly) "little humans."

"Wow," Willow said, her eyebrows arched in a grotesque combination of disgust and disbelief.

"Would you like to come in?" Derek said.

Summer wanted to elbow him.

"That would be lovely," Willow said.

When Summer didn't move out of the way on her own, Derek steered her back to the living room.

Willow followed them, her arms out as as if she were walking through waist-deep water. "This place is a catastrophe. It looks like Pearl Harbor in here."

Willow stood in the center of the room, turning in a slow circle.

Summer sighed, thinking about the cluttered kitchen counters and smoke-filled living rooms of her youth. For the briefest moment, she looked around her own house as if she were a stranger seeing it for the first time. Against one wall, a gazillion toys sat in a heap. Six empty cups stood on the dining room table amongst dried-on spaghetti noodles and fresh puddles of chicken broth.

"Well, with four kids—" Derek said.

"I don't know why you'd have another," Willow interrupted. "Or is this one an accident?"

"Mom, seriously," Summer said. Hands on her hips, she turned to face her mother.

"Aha!" Willow brought her hands together in a clap. "I knew it would be no time before you started calling me Mom!"

Now Summer threw her arms up in exasperation. "Cut the crap. Why are you here?"

"Oh, honey," Willow said. "I just wanted to see you, all grown up, that's all."

"You've seen me," Summer said. "Now let me show you the door."

"I've seen the door," Willow said. "I'd like to stay a while."

"Can you come back another time?" Summer said. "It's the kids' bedtime."

"She's inviting me back," Willow said to Derek. Then, to Summer, she said, "If it's their bedtime, surely you can talk now."

"Actually, I have to help put them to bed."

"This is the twenty-first century. Don't husbands help with that sort of thing nowadays?"

Summer groaned, and Derek barked out a laugh.

"I'll put them to bed so you two can talk," he said.

Summer sent him what she hoped was an imploring look, but he didn't seem to notice.

Willow made a big show of examining the couch cushions and brushing invisible crumbs off of them. Summer sighed again and eased herself down, massaging the spot on her right rib cage where she always got a cramp in late pregnancy.

"Please don't tell me you're going into labor," Willow said when she determined the couch was clean enough to sit on. "I didn't sign up for that."

"What did you sign up for?" The baby shifted in Summer's belly, and out of reflex, she ran a hand from under her breasts to the underside of her stomach.

"I just wanted to see you," Willow said.

Her voice sounded pouty, but Summer's anger remained burning hot. "Why now?" she said.

"Summer. You know I had a hard life. I didn't have a robot husband to help me out, to pay the bills, to put you to bed or help with homework."

"You *chose* not to have a husband," Summer said. Her voice came out a whisper-yell in her effort not to let the kids overhear the conversation. "What did you say? 'I don't need a husband. No woman needs a man.' Something like that, right?"

One of the kids squealed, and Willow winced at the sound.

"Why are you here, Mom?"

You're probably homeless and need somewhere to stay.

Willow crossed one thin leg over the other. "It looks like you could use some help around here," she said.

"We manage just fine," Summer said.

"How have you been?" Willow said, then added, "Aside from knocked up, I mean."

Summer couldn't tell whether the concern was real. When was the last time Willow asked how Summer was doing? She couldn't even recall.

"I've been fine," Summer said.

"Aren't you going to offer me a drink?"

"We have water. And milk."

"Nothing stronger?"

"No, Mom. Nothing stronger."

"Sure, I'll have some water. Thanks for offering."

When Summer returned to the living room with a glass of water, Willow was standing up, examining the pictures on the wall.

"They're beautiful children, Summer."

"I know."

"The oldest—what's her name?—she looks just like you."

Summer heard the unspoken, *and just like me,* but she ignored it and answered, "Her name's Sarah."

Softening a little, she pointed at the picture and named the other three children.

"And this one?" Willow pointed to Summer's belly.

"I'm not sure yet. We haven't decided."

"Look, Summer. I'd like to stay," Willow said. She continued looking at the pictures, examining each child's face, running a finger down the glass in the frame. "I'd like to get to know you again, get to know your husband, and your kids."

"Stay in Juniper?" Summer's sixth sense tingled. It was waking up, stretching its muscles.

"No," Willow said. "Stay here. At your house. Would that be okay?"

"YOU SHOULD LET HER STAY," Derek said an hour later as they prepared for bed.

He had driven Willow to the nearby Saguaro Inn with the excuse Summer was exhausted and the house wasn't clean enough for company. Now, Summer turned back the covers on her side of the bed and slid between the sheets. She turned her back to Derek and closed her eyes. It was cliché to wish she'd wake up tomorrow and this whole thing would be a dream. Instead, she wished she'd wake up tomorrow and Willow would have changed her mind and driven as far away as possible. Florida, maybe. Maybe even right into the Atlantic. Yes, even better. Right into the ocean.

"You're not going to answer?" Derek said.

"Nope," Summer said.

Derek climbed into bed and turned off his bedside lamp. "She's your mother."

"Not really. Your mom is my mother."

"She's reaching out."

Summer huffed out another sigh. "Now? After fifteen years? What the hell took her so long? She must want something."

"I can see why you'd think that," Derek said. "But I think you should give her a chance."

"You do, huh? You don't even know her. You don't know the damage she can cause, just by being herself. I don't want her around me, or around you, and I really don't want her around our children. She's toxic."

"Maybe she's changed."

"Yeah. Maybe she's changed," Summer said. "And maybe I'm the Prince of Persia. Goodnight."

A full minute passed, and Summer thought Derek had given up on the conversation.

"We can't afford to put her up in a hotel every night," he said just as she felt herself slipping into the welcome oblivion of sleep. "And we can't just put her out."

"I know we can't afford to put her up in a hotel every night," Summer said, cringing at the thought of a monthly hotel bill from the Saguaro Inn. "She can just leave."

"Don't you want her to get to know the kids?"

"I could give a shit."

Summer could feel Derek's tiny jolt of surprise through the bed springs. It might not register on the Richter scale, but she could feel it.

"You're not acting like yourself," he said. "Let's revisit this in the morning."

Derek dropped immediately off to sleep. Summer stared into the darkness and listened to him breathe. Because Willow's appearance, or reappearance, or whatever it was, had made her feel lonely somehow, she reached over and held Derek's hand.

The right thing to do was to let Willow spend some time here. Summer knew that. But for once, she didn't want to do the right thing. She didn't care whether she did or not. She'd rather send her mother packing. Willow and all her baggage could go ahead and take that long trip off Florida's coast, as far as Summer was concerned.

And yet. Hadn't she often seen one of Willow's expressions on the faces of one of her children? Hadn't she watched Sarah hold her book in exactly the same way Willow held hers, with one hand across the top, a pointer finger extended? Hadn't Nate picked up Willow's deep fear of thunderstorms? Luke deplored lima beans, and when someone spoke to Hannah, she cocked her head at exactly the same angle as Willow did when she tried to make sense of something.

The genetic tie was there. Could it really hurt to give Willow the chance to meet her kids, and vice versa?

Yes, Summer thought, it could hurt. Willow had hurt Summer when Summer was a child. Summer's own kids wouldn't be subjected to the same Willow experience she had, but still…

Summer's body buzzed with restless energy. She got out of bed and went into the living room. She sat down at the computer and logged into FriendZoo. For reasons she couldn't define, the posts she saw made her angry.

"Ridiculous," she muttered when she saw that one of her friends from high school had posted a video of her "genius son" reading at age four.

The baby shifted inside her body. He or she was probably going to emerge into the world as a mini stress monster, and it would be all her fault.

"Sorry, baby," she whispered.

Even though she knew it was a bad idea in her current state of mind, Summer began to type: *Your kid may be a genius, but he's a little freakin' asshole.*

It felt so good. She deleted the words and replaced them with *#genius,* then clicked *Like* and scrolled down.

A woman she had met in a support group for nursing moms had posted a selfie. Not a selfie where she was doing something fun or noteworthy, but a selfie where she was sitting in her car, looking freshly made up.

A few people had commented with things like *Pretty!* or *Nice!* but Summer didn't think she looked pretty or nice.

So she typed: *We don't give a shit what you look like when you drive your kids to school.*

Even though she deleted this comment, too, and then typed *#gorgeous* and *Liked* the photo, her stress had begun to dissipate.

"It feels so good to be bad," Summer whispered, snickering. She scrolled again.

Another woman, an acquaintance from yoga class, had posted a photo of her newborn baby, with a caption about how adorable he was.

Yikes! I hope he grows into that nose.

Now, Summer laughed, silently, a hand over her mouth. Who was ridiculous, now? She couldn't believe she was using hashtags. The baby shifted again, and Summer felt a small contraction. She deleted, typed *#babyface*, clicked *Like*, and scrolled down again.

The mother of one of Luke's classmates had posted: *Ugh. Tearing my hair out. I am so ready for this day to be over. The kids are driving me crazy. Can't wait for bedtime.*

Summer rolled her eyes. She hated posts like this because they always came from mothers who spent all day posting about how they were *#blessed* and *#grateful* and had such *#cutekids*. She began to compose a reply: *Stop complaining. You are #blessed.*

Before she could finish, Summer heard her phone chirp from the bedroom.

"Shit," she said. "I forgot to put it on silent. And who the hell is texting me at this hour?"

It was Josie: *What are you doing up?*

Summer sneaked back out to the desk and responded: *How do you know I'm up? What are YOU doing up?*

Josie: *I'm working on some plans for the community center. Go to bed. You're growing a baby.*

Summer: *I can't sleep.*

Josie: *All that mean is keeping you awake. I saw your sarcastic comments on FriendZoo. You may have them fooled but I know what you're really thinking. That kid is a genius but he's probably a little jerk.*

Here, she inserted a laughing emoji. Summer smiled and wrote back: *I thought you were working on plans for the community center, not sitting around on FriendZoo.*

Josie: *Are you Summer, or Winter?*

Summer laughed out loud at that one. *Good one.*

Josie: *Yeah, I thought so. Get off FriendZoo and go to bed.*

Summer: *I can't sleep. Pregnancy hormones.*

She didn't say anything about Willow's visit. That wasn't a conversation to have over text.

Josie: *I hereby forbid you from making even one more comment on FriendZoo tonight.*

Summer: *Fine.*

Josie: *What's wrong?*

Summer: *What do you mean?*

Josie: *You're not acting like yourself. You never post passive aggressive mean stuff, even when people deserve it. You're usually so nice.*

Summer: *I don't know.*

Josie: *Really?*

Summer: *No.*

Josie: *… (this is me, waiting)*

Summer: *I'm just stressed. There's a lot going on.*

Josie: *Luke and the heart thing?*

Summer: *That, yes. And it's worse because I can't sleep.*

Josie: *You definitely won't sleep if you're on the computer. Go back to bed.*

Summer: *Okay.*

Josie: *Love you. Everything will turn out fine, I promise.*

Summer: *Okay. Love you. 'Night.*

Josie: *Goodnight.*

Summer chuckled as she walked back into the bedroom, thinking, *Winter. That's a good one. It's my alter ego.*

OF COURSE, the first text from Josie had woken Derek, and when she went back into the bedroom, he was propped up on one elbow, waiting for her.

"Still thinking about Willow, huh?"

"Yeah," she said.

"Who was texting you?"

"Josie."

"What were you doing out there?"

"Just surfing the net."

He chuckled. "FriendZoo?"

She sighed. FriendZoo had become almost a compulsive habit. She found herself looking at her phone at the strangest times, scrolling through pointless posts. She'd once read a post that said, "I"m taking a break from FriendZoo for a while. Lately, it's like opening my fridge even though I'm not hungry, and staring at the contents just to see what's there."

That about summed it up.

"Yes," Summer said. "FriendZoo."

Derek shook his head and rolled his eyes. "So what were you thinking?"

"I don't know," she said.

He patted the bed, and she laid down next to him.

"That baby is sure getting big," he said.

She laughed. "I know, believe me."

"So?"

"I was just thinking that maybe I should let the kids get to know Willow. Not for her, but for them. You know?"

"It's not a bad idea," Derek said.

"I just don't want her to hurt them. Disappoint them. Make them crazy."

"You're here to protect them. Besides. You grew up with her, and you turned out okay. I mean, you know, considering."

She elbowed him gently, and they both laughed.

"Sorry I was a witch earlier."

"No biggie. I'm used to it."

"Shut up."

"Seriously. I think it's a good idea to give the kids the opportunity to know their other grandmother. The two of you don't have to be BFFs or anything. We don't have to spend every day or every weekend with her. But letting them get to know her, a day at a time, will be fine."

"As long as she's not still drowning herself in bourbon."

Derek shrugged. "Just lay the ground rules."

"Easy for you to say," Summer said.

"I'll help you," Derek said.

"Fine."

"Fine. Now, can we go to sleep?"

"Yes."

This was exactly why she had found Derek so appealing when they first met. He served as a calming influence. Even as a teenager, his insights were pretty profound. Tomorrow, she'd call Willow and invite her over. For a visit. Lunch. Maybe she had changed. Maybe the kids would like her.

Or maybe she is exactly the same.

"Shut up, Winter," Summer whispered into the dark.

CHAPTER FOUR

Morning came, just like it always did. Summer didn't sleep at all and she felt a tiny bit of relief when Hannah shouted, "Morning! Up!" from her crib just after six a.m.

Derek startled awake, and Summer laughed as she heaved herself to a standing position.

"You can sleep in," she said.

He sighed and turned over. She felt a tiny stab of jealousy. Why could he fall asleep so easily? That feeling dissolved when she walked into Hannah's room and her daughter reached for her, squealing happily.

"Hi, baby," she said. "Good morning."

Last night she felt pretty strong in her resolve to call Willow this morning and invite her to spend a few days at the house. But now that this morning had arrived, the sun slicing through the window to illuminate Hannah's disheveled hair, Summer started feeling doubt again.

She went through the motions, setting a handful of cereal on Hannah's high chair tray and then putting a pot of water on the stove to boil for oatmeal.

Inviting Willow to stay, even temporarily, would be like inviting her back into Summer's life ... and Summer wasn't sure she wanted that. Last night, Willow hadn't smelled of bourbon, but Summer wouldn't be surprised if she had walked over to the convenience store and bought a bottle after Derek dropped her off at the hotel. At this very moment, Summer thought as she added oatmeal to the water, she was probably waking up with a headache, shielding her eyes from the brightness of the sun and from the reality that her own daughter hadn't allowed her to stay in her house the night before.

The boys' giggles interrupted Summer's thoughts. She smiled. They were undoubtedly coming up with some prank to pull on their big sister, judging by the way they became stone-cold silent as they passed by her bedroom door on their way to the kitchen. Luke, a mischievous smile on his freckled face, sat down at the table, and when Nate elbowed him, he pursed his lips trying to hide that smile.

"What are you two up to?" Summer said.

"Nothing," they answered in unison.

"I've heard that before," she said.

"Mom, the oatmeal's boiling over," Nate said, hopping up to turn down the flame on the stove.

"Sorry. Distracted."

"Where's Grandma?" Luke wanted to know.

Summer bit back the urge to snap, "Don't call her Grandma." Instead, she took a deep breath and said, "She stayed at a hotel last night."

"Why didn't she stay here?" Nate asked.

Fortunately, while Summer began formulating her answer, Sarah screamed, and the boys, cackling, scrambled off to her bedroom to enjoy the fruits of their labor.

"They put a huge spider on my pillow!" Sarah shrieked as she tore into the kitchen, the boys just steps behind her, laughing like mad. "I thought it was real!"

Summer couldn't help but laugh as she put an arm around her daughter and hugged her close.

"Good morning," she said. "Not the best way to wake up, is it?"

"I'll get them back," Sarah said.

Summer could practically see her plotting. She took bowls out of the dishwasher and began slicing fruit, and Summer felt a rush of gratitude for her own children and the home she and Derek had created for them, however chaotic it was. The Willow question could wait, for a few hours at least.

. . .

IN ADDITION to the chess club, Summer joined the track team and the Earth Helpers club sophomore year. Derek followed suit and the two of them spent every waking hour together.

One afternoon, he invited her over under the guise of watching videos of the famous runner Steve Prefontaine, but they both knew the real reason they wanted to watch videos together was so that they could sit side by side on the couch, and maybe even hold hands. Their relationship hadn't progressed beyond friendship, but Summer felt a peculiar flutter in her stomach whenever their hands touched during a chess game, or when he jogged past her during track practice and tugged on the end of her ponytail.

Delaney and Josie teased her about how much time she spent with Derek, and Josie, who they'd made the unofficial expert on all things related to romance, said wisely, "I can tell he likes you by the way he smoothes his hair every time he sees you."

(It turns out that wasn't quite a dead giveaway. Derek's hair-smoothing habit was just that and he did it a million times per day.)

On the day of the Steve Prefontaine video, Summer and Derek walked into Derek's sunny kitchen, and his mom, Julie, grinned.

"So you're the one who's been putting that goofy smile on Derek's face for the past two months," she said. Summer blushed, but felt herself immediately warming, and then practically melting when Julie put down her iced tea and wrapped Summer in a hug.

"It's so nice to meet you, sweetie. Really. It is."

Derek mysteriously disappeared and Julie handed Summer a bowl of potatoes to wash, peel and chop. Just like that, Summer Carson became part of a family.

It was Julie who cried when she saw Summer in her wedding gown, and Derek's dad, Buck, who walked her down the aisle and gave her away. It was Julie who came to the house after each of Summer's children were born, to cook and clean and rock her tiny grandchildren while Summer napped. Julie showed up at all the kids' sporting events, school awards ceremonies and science fairs. And she was around for more than just the fun stuff. She helped with homework. She bandaged scraped elbows and put baking soda paste on bee stings. She sent kids to timeout, for goodness' sake.

Julie had stepped in, and Summer had decided long ago she didn't need Willow. And she certainly didn't need her now.

CHAPTER FIVE

Summer called an emergency Monday-evening Happy Hour meeting at Rowdy's. The scene inside the bar was quieter than usual. Whereas Thursdays were rockin', tonight, only a handful of college kids sat at the bar, and a couple of suits snacked on pub mix a few tables away.

After initial greetings, Delaney and Josie both looked at Summer, waiting. She sighed. She was the one who'd called the emergency meeting, which meant they were expecting opening statements.

"I need a distraction," she said.

When her announcement was met with stony silence, she sighed. Again. Even though the three of them had practically grown up together, the subject of Summer's mother had always been off-limits. Summer never invited the girls over, and if one of them asked any questions, she'd change the subject immediately. Over time, they'd learned not to ask—which was a relief to Summer, who wanted nothing more than to keep her home life separate from her life with her friends.

But she had to tell them now. She started with the end—Willow showing up on her doorstep—and then rewound and gave them a Reader's Digest version of her childhood. She told them about Willow's drinking and all the interesting situations it caused: Summer being left in the produce section, Willow forgetting to pick her up from school (until she wised up and started taking the bus),

Willow neglecting to sign field trip permission forms and feeding Summer cold soup out of a can for dinner. She wrapped up the story with her conundrum, and then she exhaled, took a sip of Josie's vodka cranberry (one tiny sip wouldn't hurt), and ate an olive.

After a long silence, Josie said, "I think it's time for your intervention, my sister."

Summer should have known it was coming, but still, Josie's mention of an intervention struck fear into her heart. Even though she believed The Dating Intervention (where she and Josie took over Delaney's life) and The Marriage Intervention (where she and Delaney took over Josie's marriage) had produced positive results, she didn't know if she could handle being accountable for anything else at this point.

She put her head down on the table. "I wish I could drown my stress in wine. Or vodka. Or turpentine."

"So, I guess I didn't even realize you had a mom," Delaney said.

"I know," Summer said. "Me neither."

"Seriously, though," Josie said. "What happened? How did she just show up on your doorstep?"

Summer explained how Willow had apparently spent the past fifteen years developing her research skills instead of getting an actual job. She happened to see a post from someone on FriendZoo that mentioned Summer's work as a graphic designer, and she went from there, searching the property records and then lurking around until she verified Summer was, in fact, Mrs. Gray after all this time.

"Wow," Delaney and Josie said.

Summer nodded. "Derek said we should let her stay, and he was being pretty reasonable. So she's been at the house since Friday. Ergo, today's emergency meeting. Mostly I wanted to meet with you guys so I could think about something besides my own crazy life. Like I said, I need a distraction. What's going on with you two?"

The girls looked at each other. Before Summer really had time to wonder what their silent conversation was all about, Delaney spoke.

"Jake and I are going to buy a new house," she said. "Hopefully before the baby comes. My place is too small, and his apartment is, well, a bachelor pad, so, not really appropriate for a family."

"That's great," Summer said. "How's the search going?"

"Awful," Delaney said.

Josie laughed, but forced a serious expression when Delaney gave her a dirty look.

Delaney went on, "He wants to live, like, out in the country, so our kids can run around and explore. Play cowboys. Whatever. But I want to live in town so we can walk to school, borrow sugar from our neighbors, that kind of thing. Did you guys ever fight about a house?"

Summer shook her head. "Not really. I mean, we were so head over heels, and so young. Buying a house seemed really exciting. I'm pretty sure we bought the first one we looked at."

"Do you guys ever fight?" Josie asked.

Again, Summer shook her head. "Not really. Until Willow showed up."

Summer thought about the bickering they'd done during the past few days. They bickered about whether to put the butcher knife in the dishwasher, whether to grill the chicken on Saturday or Sunday, where to put the remote control. It was ridiculous.

Delaney elbowed Josie, and Summer felt a tiny bit of apprehension sneak in.

"Look, Summer," Josie said. "I know you want a distraction. But we want an intervention."

Just as Summer had done a few months ago when she and Josie took over Delaney's life during The Dating Intervention, Delaney held up her hands as if she were admiring a big, bright movie marquee. "We call it"—she paused for dramatic effect—"The Life Intervention."

"Wow. That just doesn't have the same ring as The Dating Intervention or The Marriage Intervention," Josie said.

"No, it really doesn't," Delaney said.

Summer laughed. The sound bordered on hysterical. "I don't need an intervention."

"Um, yes," Josie said. "You do."

I probably do. Summer remembered watching Delaney's life disintegrate, and she remembered feeling like stepping in was the only option. She remembered seeing Josie's marriage on the verge of falling apart, and again, feeling like taking over was the only option. She couldn't see her own life from her friends' perspective, of course, but they had trusted her and now it was her turn to trust them. She thought of her dream vacation—in a hospital, due to injury or illness —and nodded.

"I guess I do. But it needs a better name."

"We'll work on that," Delaney said. "But let's come up with a few rules."

Josie pulled a pen out of her purse and began writing on a bar napkin. "One. You must return to yoga class."

She wrote, *Yoga* on the bar napkin. "I can already hear you: 'But I don't have childcare.' First of all, your mom is there now. Second of all, Dee and I can watch the kids for you. Two."

"Wait," Summer said. "There's no way I'm letting my mom watch the kids. I'm just saying."

"Fine. Delaney and I will watch them. Two. Date nights." She wrote *Dates* on the napkin. "Again, we will watch the kids. You and Derek must go out once a week. We don't care if you go up to the top of a mountain and make out or go to dinner and a movie. But you've got to get out of the house. Before you go crazy."

"We were going to put in a rule about sex," Delaney said. "But seeing as you're currently as big as a house, we decided we'll let that one slide."

"For now," Josie said.

"Thanks a lot," Summer said.

"Three," Delaney said. "Girl days."

Josie wrote *Girls' Day Out* on the napkin.

"I would love to, you guys, really. But I don't have time for all this."

"That's the problem," Delaney said. "You need to make time. We know you're not going to like this one, but—"

"Just say it quick. Like ripping off a Band-Aid," Josie said.

"You need to take a break from The Sweets," Delaney said.

Summer sighed. When Josie opened her mouth to speak, Summer held up a hand. "No, you're right. I do need to take a break from the band. I love it. I've loved it since we started seven years ago. I really loved it when we performed at the rodeo dance. But right now, it's not providing the stress relief it has in the past."

"That was easier than I expected," Josie said.

"I know," Delaney said. "I could see you gearing up for a fight."

Summer wanted to blame hormones for the tightening in her

throat, but she knew the onslaught of emotion came from the growing sensation of relief. The girls were stepping in at exactly the right moment, and they knew just what she needed.

"I love you guys," she said.

As Summer drove home from Rowdy's, she felt immense gratitude for her friends. Again, tears sprang to her eyes, blurring the watercolor sunset. Delaney and Josie were right. Since Willow's appearance at the front door of Summer's home, the tension had risen to almost unmanageable levels. Something had to change.

Summer cringed as she thought about her behavior over the past couple of days. She found herself snapping at Derek and the kids, leaving her keys in the freezer (and then accusing the kids of taking them), and constantly on the verge of crying or screaming or locking herself in the bedroom.

When she called Willow at the hotel and invited her over, trying to hide the reluctance in her voice, Willow said, "I just knew you'd come around. In fact, I've already showered. You can pick me up anytime."

Derek drove over to get her, and when she walked into the house, she lined up all four of the kids and inspected them as if they were livestock.

"This one looks just like you—and like me," she said as she examined Sarah's face. "Only, she got your husband's ears. Unfortunate. And this one—" she leaned down so she was eye-to-eye with Nate—"he's handsome. Lady killer. Watch out for you, honey." She whistled through her teeth. Nate grinned. Derek laughed and Summer rolled her eyes. Willow moved on to Luke. "He looks pale," she said. When he frowned, she quickly added, "And a bit mischievous." He laughed at that, and she looked around for Hannah, who wouldn't stand in a lineup if her life depended on it. "Where's that little whippersnapper?"

"That one's got a mind of her own," Derek said to Willow, as if it were a secret the two of them shared.

"Just like her mother," Willow said, winking at Summer.

Did you just wink at me? It was the first wink Willow had ever sent Summer's way.

The sound of running feet distracted Summer from saying anything to Willow, and Hannah emerged from the hall with a pair of Nate's underwear on her head and his cowboy boots on her feet. Her shirt was crusted with dried oatmeal, and her hair stuck up, cemented in place by more of the same.

"Isn't she just a handful?" Willow said, clapping her hands together. "I hope you don't have another girl, Summer. I'm not sure you can handle it."

Derek squeezed Summer's arm. Throughout the day, Willow sat on the couch taking everything in, and of course, offering commentary. Mid-afternoon when the older kids were still in pajamas, Summer threatened them with no meals for a week if they didn't get dressed. Naturally, they put on the clothes they'd worn the day before. "Oh, is that how you manage?" Willow said. "Threaten to starve them and make them wear dirty clothes? I guess that's how you afford to feed this little flock of yours, and keep up with the laundry."

When Hannah stood up in her highchair and toppled right out of it, Willow sat calmly at the dining room table, clucking her tongue.

The crying quieted, and she said, "You should really monitor her better, Summer. I'd hate for her to suffer a serious head injury because you're not watching her. Poor little thing."

Flashbacks of her own childhood played like a film reel in her mind—the time she'd spent an entire afternoon playing outside in a thunderstorm until a neighbor noticed and sent her inside, the full week she'd spent fending for herself, eating questionable produce when Willow didn't come home because she had ended up in some homeless shelter, and the time Willow left her next to those cantaloupes. Summer reminded herself that Willow had a skewed sense of good parenting.

Again, she remained silent, Derek's words from that first night on repeat in her mind: "Just give it a try. Be patient. This is your chance to reconnect with your mother. I don't want you to regret it if you don't give it an honest effort."

At one point, Summer walked into the kitchen to find Willow teaching Nate how to use a lighter to light her cigarette. Summer worked herself into a tizzy, shrieking at Willow about teaching a nine-year-old how to light a cigarette and the inappropriateness of smoking inside a house where children lived. "I didn't even know they still *made* these!" she said as she ground out the cigarette in the sink.

As she had throughout Summer's childhood, Willow acted like Summer was the irrational one.

"Using a lighter is a life skill," she said while Nate looked back and forth between the two of them as if one of them might explode at any moment. "And don't worry. I made him promise me he'd never smoke. I told him it's a nasty, nasty habit. Right, Nathan?"

"His name is Nate."

"I like Nathan better."

Willow had been at the house only three days. During those three days, Summer found excuses to spend time alone in the bathroom. She'd turn the shower on, sit on the toilet lid and either cry, belt out kids' songs in an angry growl or mutter to herself. She felt that sick longing for a car accident or semi-major illness and the resultant hospitalization. More than ever, she looked forward to the birth of this baby. Yes, she'd have to go through labor and delivery to get it, but she'd at least get an overnight at Juniper Medical Center. Maybe even two overnights. This thought soothed her as she neared home, and she found herself drifting into a dreamlike state.

When she almost rear-ended a tiny hatchback at a red light, the adrenaline dump gave her a reality check. Considering the hospital a vacation was not healthy. And her fantasies of crashing her own car or coming down with a serious illness were becoming more frequent.

The only solution: to send Willow packing.

When Summer walked through the door a few minutes later, Willow sat at the kitchen table with all four kids. Each of the three big kids stared intently at a hand of cards, and Hannah studiously mashed peas into her high chair tray with her index finger.

Summer knew the scene should make her happy, but instead, anger rose quickly into her throat and she snapped, "Where's Derek?"

Four little heads snapped around, eight eyes opening wide at the sound her her voice.

The fifth head, Willow's, turned slowly, and her eyes trailed from Summer's face down to her stomach.

"Glad you could make it back from the bar."

Summer gritted her teeth.

"Daddy ran to the store to get Hannah some biscuits. He says she's teething," Sarah said into the silence.

Summer thought—but managed not to say—*What the hell was he thinking, leaving you all here with* her?

Instead, she nodded and stalked into the bedroom to change into sweat pants. Meanwhile, she took some deep breaths. She *did* need to go back to yoga. The front door opened and she heard Derek come in. Summer waited, and almost laughed because she felt like a lioness stalking her prey. The trap was set.

Derek must have sensed it, because he took his time walking back to the bedroom.

In a whisper, she demanded, "Why did you leave the kids here with her?"

He sighed, but didn't look surprised.

"I just ran out to get Hannah some biscuits. I was gone fifteen minutes. I knew you'd be back soon, too. Take a chill pill, Summer."

"'Take a chill pill'? Take a chill pill? My husband is telling me to take a chill pill after he made the worst decision in all of history to leave my children—*my children!*—with my delinquent, alcoholic, cigarette-smoking mother!"

Summer found it difficult to maintain her low volume, but didn't want the kids to overhear her.

"Who are you talking to?" Derek asked.

"Winter. My alter ego. You wouldn't like her."

Unexpectedly, he laughed. "Is she kinky? Maybe I would."

Now, Summer laughed, too.

"I'm sorry," she said. "I just can't help but think about the time Willow left me at the grocery store. Or the time she slept through an entire weekend at a homeless shelter while I scavenged in the fridge for leftovers."

Derek moved forward as if to hug Summer, but stopped short, pretending to be afraid. She laughed and pulled him to her. He kissed her forehead and said, "I was gone fifteen minutes. If she suddenly went missing, Sarah could watch the other three until one of us got back."

Summer sighed. "What could go wrong in fifteen minutes, right?"

"Well, I wouldn't say that. But I figured it was pretty safe."

Summer found herself in a bit of a trance as they stood there, hugging. Then a yell from the kitchen broke the spell.

Nate lay on the kitchen floor, a foam sword in his armpit, howling with pretend pain. Luke stood over him, his arms raised in victory. Apparently, Luke had just beaten Nate at War.

"Knock it off, Nate," Summer said.

The mood in the kitchen transformed immediately from frivolity to frigid.

"Well, I guess I'll go have a cigarette before the bar-hopping Ice Queen freezes us all out," Willow said.

"I'll join you," Summer said.

The kids' mouths dropped open simultaneously and Summer snapped, "Not for a smoke. Just to talk. And for the record, I wasn't bar-hopping, Willow. I was at one bar, with my best friends, having a glass of water and some green olives. Not bourbon and cigarettes. Surprisingly, I don't have a taste for them, seeing as how I got a taste of them in the womb. Derek, could you please put the kids to bed?"

Derek managed to cover his surprised expression and bark out an order for the kids to get their pajamas. For once, they didn't protest. Maybe they could sense Summer's stress, or her resolve. Maybe they knew what she was about to do and didn't want to witness it. Or maybe they were just tired.

Nevertheless, they walked out of the kitchen single file without a backward glance at their grandmother. Summer was glad their last impression of her would be a good one.

Outside, Willow sat down in one of the wicker patio chairs and sighed. Summer remained standing as Willow pulled a pack of cigarettes out of her pocket and tapped it on the arm of the chair.

"Geez, I don't know how you do it with four little beasts," Willow said.

She tapped a cigarette out of the pack and Summer watched her light it in exactly the same way she had for decades. She held the cigarette between her teeth and pulled her lips back into a kind of grimace. She flicked her lighter once, twice, and on the third try it lit. Now she pursed her lips to inhale as she touched the flame to the cigarette, and Summer noticed the vertical lines along her upper lip had deepened noticeably in the past fifteen years.

"I just do it," Summer said.

As if she hadn't spoken, Willow continued, on the exhale: "I mean, they're all little chatterboxes, I'm sure you know that, and they're just chattering away talking about all the things you do for them."

Summer wondered what they'd said. She braced herself and waved the smoke out of her face. Hopefully they hadn't mentioned any of Summer's new obsessive behaviors, scouring the house for socks that matched and washing dishes until her fingers cracked and bled.

"Sarah said you started a mom and daughter book club. Is that true?"

Summer nodded.

"And Nate said you have a group of his friends over once a month for a pizza and sundae party."

"I do," Summer said. "And let me guess. Luke said I don't do anything for him like I do for the other two."

Willow laughed. "He did. But I pressed him and he admitted that he's a night owl like you and the two of you stay up late at night watching monster truck videos when neither of you can sleep."

Summer shrugged. "All true."

Although Willow had always taught her pride was a no-no, Summer felt herself smiling a little proudly.

See? I'm a perfectly capable mother.

Maybe Willow was actually coming around. Maybe they could start over. Maybe Summer didn't have to ask her to leave and never come back. A tiny sliver of hope emerged from somewhere deep in Summer's subconscious. Then Willow spoke.

"I just don't know why," she said. "I raised you not to be spoiled, and yet you're completely spoiling these kids. You're giving them the impression that the world revolves around them. That poor Hannah is going to think she's a princess the way you buy special snacks for her. Biscuits! When you were teething, I gave you a rib bone. What have any of them done to deserve this? You're raising a whole brood of entitled brats. And you're about to add another one to the mix."

Summer opened her mouth and then closed it. Of course. She'd been right all along. Willow couldn't stay. She was toxic. Irrational and toxic. She couldn't be around Summer's kids or around Summer.

"You have to leave," Summer said. "You can't stay here."

Willow coughed, and a fresh cloud of smoke escaped from between her lips. Her eyes, the exact same shade of blue as Summer's, blinked comically.

"What?" she said.

"I know you heard me," Summer said.

"But I'm their grandmother."

"Being their grandmother by virtue of the fact that you share their genes does not give you the right to come into my house and criticize my parenting."

"Of course it does. It absolutely does. You should know yourself, Summer, that your job as a parent is never done. If, as your mother"—she made an extravagant gesture towards herself with her cigarette—"I believe you're spoiling these children, making a colossal mistake, I might add, and never mind the bar-hopping, it is my duty, as your mother, to say so."

Yes, sending Willow away was absolutely the right thing to do.

Just a moment ago, Summer had questioned her own wisdom. After all, she had spent the past several weeks slowly going crazy. There was the sock-hunting. There was the hand-washing. There were those moments she secretly wished for an illness or a car accident. *And let's not forget the leaving-Hannah-in-the-car incident.*

She may be approaching the very edge of reason, but she hadn't quite reached insanity. She didn't need anyone, especially not someone like Willow, telling her how to parent her children.

"Willow—Mom," Summer said.

Willow smiled, and the split second of camaraderie made her look so pretty Summer almost reconsidered what she was about to say. No, it was best to stay the course, Summer thought. Willow's beauty was that of villains in kids' movies. She was Maleficent, not Mary Poppins.

"Yes?"

"I think it's best if you leave. And I think it's even better if you don't come back."

CHAPTER SIX

Willow had said those exact same words to Summer once. *I think it's best if you leave. And I think it's even better if you don't come back.*

Summer was fifteen. Willow, being the contradiction she was, didn't believe in ear-piercing. She believed in saturating her entire body with bourbon—to the point of poisoning—but definitely not ear-piercing. That was visible.

The topic had never really come up, probably because Willow didn't have her ears pierced and Summer didn't think about wanting earrings until Josie brought it up.

One weekend Summer and Delaney were at Josie's house, sitting on her bed flipping through magazines. Josie pointed out the earrings on a woman in a perfume advertisement and said, "You know, girls, it's a small wonder none of us have our ears pierced yet. Mama said I can get mine done now that I'm fifteen. We should go together."

Josie's mom, Carla, clucking her tongue and hiding a smile, loaded the girls into her car and drove them to the mall. A girl about their own age greeted them with a semi-wicked grin, and it was only then that Summer waffled. Heidi, the girl at the earring shop, had a neat row of piercings all the way from her lobe to the tip of her ear and Summer wondered if this initial trip would be her first step down a slippery slope.

Josie didn't even hesitate. "I'll go first."

She didn't flinch when Heidi pierced her ears, but she did hiss through gritted teeth. When it was done, she admired herself in the mirror, and then made them all laugh by pretending to talk to her crush, Mikey Jones: "Hi, Mikey. How do you like my new earrings? Come a little closer, Romeo."

Delaney went next, and insisted on holding hands with Josie and Summer. They stood on either side of her, and her death grip made Summer's knuckles sore.

She did flinch, jumping once and then again when Heidi pulled the trigger on the piercing gun. Instead of pretending to talk to Mikey Jones, she pretended to make out with the mirror, sighing and groaning until Heidi snatched it back from her.

"Your turn," Delaney and Josie said to Summer, their voices singsongy. With a flourish, Heidi motioned to the chair. Summer cringed.

"I don't know, you guys," she said as she climbed onto the chair.

"I knew we should have made her go first," Josie said to Delaney.

Delaney nodded.

Summer felt slightly offended. "Which one of us stole Mr. Richter's hall pass and hung it in Mrs. Sealy's office when you two were too scared to do it?" (Mr. Richter, the science teacher, used a huge fake spider as a hall pass, and Mrs. Sealy, one of the vice principals, was terrified of spiders. Students had heard screams coming from her office whenever she saw a live one.)

"*You* did that?" Heidi said.

"You're clearly impressed," Summer said. Heidi nodded.

"Yes, I did," Summer said. The girls giggled again, and Summer lifted her chin.

The actual piercing didn't hurt as much as Summer anticipated. A quick poke and it was over. The slow burn and longer-lasting throb were bearable. Heidi took a picture of the three of them, Summer still in the chair and Josie and Delaney leaning in from either side, all three of them puckering their lips.

It never even crossed Summer's mind to think about how Willow would respond. They were just earrings, after all. Most of the girls at school wore them (not just the slutty girls). But when Summer arrived home, flashing her rhinestone studs, Willow flipped out.

Fortunately, because Summer never let Josie and Delaney come inside, they didn't witness the verbal lashing.

Willow sat in her usual place on the couch. Summer pushed open the door. She was so lost in excitement she forgot to close it. She could feel the smile taking up her entire face. Hair in a ponytail to better show off the earrings, she approached the couch. Willow's inebriated state made her swivel ever so slowly toward Summer.

"Notice anything different?" Summer asked, turning her head slightly to one side.

Summer saw Willow notice the earrings. It registered in her eyes and she stood up, hoisting her thin frame off the couch as if she weighed a million pounds instead of a hundred. Squinting, she walked over to Summer, and leaned in close. The scent of bourbon followed her. Willow squinted.

"What have we here?"

Summer's cheeks ached from smiling. "Delaney and Josie and I all went to get our ears pierced. It's Josie's birthday and her mom said she could."

"Did your mom say you could?"

Willow's words were so slow, so perfectly pronounced, that the hairs on the back of Summer's neck stood up.

"No, but—"

"No. That's right."

Willow slapped her hard across the face. Summer's head snapped back and tears immediately stung her eyes.

"You didn't even ask me," Willow said in a voice so deadly quiet Summer backed away, afraid of what she might do next.

"I didn't know," she said. "It's just earrings."

"Just earrings, huh?"

Again, she had said the wrong thing. She continued backing up toward the still-open door. When she stood on the threshold, Willow said, "I think it's best if you leave. And I think it's even better if you don't come back."

Of course, Willow wouldn't get the reference now, almost twenty years after the ear-piercing incident. She was drunk then, and she was probably drunk now. But the words were etched into Summer's memory like tracks on a record.

Willow's evil-pretty smile faded.

"You're asking me to leave?" she said.

"No. I'm telling you to leave."

A beat of silence passed.

"Well, I guess I'll get my purse. This is what I get after years of raising you, of always putting your needs before mine. My own daughter, just putting me out."

Summer rolled her eyes. She had so much to say on that topic. So much. But instead of saying anything, she crossed her arms and waited.

Willow shrugged one bony shoulder. "I guess I'll get my purse."

"WHERE'S YOUR MOM?" Derek asked when he returned to the living room.

"Don't call her that," Summer said. "Call her Willow. She left."

"What?" he said.

"You heard me. She left."

"But why? Things were going so well. She was having fun with the kids. I can't believe she just left."

"I told her to leave," Summer said.

Derek dropped down on the couch next to Summer. "Why?"

Could she explain? Could he understand? He'd grown up in a happy, practically perfect household with happy, practically perfect parents. His mom baked mountains of cupcakes for chess club fundraisers and his dad announced the high school football games. The members of the football team had made up a secret handshake just for William Gray, and they all called, "Gray" in deep voices whenever they saw him on the field or in the halls.

Derek didn't even know what it meant to be let down in the most vital of ways. He lived a charmed life.

Winter must be emerging from her shell. I'm feeling resentful of my own husband.

"You wouldn't understand," Summer said.

Derek exhaled heavily, stood up, and went into the bedroom.

Alone in the living room, Summer wondered whether she'd done the right thing. Derek had such a strong moral compass. He always forgave so quickly, probably because he hadn't been hurt so often, repeatedly broken down. Having Willow here, at this time in

Summer's life, hadn't felt right. It added another stressor. She'd been gone for three minutes and the house already felt calmer.

Just as she was dozing off, Derek came back into the living room and pulled her to her feet. Throughout their fourteen years of marriage, neither one of them had ever slept on the couch. Holding hands, they walked into the bedroom.

Summer fell asleep with her head nuzzled into Derek's neck. This, she thought, is exactly how things should be.

CHAPTER SEVEN

Tuesday night felt just like any other weeknight. Willow's absence had decreased the tension considerably, Summer thought, and her mood felt light as she prepared for her date with Derek.

The doorbell rang, Chuck barked, and everyone scampered to the front door to open it for Delaney and Josie, and Josie's puppy, Delilah, who greeted Chuck by pouncing on him and sending his soft, floppy body rolling across the living room. They knocked Hannah off her feet, surprising her into silence, and Delaney scooped her up before she could start wailing. The boys immediately started sword fighting with Josie, and Sarah lured the puppies into the backyard with treats.

"You look nice," Delaney said to Summer.

"Thanks," Derek said. "I think so, too. I put a lot of time into this outfit."

Summer elbowed him.

"Thanks for doing this, guys," Summer said.

"Are you kidding?" Josie said between slashes of her foam sword. "We couldn't stand to see you so stressed out. *We* need you to relax as much as *you* need you to relax. You're going to send yourself into pre-term labor."

"Where's your mom?" Delaney said. Hannah squirmed in her arms and Delaney set her on the floor. She immediately lifted her arms, asking to be picked back up.

"Gone," Summer said. "And don't call her that."

Delaney and Josie looked at each other, but didn't say anything.

"I saw that," Summer said. "Trust me, we're all better off."

"Aunt Dee," Sarah called from the kitchen table, "I need help with my biology homework."

"I'll do my best," Delaney said. "No promises."

"But you do biology every day of your life," Sarah said. "You're a veterinarian."

"True," Delaney said.

"What are we feeding these hooligans?" Josie asked.

"There's bean stew in the slow cooker," Summer said.

"Dangit," Nate said. "I thought we were having a pizza party."

Summer laughed. "You are. I was just kidding about the bean stew. The delivery guy should be here in ten. There's cash on the counter."

The boys ran off, whooping and hollering, "Pizza!"

Josie tossed her keys to Summer. "Take my car. Just in case we need to rush Nate to the emergency room when I slash his arm off."

Summer shrugged. "Okay."

She'd choose Josie's SUV over her own econo-van any day.

Summer and Derek called, "Bye, kids!" and Summer felt like skipping out to the car.

When Josie shut the front door behind them, Derek turned around and pressed Summer up against it. She giggled, but stopped right away when she saw the intensity in his expression. With his hands on either side of her head, he leaned in for a kiss. It started out slow and gentle, but heated right up to steamy after a few seconds. When he pulled away, Summer laughed a little breathlessly. "It's been a while, hasn't it?" she said.

"Man, I feel like that was our first kiss all over again. Remember how long I waited for that?"

"Oh, I remember," she said. "You weren't the only one waiting. And now we're not the only ones waiting for dinner. This baby's hungry."

The baby opted for The Red Lantern, as Summer's babies always did in utero. She couldn't get past the craving for cashew chicken and fortune cookies.

"So why did you make Willow leave?" Derek said when they were seated.

"I notice you waited until we actually got here before you started interrogating me." The server brought them water, and Summer was grateful for the interruption. "Ready to order?" Summer said.

They ordered, Derek watching Summer carefully the entire time. When the server walked away, Summer said, "Let's not talk about that tonight, okay? This is supposed to be a fun, relaxing evening. No pressure. Willow ruined my entire childhood. She absolutely does not need to ruin this date night."

Derek nodded. "Okay," he said. "Okay. Do you think Delaney and Josie would notice if we didn't come home tonight? We could get a hotel room."

He waggled his eyebrows at her, and she giggled.

"That kiss really got to you, didn't it?"

He waggled his eyebrows again.

Wow, I didn't realize how badly I needed this.

"So do you remember our first kiss?" Derek said.

The server returned with bowls of egg drop soup, and Summer blushed.

"Of course I do," she said. "How could I not?"

"True."

"You were so nervous."

"It was my first kiss!" Derek said a little too loudly. They both flinched at the volume, and then laughed.

"We went to the lake that day," Summer said.

"I do remember," Derek said. "I remember quite clearly."

"You had just gotten your license, and you were so nervous about driving. Or so I thought."

"But I was really nervous about kissing you. I'd decided. That was the day I'd kiss you. I had a license, I had a girl. All I needed was a kiss."

"That's what you were thinking?"

Derek nodded. "Yep."

"You entered into manhood that day, my love," Summer said.

"No, I didn't do that for a few more months. Until that night at the drive-in."

"I am scandalized. Truly."

"You were, then. And your current state proves you have been ever since."

Summer snorted. "Proving your manhood time and time again."

Delaney and Josie were right: dating her husband was a must. After dinner, Summer felt relaxed. Calm. Maybe even a bit frisky.

They drove home in Josie's car, the windows down and rock music blasting. Tomorrow Summer had to visit with the pediatric heart specialist, but for tonight, she pushed her fears aside and enjoyed her husband. He looked over at her and grinned, then took her hand and kissed it. They could handle anything, she thought, as long as they were together.

After thanking Delaney and Josie profusely and seeing them out, Summer and Derek got ready for bed.

"It's so nice having the kids in bed already," Summer said.

"We should really do that more often," Derek said.

"True," Summer said. "We always say that, but we should really do it."

Derek turned back the covers and then came around to Summer's side of the bed and began massaging her shoulders.

"Want a massage?" he said.

"Like, a massage? Or a mas*sage*?"

He kissed her neck and she shivered.

"The latter," he said.

"I would love one," she said.

CHAPTER EIGHT

WEDNESDAY MORNING, SUMMER WOKE UP FEELING SICK AND IRRITABLE. Because the heart specialist was a specialist, she'd had to take the appointment time they gave her, which meant she was stuck taking Hannah with her. Not that she minded, but Hannah would undoubtedly be walking all over the office, eating the pages of waiting room magazines and anything else she could get her grubby little fists on.

Of course, Derek left for work before the kids even got up, and the morning routine wasn't routine at all. Or it was, if Summer considered the lost socks, lost shoes, lack of clean clothes and complaining about going to summer camp.

"You don't know what camp is like for me," Nate said. "Or else you wouldn't make me go."

"Mo-om," Luke said. "I don't have any clean jeans."

Summer felt like yelling, "You're lucky you even get to go to camp! I had to fend for myself! And I just washed eight loads of laundry yesterday. Don't tell me you don't have any clean jeans!"

But she didn't.

She managed to keep it together (and by keep it together, she thought, she meant that she didn't eat any of her young) until she pulled through the camp's drop-off driveway, but as soon as she watched her kids walk away, Sarah's hand on Luke's shoulder to guide him through the gate and Nate, who always ran ahead, waiting patiently for them so they could walk into the building together, she lost it.

What if Luke did need surgery? What if his condition was permanent? What if he died on the table? What if he died after surgery because of a blood clot or an infection or those other mysterious complications? She hated that word, complications. Her life was a complication.

She tried to calm herself with yoga breathing and gentle reminders that she had no control over this situation, but panic set in, an inflating balloon in her chest. The appointment wasn't for another hour, so Summer had to wait. She hated waiting. Driving around in this condition certainly wasn't prudent, so she went to the little coffee shop down the street.

"The usual, Mrs. Gray?"

Summer flinched. She hadn't even realized she'd walked inside.

"Are you okay?" Eddie, the kid who worked the espresso machine every Wednesday morning, peered at Summer from behind the register, his brow wrinkled in concern.

"I'm fine," Summer said, hoping her smile cut down on the angry tone of her voice.

"Why are you handing me a diaper?"

"Shit."

Summer stuffed the diaper back into her purse and rummaged around for her wallet.

"You know what? Coffee's on me today. And Hannah's granola bar."

"Oh, Eddie." Summer felt the beginnings of a big cry, so she thanked him and rushed outside to the patio. Hannah immediately climbed atop the ride-on horse and began bouncing.

Eddie delivered Summer's decaf latte and gave her arm a gentle squeeze.

"You're going to make a great husband one day," she said to him, patting his hand.

He made a show of bolting, and she managed a smile. Hannah kept bouncing. And bouncing. The squeaking of the horse's springs put Summer into a kind of trance, and she sipped her latte, repeating the silent mantra, *inhale, exhale.*

The time passed so slowly Summer felt like she was in a parallel universe. Or a fishbowl. She sat at the little table, her legs crossed, and her foot bouncing and shaking in a way that would drive her crazy if someone else was doing it. She checked her phone compulsively, every minute or even more frequently.

Hannah bounced.

Eight forty-five finally rolled around, and she gathered Hannah off the horse and carried her to the car.

"Let's go see what the doctor has to say," she said to her daughter.

"Dr. Tippy Toes?"

Why did even that make her want to cry?

THE HEART SPECIALIST obviously made a lot of money. Dollar signs flashed in Summer's mind and she hated herself for thinking that way. If Luke needed heart surgery, how would she and Derek afford it? She winced when she noticed the real leather chairs lined up along the walls, and dug a wipe out of her purse to clean Hannah's hands before she could slime the cushions.

A table in the corner held a single serve coffeemaker, but apparently the office staff didn't stock decaf. Summer sighed. Not that she really needed any more coffee. She just wanted something to do with her hands. Celebrity gossip magazines covered the surfaces of another small table, but Summer knew she'd just get angry reading speculation about romantic feuds and plastic surgery. Did any of that crap really matter? She sat down and tapped her fingers on her legs while Hannah ran from one end of the room to another shouting, "Tippy Toes!" over and over.

Fortunately, no one else was in the waiting room at the moment, and the evil Winter had the audacity to suggest that perhaps it was because all of this doctor's patients had died. After what seemed like hours, a nurse opened the door and called Summer's name. She stood up, briefly wondered where Hannah was, and then sighed with relief when she realized she was hiding under a chair.

They walked through a labyrinth to a fancy conference room so sterile-looking and dust-free Summer felt like she'd entered another dimension. The nurse told her the doctor would be just a moment, and closed the door behind her. Summer pictured her own house, cluttered and dusty, footprints on the cabinets and handprints on the floor.

How could this doctor even understand her? How could he understand where she was coming from? How worried she was? Hannah seemed to sense Summer's anxiety and climbed onto her lap.

Someone knocked gently on the door, just two taps, and then opened it. Before Summer could finish her thought about why someone would knock on a door inside his own office, she felt her train of thought screech to a surprise-induced halt. The doctor was a woman. A woman not much older than herself. Tall, with chocolate-colored hair and bright green eyes.

"I'm Doctor Karlsen," she said, holding out a hand to shake. Summer noticed her short, square fingernails were quite clean.

"Summer Gray," Summer said.

"Are you okay?" Dr. Karlsen asked.

"I'm f—no. I'm not okay."

"Freaked out, right?"

"Right," Summer said. She heard the waver in her own voice and swallowed it.

Instead of walking around the conference table and sitting opposite Summer, Dr. Karlsen sat in the chair next to Summer's and smiled at Hannah. When Hannah squealed, the doctor grinned at her before returning her attention to Summer.

"I get it," she said. "I'm a mom, too. I'm not going to patronize you with cliché phrases like 'don't worry, it'll be fine,' and 'I've done a million heart surgeries,' because Luke is your baby. Yes, he needs surgery." She didn't pause to let the news sink in, but instead plowed ahead. "He has a congenital defect on one of his valves and it needs to be replaced. If we don't replace it, he could go into cardiac arrest. But I want you to know he's going to be in good hands, okay? Yes, he needs surgery. But the good news is that a valve replacement is a routine procedure with very little risk for complication."

"But, I mean, it's open heart surgery, right?"

The doctor nodded. "It is, yes."

"How many have you done?"

"Hundreds."

Summer had hundreds of questions, which she asked, and Dr. Karlsen answered them all thoroughly, calmly and patiently.

"Think about it this way," the doctor said. "This surgery, now, when he's healthy, gives us more control over the situation. If he doesn't have the surgery now, he'll go into cardiac arrest at some point. You won't know when. Then we're playing catch up, being reactionary. The surgery keeps us ahead of the game. By being proactive, we maintain control. He's fine and the heart works great. The reward outweighs the risk by a long shot."

Summer nodded. When they both stood, Hannah on Summer's hip, Dr. Karlsen opened her arms for a hug. Hannah patted her shoulder, making Summer smile.

"My staff will schedule the surgery, okay? Brittany, at the front desk, will call you. When are you due, by the way? I guess we should schedule around that, right?"

Maybe this fancy specialist *would* understand.

"Next week," Summer said.

"It's your third?" Dr. Karlsen said.

"Fifth."

"Oh, my! And I thought two were a handful."

Summer laughed. "Two are a handful. Three are two handsful. Anything after that is icing on the cake."

"All right. Well, I'll talk to Brittany and make sure she schedules it a few weeks out, to give you some time to recover."

Summer shrugged. "Having us both in the hospital at once would be helpful for visitors."

Summer walked back to the car with a new sense of calm about Luke's surgery. Hannah babbled happily in her arms, and continued pointing out colors—of flowers, the sky, the leaves on the trees—as Summer buckled her into the carseat.

Derek answered his phone on the first ring.

"So he does need the surgery," Summer said without preamble. "He has a congenital defect on one of his valves, so that valve needs to be replaced. The doctor says it's pretty routine and complications are rare."

She exhaled, waiting for a response. When she didn't get one, she realized Derek was crying.

Just when I was feeling this amazing sense of peace.

"I know," she said. "It's scary. But I really liked this doctor, Derek. She's a mom, too. She—"

"The fact that she's a mom doesn't mean she's any good at what she does," Derek said.

"No, of course not. You're right. But she understands our anxiety. She answered all of the questions we came up with. Very thoroughly, too. It seems like she knows what she's doing."

"It seems like it? I mean, did you actually get, like, I don't know, a success rate from her or something?"

"No, Derek. I trusted her as soon as I saw her."

"You trusted her based on how she looks?"

Usually, she'd joke that she trusted Dr. Karlsen based on "The Vibe," the metric by which she judged all people within seconds of meeting them. And Derek would say something like, "Oh, the mysterious vibe." She'd say, "It's very accurate, too."

But today wasn't the day to joke about The Vibe. So she bit her tongue, even though Winter wanted to tell him, *You didn't even meet her. You weren't even there.*

A startling thought flitted into Summer's consciousness: Winter was showing up at all the wrong times.

"You're right," she said instead. "Evaluating someone's appearance is not the best method for determining a heart surgeon's level of ability. But she comes highly recommended by Dr. Tippy Toes, and she seemed very knowledgable. We can get a second opinion if you like, but Dr. T. heard the heart murmur and he thought it was a valve problem, which is exactly what Dr. Karlsen says it is. So their diagnoses match. They did the scan and everything, too."

As she justified her trust in Dr. Karlsen, Summer began to feel resentful. Derek hadn't come to the appointment. She'd told him she could handle it, and he had just agreed. He'd even said something about trusting her, something exactly like, "I trust you." Yet, he didn't want to trust her analysis of the surgeon. He should be reassuring her, not questioning her.

"If you're so concerned about it, why didn't you come to the appointment with me so you could grill her yourself, get her success rate, ask her to pledge Luke's survival on the life of her own first-born?" Summer said.

She stomped on the brake pedal, jerked the van into reverse, and backed out of the parking spot without looking, nearly hitting a light pole and then slamming on the brakes again. Then, shaking from adrenaline, she drove slowly out of the parking lot.

"You know I couldn't. I can't take time off work, yet, especially if I'm going to have to take time off for the actual surgery."

"Then you should trust me to make the decisions based on what I learn at the appointments."

"Touché. You're right. I'm sorry. I'm just stressed."

The light at the intersection of Birch and Pinecone Roads turned red, and Summer put her forehead on the steering wheel. They were both stressed. She knew it was stupid to get upset with Derek. He had the right to ask questions.

Summer wondered for the briefest second whether their marriage would make it through this. Her own rational mind said it would. Winter, though, her teeth bared, said it wouldn't. A child's illness often pushed his parents apart, to opposite edges of the plane of mental stability.

Another driver honked. Summer jumped, noticed the light had turned green, and accelerated with extra caution.

CHAPTER NINE

After her appointment with Dr. Karlsen and the subsequent argument with Derek, Summer picked the kids up from summer camp early. She'd decided to take them for ice cream to tell them about Luke's impending surgery. The fact that Luke handled the news so well only made her feel worse. He had no idea what could happen. He had no idea these next few weeks could be the last weeks of his life.

He just sat there in the booth at the ice cream parlor, his blue eyes —identical to hers—blinking a few times before he nodded. "Okay," he said. "Can we go home and sword fight now?"

Summer nodded, gathered up the kids and drove them home, where the anxiety of the past couple of weeks took over yet again.

She had begun to see everything as a hazard. She locked Chuck in his dog crate so he wouldn't trip the kids. She overcooked the meat at dinner to ensure she killed any bacteria it harbored. She washed the bedsheets every day, on the hottest setting.

Without telling Derek, because she knew he'd think she had lost her mind, she set up the baby monitor in the boys' bedroom so she could listen to Luke breathe at night. She hid the speaker under her pillow and turned it up to full volume after Derek fell asleep. Now, in the bedroom folding laundry, she could hear Nate and Luke talking in their bedroom.

"Are you scared?" Nate asked.

"Nah," Luke said. "I mean, Mom says the lady is a good doctor. And I'm a tough kid, so."

Luke often ended his sentences with, "so," and a shrug. She pictured him now, probably sitting on his bed loading a gun with foam darts, his fingernails dirty (she should really scrub them to make sure he didn't transfer bacteria to his immune system) and the afternoon sunlight making his blonde hair white.

Hannah's birth had unseated Luke as the youngest, but Summer still thought of him as her baby. She burst into tears again, then laid down on the bed and buried her face in the pillow.

Of course, Winter chose that moment to pipe up: *You should be scrubbing the kitchen counters right now, not crying into your pillow. Get yourself together, woman.*

"You're right," Summer said. "I should be scrubbing the counters. Why haven't I done that yet?"

She heaved herself off the bed and blew her nose.

The kitchen counters were a breeding ground for bacteria. Before she could scrub them, she had to empty them off. For some reason, her children (and her dear husband) thought the counters should serve as the dumping grounds for anything they didn't know what to do with.

"Kids! Come into the kitchen, please!"

For once, they listened immediately, probably because she'd let them come home early from camp and also because she'd fed them ice cream. For once, they did as she asked right away, and carried their various things to their bedrooms. Sarah had left a few books on the counter, and the boys had stashed their ninja throwing stars there. Hannah couldn't reach the counter, but someone (probably Derek) had set some of her ponies down next to the throwing stars.

Even though the kids didn't complain about the quick clean-up, Summer felt herself growing increasingly irritated with all of them, and with Derek, too. Why couldn't they just put stuff away? Didn't they realize she was going to have to clean it all up later? Or force them to do it? By the time Derek walked in the door on Wednesday night, she was hankering for a fight.

"How was your day?" he said.

Winter piped up inside Summer's head, listing every event of Summer's own day, including diaper changes and bathroom breaks.

Although the words didn't come out of Summer's mouth, Derek looked increasingly frightened of what she'd say. Summer knew Winter was out of control, but it felt good to imagine ticking these items off on a long list.When Winter got to the counter-scrubbing, adding "but only after having everyone come in here and pick up the gazillion pieces of junk they'd left on the counter, for some inexplicable reason," Summer sighed.

"It was fine."

As if he could read her mind, Derek said, "I'm sorry you had a rough day. And I'm sorry you had to go to the surgeon's office by yourself. Okay? I thought I was doing the right thing by staying at work. But obviously I wasn't. I know you're stressed. But remember, we're in this together."

Summer reached out for her husband, and just like that, Winter dissolved like an apparition.

That night, Summer laid awake all night listening to Luke's breathing on the baby monitor. Because Derek was covering an early shift for a co-worker, he left before sunrise. Summer got out of bed feeling like a zombie and wanting nothing more than to stay home with her kids.

JOSIE TEXTED Summer before she'd even fed the kids breakfast: *Don't go to Rowdy's tonight. We have a surprise for you. We'll pick you up at 4.*

I can't go anyway, Summer had texted back. It seemed more important than ever to spend time with the kids.

You're going, Josie had responded. *Don't try to get out of it. You need it. See you at 4.*

Between crying jags and loose laundry collection, Summer spent the next several hours wondering what Josie and Delaney were up to. Surely they weren't taking her to some strip club before the baby's arrival. They couldn't be. Or, maybe they were. It'd be a nice change of pace. A little lap dance from a thong-clad guy with a six-pack never hurt anyone.

The doorbell rang at exactly four p.m. Summer barely heard it over the vacuum. Derek had taken the kids outside, and she'd put some tamale pie in the slow cooker for dinner before returning to her frenzied cleaning.

Summer had forgotten Josie and Delaney were coming. She glanced down at her outfit and realized she'd have to change. Hannah had smeared oatmeal on her shoulder and oh, geez, how had she not noticed that coffee stain on her right boob? She grimaced, then shrugged, then grimaced again when she caught a whiff of her body odor.

Delaney and Josie would just have to wait while she freshened up. They'd understand, in large part because they wouldn't want to be seen with her looking or smelling like this.

The sudden silence when she turned off the vacuum left her ears ringing. She pushed a strand of greasy hair out of her face and went to open the front door. Was she even wearing a bra? Nope.

Before she reached for the doorknob, the door swung open. Summer stepped back and yelped in surprise. It wasn't Delaney and Josie. It was Willow. She gave Summer a once-over before breezing in.

"Honey, you look like a mess. I hope it's okay I just opened the door. I rang the bell but no one answered it for quite some time. What are you doing in here? It's a disaster."

The high heels gave her back end a little sway and Summer stood back to watch Willow's ridiculous sunhat cruise through the living room. Summer's mind played her a recap of all the scrubbing, wiping, scraping and vacuuming she'd done all day. Willow should be wearing white gloves and trailing a finger along every surface, testing for dust. Summer wrung her hands.

I'm wringing my hands.

She dropped them at her sides.

"Did Derek—did I—did someone invite you over?"

"No, honey! Heavens, no. You made it clear you didn't want me here. But it seems as though you need me. And you know, I got to thinking."

She's going to apologize. Finally. After all these years.

Summer's heart beat faster. What would Willow say? Would she apologize for the drinking? For ignoring Summer for years? For leaving Summer next to the cantaloupe?

"This is the perfect time for me to be here. To spend time with the kids. I can help with them when you have this baby. God, you must be getting close."

An apology was too much to hope for, apparently.

"Willow—"

"Mom. Call me Mom, honey."

"Look, I—"

The doorbell rang. Summer didn't know whether to laugh or cry.

Why couldn't they have arrived just five minutes earlier? Summer would have evacuated as quickly as possible, and never would have known about Willow's impromptu visit.

This time, she expected the door to open before she answered it. Delaney and Josie never bothered waiting. Sure enough, they walked right in. They looked so much like angels Summer's breath caught. The afternoon sun made Delaney's hair golden, and Josie's skin radiant. Josie had her head tilted back as she laughed at something Delaney said.

When they saw Willow, they stopped. Froze.

"Is this—" Delaney said.

"Your mom! It's your mom!" Josie said. "It's about time! We get to meet your mom!"

"Dead ringer!" Delaney said. "You guys look exactly the same."

Summer shrugged.

"Guys, this is Willow. Willow, this is Delaney, and this is Josie. Willow was just leaving."

"I was?" she said to Summer. Then she turned to Delaney and Josie. "I wasn't, actually. It's so nice to meet you, girls. I can't say I've heard anything about you, but…"

"Woman, you need a shower!" Josie said.

Summer nodded, and rushed out of the room. As she did, she heard Delaney ask, "So how long are you in town for?"

Fifteen minutes later, Summer reemerged in a pair of capri pants and a bright blue tank top that made her look less like a circus tent than any of the other maternity tops she owned.

"Wow. You look—" Willow said.

"Much better," Josie said. "We've just been having such a nice chat with your mom!"

Summer refrained from rolling her eyes.

I'll bet.

"But now we have to go," Delaney said. "We have an appointment."

"Shall we see you out?" Josie asked Willow.

Willow looked at Summer with some misguided sense that Summer would ask her to stay. Summer looked away. With that, the girls ushered both Willow and Summer out of the house.

"You know, it must be a shock for her, seeing me pregnant. And not only pregnant, but really pregnant," Summer told the girls as Josie pulled away from the house. "It's the fifth time, and I must say, I'm bigger than ever."

Josie reached across the center console to pat Summer's knee. Her elbow hit Summer's belly. "Sorry, baby," she said.

They all giggled.

"So that was awkward," Delaney said. "What was up with that?"

"I have no idea," Summer said. "She just showed up. Can we talk about something else? Thinking about Willow is raising my stress levels. What's with this mysterious appointment? Is it too much to admit I was hoping we were going to a strip club for a lap dance?"

"I wouldn't subject my new nieces or nephews to that," Josie said.

Delaney rubbed her belly. "Jake and I are going to buy a house," she said.

Summer closed her eyes and leaned her head back on the seat, grateful for the distraction.

"That's great. Did you guys find one you agree on?"

"Well, no," Delaney said. "Not exactly. But I was thinking we could go look after this."

"Where are we going?" Summer asked again.

"Mani-pedis, Mama," Josie said. "We can't have your nails looking like that in the delivery room."

"I can't even see those puppies. Are they bad?"

"The worst," Delaney said.

Summer grimaced. She hadn't even thought about her toenails. "Thank goodness you guys are looking after me. You're such good friends. And then we're going house hunting?"

"Yeah," Delaney said. "If you're up to it."

"I'm up for anything," Summer said. "Where do you want to

look? I love your neighborhood. Maybe just find something a little bigger around there?"

"That's what I was thinking," Delaney said. "But Jake loves being downtown."

"You practically are downtown," Josie said. "I mean, like, a hop, skip and a jump."

"I know. But he's right downtown. You know?"

Josie muttered something about men in Spanish, and Summer grinned as she drifted off to sleep.

She jerked awake when Josie parked at the curb in front of the nail salon. She'd almost rather stay in the car and sleep than worry about her toenails. But she had to do this, for Josie and Delaney.

"Your hands are dry. Really dry," the manicurist snapped when Summer finally settled on a folding chair that hurt her back and cut into her legs, making her ankles swell.

"I know," Summer said, trying to stifle a yawn. "I was cleaning all day."

"You should not be cleaning right now. Chemicals hurt the baby."

Winter's hackles rose. Of course she wasn't using chemicals. "I use vinegar," she said. "Totally safe."

It was a good thing they were here, Summer thought. Her fingernails were in bad shape. The feeling of the manicurist rubbing her forearms and fingers nearly put her to sleep again.

"Why were you cleaning all day?" Delaney asked from across the room where she sat in a massaging chair, her feet in a tub of warm water. She set her magazine on her lap and Summer laughed at the perplexed look on her face.

"Nesting," the manicurist said.

All the women in the nail salon nodded, some of them making "mmhmm" noises.

"Weird. Will I do that, too?" Delaney wanted to know.

They all nodded again.

"I guess I need a house to nest in."

"We'll find you one," Josie said. "Just give me a mission. I'm on it. You won't be homeless when you give birth."

Delaney and Summer laughed, but stopped immediately when one of the nail techs glared at them. They spent the rest of their appointment in near-silence.

"I do feel so much better," Summer said a half-hour later when they stood on the sidewalk admiring their toenails. "Thanks, you guys."

The girls squeezed her in a quick hug. "You'e welcome."

"Now. House hunting?" Josie said.

"Let's eat dinner, first," Summer said. "I'm starving. I think I forgot to eat lunch today."

"Did you eat breakfast?" Josie's tone was conversational, but Summer could hear the edge underneath it.

"I think so," Summer lied. "Come on. Let's go."

Summer knew she hadn't eaten breakfast, but she felt guilty enough about it without having Josie chastise her. And anyway, she was eating now, right?

AFTER DINNER, the girls met the real estate agent, a tiny gnome of a man with slicked-back hair and short fingers who claimed his name was Jack Jackson, at one of the houses on Delaney's short list.

"See?" Delaney said as the four of them stood in the living room. "This is perfect. It's perfect. But Jake would hate it. The rooms are too small and the ceilings are too low."

The house, a Victorian just a few blocks down from Delaney's current home, was apparently a few blocks in the wrong direction. It was farther from the heart of downtown than Jake would like. According to Delaney, though, it had everything: three bedrooms, a yard for the puppy, Sweetie, and a big tree out front where they could hang a baby swing.

"Would he *really* hate it?" Josie asked. "Or just the location?"

Jack Jackson piped up: "The location is perfect!"

Josie rolled her eyes. Jack Jackson's phone rang, and he held up a finger and stepped outside.

Delaney sighed. "I don't know. We can't agree on anything. The houses he likes are all sharp corners and stainless steel. Hardly the kinds of places to bring a baby home to."

Summer laughed. "Look at her body language," she said to Josie. "So dejected. You'll find something, Delaney. It just might take a while."

"Well, we only have, like, a month!" Delaney gestured to her belly.

"You know, finding a house after the baby's born wouldn't be the end of the world," Summer said. "He or she won't be crawling around for at least six months, so you don't have to worry about those sharp edges right away."

"What about nesting?" Delaney wanted to know.

"You can nest anywhere," Josie said. "It's just cleaning and stuff. Right, Summer?"

Summer nodded. "It's true. We can keep looking, but maybe you should just resign yourself to finding a house when the baby is a few months old. Just relax and let the Universe take care of it."

You should take your own advice, Winter whispered.

"Maybe," Delaney said. "It's something to think about, anyway. I just feel anxious about this."

"Well, let's go look at the last house on your list," Summer said. "Where did that guy get to?"

"Who, Jack Jackson?" Josie said.

Summer snickered as they walked outside to find him.

The next house stood just a block from downtown—definitely within walking distance of the square and the fountain.

"But I feel like it's too small," Delaney whined. "I mean, the third bedroom is practically a broom closet."

"Okay," Summer said. "You know I love you, but you're being kind of a baby about this. The houses you're looking at? They're perfect for raising a baby. You should see the trailers I grew up in. Crappy, falling down, leaky roofs. It's a house. It has four walls and, according to the listing, a brand new roof. You're making much ado about nothing."

Josie gave Summer a strange look—equal parts perplexed and annoyed—and said, as if Summer hadn't spoken at all, "That could be Jake's office."

Summer noticed a twinge in her belly, and rubbed it with her thumb. It didn't go away. It figured. She *would* go into labor in a stranger's house. This entire pregnancy had been like that.

First, Derek had lost his job practically at the same time as she was peeing on the pregnancy test. Then, he'd gotten a new, demanding job that kept him away from the house during her entire first trimester, when it was all she could do to keep from living in the bathroom, draped over the toilet. Then Luke had started having weird symptoms, saying it felt like he had a moth in his chest.

Her uterus tightened at that thought. Definitely the start of labor.

"You've been acting weird all afternoon," Josie said to her then. "And you just made a weird noise."

"Have I?" Summer said. "And did I?"

"Yes, and yes," Delaney said. "What's going on?"

At that moment, Summer's water broke.

For the first time ever, it was a huge gush. All over the floor of this adorable house's living room. The carpeted floor. All three of them stood there, Delaney and Josie staring at Summer and Summer looking down at the soggy carpet. Why hadn't Summer thought to carry a jar of pickles with her?

Delaney clapped a hand over her mouth.

"*Dios mío*," Josie whispered.

"What the hell are we going to do?" Delaney said.

Summer stood there, her arms raised in an *I-don't-know* gesture. The grandfather clock ticked loudly.

"Oh, my," Summer said after a long silence. "Oh, my."

"I'll call the exterminators," Josie said.

Summer laughed then, loudly. She put one hand on her belly, one on her forehead, and cackled. "Well, I never."

She knew she should feel embarrassed that she'd just made a huge mess in a stranger's house. She thought she should feel guilty for taking the attention off of Delaney's house hunt. But all she could feel at the moment was relief. Finally, a trip to the hospital. A break. Two days alone.

"Do you want me to take you to the hospital?" Josie said.

Summer wanted to jump up and down, to scream like her teenage self and throw herself at Josie's feet, begging to be taken to the hospital. But she needed her hospital bag, and the package of chocolate chip cookies she'd stashed at the bottom. The package she planned to eat, all by herself. With some reluctance, she said, "Not yet. Just take me home."

Josie nodded. "Let me call a cleaning service."

The real estate agent came back inside, saw the scene, froze and walked back outside. Josie made the call, and Delaney guided Summer out to the car.

"You stay here," Josie said to Jack Jackson on the way out. "The cleaners are on the way."

He didn't answer.

All three of the girls laughed like lunatics as they drove away.

CHAPTER TEN

THE CONTRACTIONS CAME ON STRONG. SUMMER KNEW THIS BABY WOULD come fast. When they arrived at her house, she grabbed her hospital bag and handed Josie and Delaney the minute-by-minute schedule she'd typed out for the kids. She climbed into the van.

"Are you ready?" Derek asked, squeezing her thigh and grinning at her before backing out of the driveway.

"Do I have a choice?" she said.

His laugh, nervous and excited at the same time, made her smile. He put the car in Drive and she rolled down the window. A ribbon of her hair escaped and fluttered in the breeze.

"You're so beautiful. I'm so happy you're the mother of my children," he said.

Although his words made her feel unreasonably emotional, she said, "Don't get all mushy on me. I've got to push a baby out."

They held hands the rest of the way to the hospital, where Summer fell onto the bed with a deep sense of relief.

"This is what I've been hoping for," she said to Derek as the nurse strapped the monitors around her body.

"You knew it was inevitable, right? You've done this four times before."

"No, not the labor and delivery, smartass," Summer said. "The vacation."

Derek quirked an eyebrow, and the nurse laughed.

"I hear you, honey. Sometimes getting a few nights' rest in a hospital is exactly what you need, even if you gotta give birth to do it."

Derek didn't answer, but shook his head. Summer couldn't tell whether he was amused or disturbed. She chose not to open the door on that conversation. One tiny crack and all the stress and anxiety could come pouring out.

"I love the hospital bag," Derek said when the nurse left. "It's the only time I get to eat salt and vinegar potato chips. Want anything?"

Summer laughed. "My junk foodie, reformed, until he relapses when we hit L and D. No, thanks. I packed cookies but I'll have some later. I'm going to take a little nap. With my beautiful toenails."

As she drifted back and forth between consciousness and sleep, Summer half-dreamed, significant moments rising to the surface like bubbles.

There was the first time she saw Derek in a pair of Wranglers. Not coincidentally, they'd had sex for the first time that same evening. The weather was brutally hot, so hot it seemed like the air was sweating. She rode her bike up to his house, and he didn't hear her approach.

Those Wranglers hugged his backside, and his bare back looked so muscular, especially as covered with sweat as it was, that she couldn't help but stare. She forgot she was riding her bike, and the front tire hit a piece of firewood that hadn't made it to the wood pile. The impact launched her over the handlebars, and she landed flat on her back.

Of course, the sound of the crash was enough to get Derek's attention, and he turned around just in time to see her flipping through the air. As she laid there on her back, blinking into the hot, blinding sun, he stood over her, looking like some kind of god.

"Wow," she breathed.

He'd laughed then, a loud, raucous laugh that made her fall in love with him that very instant. Then he'd pulled her to her feet, kissed her gently on the mouth, and picked up her bike.

Now, a decade and-a-half—and five children—later, the nurse came in to check her, and smiled. "You'll have this baby in your arms within the hour."

Summer nodded and looked over at Derek, who was watching

her, staring right at her, his open book apparently forgotten on his lap.

He's so damn sexy. I wonder whatever happened to those Wranglers.

She smiled at him and fell back into her half-conscious state.

There was the moment Summer realized she couldn't allow herself to care whether Willow was in her life. She wouldn't care. She refused to.

It was the day Summer and Derek shared their first kiss. Summer came home jubilant. She could feel her own skin glowing, her body pulsing with this new, sparkly, magical feeling. He kissed her once more at the front door, his fingertips resting above the ear behind which he'd just tucked a strand of her hair.

She wanted to laugh and cry and dance all at the same time. So when she walked through the door after watching him drive away, she felt like she might burst if she didn't tell someone. Naturally, Willow was the first person she wanted to tell.

But Willow was only half-coherent. She laid on the couch, eyes mostly closed. So Summer did an about face and walked right out the door. She rode her bike to Josie's house. Josie called Delaney, and Josie's mom, Carla, made them all cookies while Summer talked nonstop about Derek and the kiss.

She wanted, more than anything, for her own mother to make her cookies and sit across the table from her, eyes twinkling with empathy and excitement and amusement and probably memories, too. But it was at that moment, when Carla reached over and squeezed her hand, that Summer knew she had to stop relying on Willow for anything.

A mother's impact on her children isn't in the big moments, Summer thought then. It's in the small moments. Summer didn't care if Willow showed up at chess tournaments or bought her that first box of tampons. She didn't care if her mom walked her into school on the first day or even sat in the audience at high school graduation.

But she craved her mother's attention like Derek's goat, Poppy, craved petting. She wanted her mother to ask how her day was, to get to know her best friends, to sit and talk after school or watch movies on the weekends.

But just like Poppy bumped her head up against someone's hip over and over again without getting the reaction she wanted, Summer continually bumped against Willow's disinterest. Didn't all mothers fail their children somehow?

Summer came back into full consciousness wondering how she would fail this new baby, and all her other children.

When Sarah, Nate, Luke, Hannah and this new baby had their own families, what would they recall about her parenting? Probably that she never let them drink soda. Or that she made them eat raw carrots rather than potato chips.

"What will they remember about me?" she asked Derek.

"That you loved them."

He always said the right things.

THE BABY WAS BORN at seven fifty-nine p.m.

She came out screaming and bright pink, and Summer blinked back tears of laughter at the intensity of her new daughter's emotions.

"It's so nice to meet you out here," she said to the baby, who quieted the moment the nurse set her on Summer's chest.

Derek leaned over to look at the baby, and Summer shifted her so he could see her face. "She's so beautiful," he whispered, kissing first Summer's forehead and then the baby's. "What shall we name her?"

"Xena, Warrior Princess?" Summer said.

"She has the lungs for it," one of the nurses said.

Summer tucked the blanket under the baby's chin so she could see her face. She had Sarah's pointy ears and Nate's cat-like eyes.

"How about Olivia?" Derek said.

"That's cute," Summer said. "I'll think on it."

When the nurses left, Derek sat down in his chair with a huge sigh.

"Wow. It's almost like *you* just gave birth," Summer said.

He laughed. "I don't know why, I was nervous this time. I'm always a little nervous, but you've been acting so ... I don't know, so strangely."

Shit. "I have?"

"Cleaning the grout on the kitchen counters with your fingertip?

Scraping it with your fingernails? You don't usually do that stuff, even when you're nesting."

"I did that?" Summer knew she'd done it. She'd been so disgusted when she realized she could scrape a yellowish film off the grout even after spraying the crap out of it with her vinegar cleaner and wiping it until the paper towels disintegrated. She couldn't bring a new baby home to that yellow film. And she certainly couldn't bring a heart surgery patient home to that yellow film. She didn't say any of this to Derek, though. He'd think she was crazy.

"See?" he said.

"I'm fine," Summer said. "Just a bit anxious lately, that's all. Just keeping the germs down."

"Well, I've still got an eye on you," Derek said. He stood up. "Do you think I can hold that baby now?"

"I suppose."

She transferred the swaddled, sleeping baby into Derek's arms and he returned to his chair. "Olivia. Do you like that name?" He waited for a moment, and then looked up at Summer. "She said yes."

"I like it, too," Summer said.

They sat in silence for a while, Derek staring at the baby's face and Summer staring at the two of them. She wondered what the kids would think of the baby. Sarah would undoubtedly fawn over her, wanting to hold her and pointing out every little thing she did as, "like, the cutest thing *ever*."

The boys would be ambivalent until she could sword fight. They'd only just taken an interest in Hannah. She smiled as she pictured Hannah toddling around, waving a sword that was longer than she was tall.

Not for the first time, guilt made a sneaky appearance. Throughout this pregnancy, she had repeatedly questioned whether having another child was the right choice. Five was a lot. With four, each parent could wrangle two children. But five? Wow.

Although, Summer thought, Sarah was practically self-sufficient, and she didn't need much wrangling. Nate, too. Luke would need a lot of attention in the coming weeks, though. And Hannah. She was still a baby, herself.

A new wave of anxiety combined with lack of sleep and the tail end of the adrenaline rush to make Summer very tired all of a sudden.

"I think I should nurse that baby and then get some sleep," she said to Derek.

He kissed Olivia's rosy cheek and handed her to Summer.

"Do you still want me to go home tonight?" he asked.

"Yeah, maybe stay here a couple of hours? And then I think we should let Delaney and Josie off the hook, don't you?"

He nodded. "Although, I can see what you mean about the vacation. It's so quiet here."

Olivia nursed like a champ, and Summer and Derek sat in relative silence, listening to her snuffling and grunting. When she fell asleep, Derek said, "I'll take her now so you can sleep."

Of course, sleep came instantaneously, and it felt like only a second had passed when Derek woke Summer up. He kissed her on the forehead and said, "It's been three hours. I figured you'd want to nurse again. I'm going to head out. Well done, my beautiful birthing machine."

Because Summer knew Olivia was their last baby, she felt an overwhelming need to memorize every single detail, to burn each one onto her brain with laser precision. The tug of the baby's mouth at her breast. The way she opened and closed her hand on Summer's ribcage as she nursed. The sounds she made, little piggy grunts. The way her long eyelashes laid against her cheek and her itsy bitsy, wrinkled feet curled up. And that new baby smell.

Summer felt the tears on her cheeks before she realized she was crying.

After the births of the other four children, Summer had thought about Willow, but only very briefly. Now, though, thanks to Willow's recent reappearance in her life, questions came unbidden into her mind.

Had Willow wanted Summer? Had she admired her for hours the way Summer admired each of her children after birth? Had she wondered whether Summer would grow up to be a veterinarian or a musician or an artist? Had she felt this overwhelming, almost suffocating feeling of hope that Summer would find happiness?

Or had she felt detached and distant?

You could always ask her, Winter breathed in her ear.

Summer didn't want to ask Willow. She didn't even want to speak to her.

Olivia nursed away. Summer pulled the little blue-and-pink striped cap off her head to look at her hair. Now that it was dry, it looked the same color as a brand new penny. She'd always wondered if she'd have a redhead. Red hair ran in Derek's family, but so far, the kids had all gotten Summer's white-blonde.

She grinned and stroked the soft, downy hair. "What a surprise, Miss Olivia," she said.

After a little while, she put the baby back in the bassinet and laid down to take a nap. It didn't really matter, she thought, whether Willow had experienced these same feelings. What mattered was that Summer did. What mattered was that Summer's children knew she loved them, more than anything else in the world. Well, along with their Daddy. With the faces of Derek and her children clear in her mind's eye, Summer fell into a deep sleep.

The dream-memories came and went all night long, and every time Summer fully awoke, she felt disappointed morning hadn't yet arrived. During a three a.m. nursing session, her head bobbed her out of a vision of giving birth to Sarah, how scared and elated she and Derek had both been, and how they'd been so proud at the hospital. Their first child, their daughter, was perfect. She was alert and had a strong grip, she went limp with sleep every time someone held her, and she didn't make a peep.

Driving home from the hospital, Summer sat in the back seat with Sarah, the baby's fist curled around her index finger.

"I know it's just a reflex," Summer said to Derek, watching his eyes in the rearview mirror. "But I feel like she's holding my finger because she loves me."

"She does love you," he said. "You're her mommy. Little girls adore their mommies."

Then they'd gotten home and Sarah had screamed her perfect head off around the clock. Derek and Summer had been so wildly in love with Sarah, they hadn't minded the screaming at all. They took turns pacing the house with their bundle, singing, "The Cat Came Back" every single night for the first six weeks.

Miraculously, the crying stopped. Something just clicked. Nate,

Luke and Hannah had been so much easier, but Summer never forgot those first six weeks of Sarah's life.

At four a.m., Summer jerked out of a surreal half-dream about her mother sitting on the couch, holding Olivia and orchestrating some kind of weird marching band with the older kids.

At ten minutes after five, it was a crystal clear memory of Derek walking towards her, his grin as wide as the Arizona sky. Where were they? Why was he smiling like that? She wasn't sure. But she was sure about how she felt at that moment. Her body vibrated with pure joy. Laughter wanted to bubble its way up to the surface. She wanted to run to him. But something stopped her.

At six, she ordered breakfast with a cup of coffee and admired her new daughter while she waited.

Olivia was definitely a redhead, which at once terrified and excited Summer. Her toenails were shaped exactly like Derek's, rounding over the tops of her toes. Her nose turned just slightly down at the tip, like Luke's.

What if God, or the Universe, or whomever, had given her Olivia as a kind of consolation gift for taking Luke away? Summer pushed the thought out of her mind and tried to place Olivia's mouth. It wasn't quite like Derek's, with the full lower lip and small upper lip. It wasn't like her own, a kind of permanent smile.

It was really familiar, though.

Someone knocked on the door before she could place it. Breakfast. And coffee. When the orderly left, it hit Summer: Olivia's mouth looked exactly like Willow's. Of course it would. It was a beautiful little mouth, full and round like a pouty little "O," but for goodness' sake. Couldn't the child have gotten her mouth from someone else?

Summer sighed.

Olivia's chin looked exactly like Nate's, and her hands were blocky like Sarah's.

"You'll never be a pianist," Summer told her. "But that's okay. Pianist is a weird word anyway."

Olivia didn't seem to mind and Summer decided she was an easygoing child.

A nurse came in to take Olivia to the nursery for an exam—"Dr. Thibedeau is here so we're lining all the babies up!" she said with way too much cheer in her voice—and Summer showered and indulged in a cookie.

Derek texted Summer an hour later: *The kids are anxious to meet their new baby sister. Can we come over?*

Summer responded: *She's anxious to meet them, too. :)*

They arrived in a cacophony of fake sword fighting sounds and squealing, squeaking of shoes on the tile floor and loud big sister "Shh" noises. *You can always tell when the Gray family shows up.*

Within seconds, Summer was surrounded by her five children. Hannah clambered right onto Summer's lap with no regard for the baby, and Sarah squeezed in next to Summer. The boys sat on their knees on either side of Summer's legs. While Hannah squeezed Summer's cheeks, saying, "I MISS you, Mama," over and over again, Sarah stroked Olivia's head and the boys leaned forward to peer at her. Summer looked over their heads at Derek, who smiled back.

"You know," he said, "I think I'll just run over to Rowdy's and have a drink. You got the kids? I'll be right back."

It was probably lack of sleep that put them both into fits at this. The kids looked at Summer, stunned, as tears rolled down her cheeks and her voice leaked out of her like helium being let out of a balloon.

"You're hysterical. I've seen this before." A nurse walked in, and stood in the doorway. "Any parents who pass the three-kid mark always end up hysterical at some point."

This only made Summer and Derek laugh harder.

"Beautiful family," the nurse said, looking at each of the kids in turn. "I'll come back in a little bit. Seems like you're doing fine."

Summer managed to squeak out, "Thank you," as the nurse walked away.

It was only then that Summer noticed Hannah wasn't wearing shoes. With the exception of Sarah, the entire family looked like it had just walked out of the apocalypse.

All three of the younger kids' hair stood straight out from the backs of their heads, tangled from sleep. Hannah and Luke had peanut butter smeared on their cheeks. Nate had a toothpaste stain on the front of his shirt, and holes in the knees of his jeans.

"Did you even look at these children before you brought them out of the house?" she asked Derek, and a fresh wave of giggles overtook them.

"They've lost it," Nate said, and Sarah nodded sagely. Luke added, "She's always said we'll send her to the looney bin, but I think it's safe to blame the breakdown on the new baby."

"It's already happening," Derek said. "Olivia's going to get blamed for everything."

Summer kissed the baby's head. "Want to hold her?" she asked Sarah, who nodded and laid Olivia against her shoulder.

With the extra room on her mother's lap, Hannah spread out, laid back and closed her eyes. The boys scooted closer to Sarah. Luke pulled Olivia's hat off and the big kids gasped.

"Red hair!" Sarah said. "I love it. That's so cute! It's, like, the cutest thing *ever*!"

"There's a girl in my class with red hair," Nate said. He seemed to have more to say, but he shut his mouth and looked down at his hands.

"And?" Derek said.

"And she's always getting in trouble," Nate said. "I heard Mrs. Ranger talking to the librarian about how she's a handful because she has red hair. And the librarian said, 'Well, you know how redheads are.'"

Summer and Derek looked at each other. Derek shrugged, so Summer shrugged, too.

"Well, I guess we'll find out," she said. She tried to keep her voice light, but she couldn't shake the tiny bit of uneasiness that crept in.

CHAPTER ELEVEN

W‍HEN D‍EREK TOOK THE KIDS HOME AFTER ABOUT A HALF-HOUR, Summer felt like she could float in the silence. She immediately felt remorse at that thought, and was grateful when the nurse interrupted Winter's scathing remarks.

"Quite a brood you've got there," she said as she walked in. "You really have your hands full."

"You know," Summer said, "I read this article once where the writer was saying parents should answer, 'Full of love!' or 'Full of joy!' But you're right. I do have my hands full." She heard her voice crack and cleared her throat. "I'm not sure I can handle this."

"You're a pro by now," the nurse said, strapping the blood pressure cuff around Summer's arm. "You'll settle right in."

All at once, words started pouring out of Summer's mouth. She told the nurse about Luke and his heart surgery, about how Willow had just resurfaced after fifteen years and how Summer was struggling to forgive her for being a terrible mother.

Halfway through, Olivia started to cry, and the nurse took her, reswaddled her, and handed her back to Summer, all the while nodding or shaking her head where appropriate as she listened to Summer talk.

"You do have a lot going on, honey," she said when Summer wound down. She handed her a tissue, and Summer blew her nose loudly. "But you'll be fine. We just carry on." She shrugged. "That's what we do. Still, I'm going to give you some pamphlets before you leave, okay? I'll go get those now. Just some information about post-partum services."

Summer nodded, wiping her nose and dabbing at her eyes. The nurse paused in the doorway, then came back and wrapped Summer in a tight hug. "You'll be fine, honey. Okay? I promise you."

She walked out, and almost bumped into Derek's mom, Julie, who was coming in.

"Oh, sweetheart, let me see that baby."

She took Olivia from Summer, and sat down on the edge of the hospital bed. "Beautiful," she whispered as she admired her newest granddaughter. "Just gorgeous."

Then, she barked out a laugh. "Oh, what was I thinking?" She patted Summer's leg. "You're beautiful, too, sweetheart. Just like always."

Summer laughed, but the laughter dissolved into tears.

"Oh, honey, what's the matter?" Julie asked.

Summer ran through her list of concerns in a manner much more organized than the spew she'd issued forth for the nurse. At first, Julie didn't answer. She often liked to ponder troubles before offering advice or comfort.

She rocked the baby, tapping her foot to some melody. Probably The Beatles, Summer thought. After the birth of each child, Julie selected a theme song from The Beatles' repertoire to become that child's theme song.

Olivia's should be "Help!"

"Shut up, Winter," Summer said quietly.

For Sarah, Julie chose "I Saw Her Standing There." Nate's was "Here Comes the Sun," and Luke's was "Hey, Jude." Hannah's was "I Want to Hold Your Hand."

"You know, honey," Julie said after a long silence, "it wouldn't hurt to reconnect with your mom."

Summer took in a breath to respond, but Julie held up a hand. "Just hear me out. We don't always get second chances in this life. I believe Willow is here for a reason. You may not be able to see it just yet, but I'm sure it's there. You don't have to answer right now. I don't want to upset you while you're recovering from childbirth. But

I don't want you to do something rash and regret it later. You might not get another chance to make it right."

Summer nodded.

Julie said, "And I think Miss Olivia's song will be, 'She Loves You.'"

Delaney and Josie arrived that afternoon.

"I just couldn't help myself," Josie said, rushing into the room and thrusting a gift bag at Summer. "I bought her a coming home dress. I know I already gave you the gender neutral sleeper, but you know I can't resist dressing up a baby girl."

"I smuggled in some champagne, too," Delaney said, holding up a huge purse. "Let's hurry up and open it while it's still cold." She glanced behind her at the open door. "And before an enforcer comes in and confiscates it."

Summer oohed and ahed over the lacy purple dress, sipped the champagne like the luxury it was, and admired Olivia along with the girls, but she still couldn't shake the feeling of anxiety that was building somewhere deep in her core.

"You look exhausted," Delaney said.

"Shut up, Dee. Of course she does," Josie said. "She just gave birth, like, eighteen hours ago."

"I didn't mean it like that," Delaney said. "I was going to say, why don't you take a little nap, and we'll sit here and hold Olivia?"

Summer nodded. "That sounds divine," she said.

Only, she found that when she closed her eyes, she couldn't sleep.

When she gave up and opened her eyes, pretending to be waking from a nice nap, Josie was rocking Olivia, whispering to her in Spanish.

"I hope you're not telling her all my secrets," Summer said.

Josie laughed. "No. Just imparting all my girl wisdom."

"Don't you think she's too young to hear about boys?"

"Speaking of secrets," Delaney said from her spot on the couch. "What is up with your mother?"

"That's the last thing I want to talk about right now," Summer said. She sighed. "Besides. I don't know how to answer."

"I think you need to reconcile with her," Josie said.

Summer shook her head. "You can say that because your mom

was a decent person. Willow isn't. Never was. I don't want her poisoning my life."

"I get that," Josie said. "But what if, God forbid, she dropped dead tomorrow? Would you be sorry you hadn't made up with her?"

Josie's own mom had died suddenly, about seven years ago, from a brain aneurism. She was making tamales, and Josie found her on the kitchen floor.

"We obviously had two entirely different experiences with our mothers," Summer said. "Your mom was more of a mother to me than Willow ever was. If she dropped dead tomorrow, I'd probably be relieved."

Delaney's eyes went round, and Josie sucked in a breath and made the sign of the cross. More guilt. More remorse.

"Sorry," Summer said. "I don't mean to sound insensitive. But it's true."

The girls were quiet for a minute, and then Josie stood up. She handed Olivia to Delaney, moving briskly from rocking chair to couch. Then, she approached the side of the hospital bed, put a hand on Summer's shoulder and leaned down to kiss Summer on the head.

"You know I love you. But think about this, okay?"

Summer nodded.

"I'll be in the car, Dee," Josie said to Delaney.

Once she was gone, Delaney made a show of adjusting Olivia's hat. Summer pulled her knees up and put her head on them.

"I can't believe I said that," she said.

Delaney didn't answer for a while. Then she said, "We've all walked our own paths. You know Josie's sensitive about it. I know you haven't gotten any sleep, and you just pushed a baby out. Josie knows, too. That's why she didn't eat you alive."

Head still on her knees, Summer chuckled. "Thank goodness for that."

"Summer?" Delaney said.

"What's wrong?" Summer's new best friends, The Worst-Case Scenarios, made her head snap up. Had Olivia stopped breathing? Had Delaney dropped her? Everything looked fine.

"How will I know what to do?" Delaney said.

Summer sighed with relief. "What do you mean?"

"I mean, when I have this baby. How will I know what to do with it?"

"You just will. You just do."

"Easy for you to say. You're a natural," Delaney said.

Summer sensed Delaney was near tears and she smiled, pretending as hard as she could that she felt confident. "At first, it's just a schedule, you know? It's just meeting her needs. Feed, change, swaddle, rock. Cuddling is natural. Feed, change, swaddle, rock. Lay her down. Take a shower before she cries. Feed again. Feeding, feeding, feeding. Change. Rock. Swaddle. Feed. Change. Change."

When Delaney made a face, Summer quickly added, "You've seen me with mine a million times. You already know the basics. It's just doing it. And once you've been doing it for, like, a few days, you totally have it down. I mean, a few days feels like a few years. You feel like you've been doing it forever. And ever."

She left out the part about never feeling like you really had it down. She could fill Delaney in on that later.

When Delaney left, tucking Olivia into Summer's arms with a deftness that proved she'd be a good mother, Summer savored the silence. It didn't last long.

An hour later, her next visitor—an unwelcome one—walked in.

Summer should have known Willow would come to visit. She could be very conniving, and she had probably staked out Summer's house the previous evening after Josie and Delaney whisked Summer away for a pedicure. When Summer and Derek left in the van and didn't return home, Willow likely assumed Summer had gone into labor.

Then, she'd waited for a couple of hours before calling the hospital and asking to be connected to Summer's room. Summer could just picture it: Willow, her eyes slightly bleary from bourbon and her fingers moving almost lazily over the phone's keyboard as she dialed the number for the hospital.

"Summer Gray, please," she would slur into the phone. "Labor and delivery."

She'd break up the word delivery into a song, making each syllable its own beat. The nurses who answered the phone would put her through, but of course, Summer wouldn't answer. She was in labor. Willow didn't care whether Summer answered. The fact that the nurses rang a room was confirmation enough that Summer was there.

She bided her time, and then she waltzed into Summer's room with one arm bent at the elbow, her hand in the air as if she were holding a cigarette.

Very glamorous.

"Why didn't you call me when you went into labor?" she said.

What a greeting.

"Why would I?"

"Can I see the baby? I predicted it was a girl. Did it turn out to be a girl?"

Summer sighed, and almost smiled, despite herself. "Yes. Olivia. Of course you can see her. She's right there."

Willow had the good sense not to pick the baby up. Instead, she stood next to the bassinet, her hands on one edge of it, and looked down at her.

"She's perfect," she whispered. "She looks exactly like you did when you were born."

All those questions came flooding back to Summer.

You remember what I looked like?

How did you feel when you held me?

What promises did you make to me? Did you keep them?

Did you love me?

Did you even want me?

But she kept them to herself.

Willow took a breath as if to continue, and Summer hoped, for a split second, that she might address some of those questions. But she should have known better.

Willow went on: "I can't believe you have five children, Summer. I mean, it's like a school of fish. What do you even *do* with so many children?"

Summer sighed.

"Oh, I'm sorry," Willow said. "I didn't mean it like that. They're all beautiful. So beautiful. Such a treat. I can see why you want to keep having them. But this one's your last, right?"

Summer wouldn't have imagined the conversations could get worse, but, she later reminded herself, thinking a situation can't get worse is often the biggest mistake.

CHAPTER TWELVE

The vacation was over.

Summer loved her house and the home she and Derek had built inside it. She loved her husband and her children.

She also loved being in the hospital. She loved the quiet. She loved not having to cook or do dishes or fold clothes. She loved having food delivered. Of course, she had to return to reality at some point. That point was now and as Derek pulled the van away from the hospital entrance, Olivia in the back in her carseat, Summer started to cry. Again.

"I'm unaccustomed to these crying jags," Derek said. "Are you okay?"

Summer wanted to answer that no, she wasn't okay. She was exhausted. She was scared for Luke. She was scared that caring for Luke would take away from her time with Olivia, and Olivia would grow up believing she was unimportant. She would seek mens' attention, root it out like candy, and grow up to be a prostitute. It would be all Summer's fault.

But instead of saying any of these things, Summer said, "I'm just so happy to be bringing Olivia home."

Derek nodded and patted her leg. He looked as convinced as she felt.

Chaos. Summer felt like she was walking onto a battlefield or the site of a hazardous materials spill. Or a battlefield where there had been a hazardous materials spill. During the apocalypse. Surely zombies would come around the corner at any moment.

To his credit, Derek had kept up with washing the laundry. A mountain of clean, unfolded clothes covered the entire couch. Josie and Delaney, who had sat with the kids while Derek picked up Summer and Olivia, were hard at work in the kitchen, scrubbing dishes.

Summer froze in the entryway.

"I thought I told you to use paper plates while I was gone," she said.

"I couldn't find them," Derek said.

Hysteria threatened. Summer could feel it in her stomach, expanding, threatening to choke her.

Teeth ground together, she said, "I told you they're on top of the fridge."

Derek shrugged—not in a careless, blasé way, but in an I'm-at-a-loss-and-know-there's-nothing-I-can-say way.

Summer took some deep yoga breaths and turned away from Derek. She noticed Delaney and Josie carefully ignoring them (but taking note of every single movement, every action, out of the corners of their eyes).

She took some more deep yoga breaths. "I need to sit down. Only, there's nowhere to sit."

Behind her, Derek sighed. "The kitchen table?" he offered.

In the kitchen, Delaney and Josie froze. Josie turned off the water at the sink and hurried in a decidedly non-hurried way over to the kitchen table. When she turned around, her arms were completely full of stuffed animals and weaponry.

"Have a seat, Summer," she said, way too brightly. "I am just adjourning this meeting of the stuffed animal ninja convention."

Then she yelled, "Boys!" and offloaded the toys when they came rushing in from outside. Summer sucked in a breath when she saw that their muddy feet—and the puppy's—were leaving tracks all over the floor, which she'd scrubbed shiny only a couple of days before. She picked her way through the living room, over the cups and saucers and fake coffee cake from Hannah's tea set, and sat down at the kitchen table.

"How are you?" Delaney asked.

"I'm okay," Summer said. "I'm feeling pretty good."

The tension in Delaney's shoulders eased.

See? I can do this. Fake it 'til I make it.

"Actually, I'm feeling great," Summer said.

Delaney turned around, very slowly, to face her. "Really?"

Summer shrugged a shoulder. "Considering. You know."

Sarah was busy taking Olivia out of her carseat while Hannah watched, fascinated. Derek had disappeared.

"Did a bomb go off?" Summer asked.

"We had hoped to have this all cleaned up before you got home," Josie said, "but that didn't really work out. It's a lot of work keeping up with four kids."

There's that hysteria again.

At the look on Summer's face, Josie quickly added, "I mean, every time we made headway on one thing, like taking out the trash, someone interrupted us. Luke needed a bandage for his knee. Sarah needed help with her homework. Nate needed stitches. Okay, just kidding. Not that last one. Anyway. We couldn't keep up."

Summer put her head down on the table.

"I mean," Josie said, "we're not as skilled as you are. That's all."

"And then we were talking about when you come home," Delaney said, "and how we think you should hire a housekeeper."

The hysteria bubbled right up and out of Summer's mouth. She sat up and laughed. Her head tilted back, involuntarily, and she howled.

"You think I should hire a housekeeper?" She wiped tears from her eyes.

Josie and Delaney stood side by side at the counter. They turned, simultaneously, so they were leaning with one hip against it, arms folded.

"Yes," Josie said, drawing the word out slowly. "You're going to be nursing a new baby. You have a one-year-old and three kids who will be going back to school really soon. You have to cook. You have to work. You have to chauffeur kids. Derek's working. Why not hire a little help?"

Summer shook her head. Her alter-ego Winter emerged and said, "You really don't know what it's like to raise four children, do you?"

The girls looked a little wounded, and Summer felt herself soften.

"The problem with a housekeeper is that I'd end up paying her to pick up my kids' toys just so she could get to actually cleaning the house. She'd spend as much time clearing off the floor as she would vacuuming. She'd spend more time clearing homework papers and little toys and used tissues off the kitchen counter than she would actually spend doing dishes. See what I mean?"

Josie nodded. "We see what you mean."

Delaney added, "In fact, we've experienced that phenomenon ourselves."

"See?" Summer said.

"But what if you made, like, a chore chart or something?" Josie said.

"Don't you think I've tried that?" Summer said, spluttering. "These kids can't pick up their own feet, let alone a bunch of crap off the floor. The last chore chart we made ended up in the toilet."

"We're just trying to help," Delaney said. "We were just brainstorming, that's all. I mean, when we went to get pedicures, your fingers were practically bleeding from all the cleaning you were doing. We just don't want you to overdo it."

"It's okay to ask for help," Josie said. "We already know you're Super Mom."

All three of them jumped when the doorbell rang.

When Summer and Derek brought Sarah home, Julie sent them a singing telegram. When they brought Nate home, she sent them a basket of movies, snacks and champagne. With Luke, it was a greeting card stuffed with gift cards for restaurants and movie theaters so they could go on a date. Finally, when Hannah arrived, Julie sent them a huge bouquet of flowers and a bottle of fancy whiskey, with a little note: *To the best parents I've ever known. You're gonna need this.*

So when the doorbell rang the same day they brought Olivia home, Summer felt a glimmer of happiness. Maybe Julie had sent her some sleeping pills. To give the kids. Summer glanced around to see if anyone had noticed her train of thought. She was relieved she hadn't said it out loud. She'd never really give them sleeping pills. Would she? The idea had some merit.

Derek emerged from the back of the house to answer the door. Summer couldn't wait to see what it was. This was almost like

Christmas morning. She stood up, and sat down abruptly when she saw who was there.

Willow.

She'd let Derek deal with it, she thought. Then she heard him inviting Willow in. She heard her say something, and could tell from the tone of her voice it was scathing. Probably about the state of the house. Or Derek's shirt, which was stained with spaghetti sauce. "Well, I've been on my own with the kids for a couple of days," Derek said, his tone bordering on apologetic.

Summer felt a strong urge to get up, fold laundry, pick up toys, stack books or grab the sponge out of Josie's hand and wash some dishes. But she remained seated.

Willow walked through the living room, craning her neck like a bird. "Where's Summer?" she said, but spotted her before Derek answered, and then picked her way into the kitchen.

"Hi," she said, leaning against the kitchen doorway and folding her arms. "This place is a mess. You must feel so overwhelmed."

In her peripheral vision, Summer saw Josie inhale and hold her breath. Warning bells sounded.

"That's why we're here," Josie said. She held up the sponge. "We're helping out."

Willow raised her eyebrows and let her eyes scan the kitchen countertops. "Well, you're not doing a very good job, I dare say, ladies."

Josie stared at Willow for a long moment, and Summer could practically hear the thoughts going through her mind. Surprisingly, she didn't respond.

"Wow," Delaney whispered. "I've never seen Josie speechless. Ever."

"Summer, I have some concerns," Willow said. "You've never been a very good housekeeper, and now you have five little urchins working against you. Plus this guy." She jerked her thumb in Derek's direction. Now he was speechless. "I know how men are," she said when she saw the surprised expression on his face. "You need help."

"I was thinking of hiring a housekeeper," Summer lied, grasping onto the girls' idea as if it were her own.

Willow shook her head. "No. What you need is someone to mind the kids while you clean."

Josie found her voice. "We'll help her, Mrs.—Willow. That's what we're here for. We were here when she had Sarah, and Nate, and Luke and Hannah. And we're here for her now. We can mind kids and do chores. And Summer may not be the best housekeeper, but you know what? She's a good wife and a damn good mother. She and Derek are doing everything right. These kids are happy. They're healthy, they eat good food and they're dirty all the time. More importantly, they're kind. Which is more than I can say for you. So it may look like Summer needs help, but I'll tell you what. She is doing just fine—no, spectacularly—without it. Instead of tearing her down, you should be telling her how proud you are."

Willow didn't bother looking surprised.

"Damn right I'm proud," she said. "Everything she does right is a reflection on me. I fed her only organic food when she was growing up. I always provided her with a safe home. She was happy. She was healthy. I mean, she must be healthy, right? She can procreate like nobody's business. But the one thing I could never drill into her head was how to clean a damn floor. She wasn't a good housekeeper as a child, and she isn't one now. And that's why she needs help. Which is why, as of today, I'll be staying here."

In the silence that stretched like already-chewed bubble gum after Willow's announcement, Summer had yet another vivid flashback of her childhood.

The memory of Willow's lesson on cleaning floors, or work ethic, or both, flared to life in brilliant colors and sounds. Summer was eight or nine. Willow went to "run errands," and told Summer that once she cleaned the kitchen floor, she could ride her bike to the creek. Summer spent an hour on her hands and knees, scrubbing the floor with a rag. She had the radio on, and scrubbed in time to "Don't Worry Be Happy" and "Heaven is a Place on Earth."

When she was done, she emptied the bucket in the backyard like Willow had taught her to, hung the rags on the clothesline and rode to the creek. She spent what felt like a long time sending little leaf boats down the current, and then another long time laying on the bank, listening to the water.

The sun began to set, illuminating the leaves on the trees and making the water sparkle. Summer rode home. She walked into the house, relishing the feel of the fan blowing cool on her sunburned skin. Deadly quiet met her, and she felt the hairs on her arms prickle with apprehension. Was it at that moment Summer realized "running errands" was actually a euphemism for going to buy bourbon?

"Where have you been?" Willow's voice sounded eerie, ghostlike. Summer couldn't tell where it was coming from.

"I rode down to the creek. You said I could. After I—"

"After you cleaned the floor, yes. After. You. Cleaned. The. Floor."

Summer knew the floor was clean when she left. She checked it before sliding into her flip flops and riding away. She didn't say as much, but when Willow grabbed her by the upper arm and marched her into the kitchen, she knew what had happened. Willow had come home, made herself a drink, and dripped a trail of water or bourbon on the floor. Then she'd tracked it all the way from the counter near the refrigerator to the living room.

Willow pointed out every droplet of dirty water, every smudge, and the single Summer-sized footprint.

"Clean it again," she said, her words cutting into Summer's conscience so smoothly she believed for a moment the bourbon trail was her fault.

Then, as Summer obeyed, her arms burning from the effort, Willow stood over her, inspecting every stroke as if their lives depended on having a clean floor. Between gulps of her drink, she spit her words out in time to Summer's scrubbing: "This. Is. Why. We. Have. Cockroaches. Mice. Flies. This. Is. Why. We. Live. In. Filth. Becauseyouarealazygirl."

The fear of her teardrops landing on the floor was the only thing that kept Summer from crying. Inside, she could feel the tiny embers of an emotion she rarely experienced: anger. Willow said she could go to the creek. Willow came home to a clean floor and then messed it up herself. Now she was blaming Summer. As the words comprising Willow's accusations tumbled together, Summer began to hate her mother.

The grown-up Summer stood in the kitchen of her adulthood, her body sore from giving birth, her heart pounding way too fast, her vision going black around the edges. The anger was back. She wouldn't allow Willow (or her poisonous vibes) to remain in this house.

"You will not be staying here," she said quietly, the floor-scrubbing rhythm providing a beat for her words. "Leave my home."

Again, Willow raised her eyebrows. Summer hated that expression. She wished she could tear those eyebrows right off that smug face.

Inexplicably, Derek chose this moment to step forward. "I think she should stay."

No, he hadn't seen the film reel in Summer's mind. No, he had no idea, not really, of Willow's true personality. Summer had never shared the details with him. And no, he probably didn't want to get punched in the face. Summer felt her fist curl at her side.

Where is all this imagined violence coming from? Oh. Yes. Winter. Welcome back, sweetheart.

"Well, you think wrong," Summer said to Derek. Willow's expression became even more smug. As if that were possible.

"We could use the help," Derek said. "I can't take much more time off work, and won't it ease your mind to have someone to help with the cleaning and cooking?"

"Someone *else*, maybe!" Summer said. "She can't even cook!" She flinched at the screechy sound of her own voice.

"It's been fifteen years since we've spoken, honey. I've learned a thing or two," Willow said.

Is it my imagination, or does she actually look hurt that I don't want her here?

Summer sighed. Neither Delaney nor Josie had moved. Not an inch.

"I'll tell you what she'll do," Summer said to Derek, to the girls and to the room. "She'll sit on the couch with a cigarette in her hand, giving our kids lung cancer, watching some stupid soap opera, demanding that I bring her food and criticizing every move I make. She won't help. She isn't capable."

"We could use the help," Derek said again. Summer found herself hating Derek, too.

This is a first, Winter said to Summer, and Summer pinched her own arm to shut Winter up.

"We don't need help!" Summer said.

"Yes, you do," Josie said.

"Oh, no. Not you, too," Summer tried to whirl toward Josie like she'd read about people doing in books, but her body was too tired to whirl. Instead, it did a slow revolution.

"You've just seen a perfect example of how she can be," Summer said.

"You know my opinion," Josie said.

Josie's opinion was that Summer should try to reconnect with Willow. But Josie was thinking about her own mother, who'd been a kind and loving saint compared to Willow.

"It's not the same at all," Summer snapped.

"Looks like you've been outvoted, honey," Willow said.

"Outvoted about what?" Nate flew into the room, sensing an injustice. "I didn't get to vote!"

"There was no vote," Summer said. "You didn't miss anything."

"Well, then, what are you guys talking about?" Luke said.

"When did you get here?" Summer asked him.

"I sneaked in, like a ninja," he said.

He grinned at her, and her resolve softened. She still wanted to punch Derek in the face, though. And Willow, too. And, for that matter, Josie, with her righteousness. She wanted Willow here about as much as she wanted someone to pull her toenails out with pliers.

But it was true: she and Derek could use the help. With Derek working, school and fall sports starting up soon, and a brand new baby at home, an extra pair of hands would be nice. But did Willow's count?

Couldn't she just stay somewhere nearby? Like, in the next state? California was nice this time of year. At any time of year, really. Utah was very pretty. Did she have to stay here?

Summer looked from Derek (who wore a mildly terrified expression) to Willow (and the smug countenance Summer so hated), to Josie and Delaney, to Luke and Nate.

What would life look like without Willow? Chaotic, noisy, messy. Exactly what Summer was used to, only, with an additional child.

What would life look like if Willow stayed? Chaotic, noisy, messy. With her biggest critic standing by, waiting for her to make a mistake.

Suddenly, Olivia started screaming. Summer took that as a sign. She made her decision.

• • •

SARAH CAME RUSHING OUT of the bedroom, carrying the wailing Olivia, and Summer's breasts reacted by leaking all over her shirt. She'd forgotten to use nursing pads.

"Whatever," she muttered, taking the baby, thanking Sarah and brushing past Willow to go sit on the couch. Hannah climbed up next to her and began rubbing Olivia's head.

This whole situation was Derek's fault, really. If he hadn't befriended Willow, if he didn't have such a kind heart, if he didn't want Summer's life to be easier (and when had she ever asked for an easier life? She was an independent woman!), none of this would be happening. Why did he have to be so ... *good*?

Josie and Delaney started washing dishes again, Josie scrubbing and Delaney drying. The boys zoomed out of the living room, and Willow started stacking papers—bills, junk mail, schoolwork—in tidier piles on the counter. Summer thought she was trying to prove her worth. No one spoke. For the second time within the hour, the doorbell rang, breaking the spell of silence.

Every head in the room turned toward the door at the sound of the bell. Derek answered the door, and Julie stood there, a brown box in her arms. Her smile faded as she took in the somber mood.

"Perfect timing," Summer heard Derek say to his mom.

Why couldn't the universe have given her Julie for a mother? In a way, it had, by allowing her to find Derek. But how had the universe connected her with Willow? It made no sense whatsoever.

"A present!" Luke ran to the door and took the box from Julie. "Grandma brought us a present!"

Julie laughed. "Wait for your brother and sisters, now," she said.

Derek introduced Julie and Willow, and Summer could practically see Julie sizing up Summer's mysterious mother. She had the good sense not to say anything. Willow, on the other hand, didn't hold back.

"So you're the one who encouraged these two to procreate so foolishly," she said as she grasped Julie's hand. "Didn't Summer tell me you have a whole flock of children as well?"

Julie smiled. To a stranger—to Willow—the smile would look innocent and kind. But Summer could see the cunning behind it.

"It's just lovely to meet you," Julie said.

"Likewise," Willow said.

Summer sighed and Olivia nursed away madly, with no idea how good she had it.

WILLOW STAYED.

The rest of them (Derek, Josie and even Julie, not to mention the kids) made it impossible for Summer to send her away.

"She can have my bed!" Sarah said, and Summer knew she'd regret it after one night sleeping in the boys' room. "She can have my bed!" Nate said, and Summer knew he'd regret it as soon as he shared the bed with Luke for one night.

"My bed!" Hannah shouted, unable to resist joining in the excitement.

In the end, it was settled that they'd blow up an air mattress in the girls' room. Sarah would sleep on that—possibly with Hannah—and Willow would sleep in Sarah's bed.

Everyone seemed so happy about it.

Even Julie, despite the decidedly cool reception she'd gotten from Willow. She was completely unfazed by Willow's lots-of-kids comment, and instead of recoiling, she opened her arms to give Willow a big hug. Of course, that didn't break Willow's icy exterior. She sniffed, eyebrows still raised in superiority, and endured Julie's embrace with stick-straight posture.

"What a wonderful daughter you raised," Julie said, and Willow relaxed a little. "I'm sure she'll appreciate your help immensely."

At that, Julie gave Summer a look, and Summer forced a smile, their conversation at the hospital fresh in her mind. *We don't always get second chances in this life. Willow is here for a reason. You may not be able to see it just yet.*

Summer could handle this. So what if it meant losing her sanity? At least everyone else would have theirs.

Julie left almost immediately after her arrival. A few moments later, Josie and Delaney began gathering their things to leave, too.

Summer didn't miss the conspicuous head-jerk Josie gave Derek, commanding that he follow her outside, but Olivia was still nursing with the ferocity of a baby crocodile and Summer couldn't get up to join them. Instead, she remained stuck in the living room with

Willow as the kids emptied Julie's box—an assortment of bubbles, sidewalk chalk and water guns—and went outside to play. Trapped, Summer wished she could dissolve right into the couch and disappear. Maybe she could teleport and end up on the beach.

"I don't understand why you're so against me staying here," Willow said. She looked around, sniffed again. Her exaggerated expressions made her seem like a caricature of herself, Summer thought. "You obviously need the help."

"Do we have to have this conversation? You're staying here. You got what you wanted. Okay?"

"I just don't understand, that's all."

Instead of screaming like she wanted to, Summer clenched her teeth. "Fine," she said in a near-growl. "You know why I don't want you staying here? Every time you speak to me, it's a veiled criticism. Everywhere you look, you see my mistakes. My shortcomings. I see them clearly enough, myself. The last thing I need is for you to point them out to me, every single day. You don't cook. You don't clean, which I'm pretty sure is the whole reason you had a child in the first place. So I hardly think you're going to be any help, unless you count character building as the kind of help I need. Personally, I think I had enough of that growing up."

For once, Willow didn't have a comeback.

Olivia finished nursing, and her head lolled back. Summer wished she could fall asleep so easily.

"Can I hold her?" Willow said.

"I guess." Summer handed the baby to Willow. "I'm going to see if I can catch Josie and Delaney before they go, to say good-bye and thank them for doing dishes."

"That Josie's a real firecracker," Willow said.

"She is," Summer said, and wondered why she felt defensive, when it was partly Josie's doing that Willow was still sitting on the couch.

She heard Delaney's voice before she made it all the way into the driveway, and its tone stopped Summer in her tracks, just behind the juniper bush next to the front door. *I'm not hiding. I just happened to stop here.*

"I'm really worried about her," Delaney was saying. "I mean, she's not herself. I think we need to get her some help."

Josie chimed in. "I mean, she's depressed."

"Do you think it's just the baby blues?" Derek asked. "She did get a bit, well, you know, a bit emotional after she had each of the other kids."

"She's been going downhill since she found out she was pregnant with Olivia," Josie snapped. "That surprise hit her like a freight train."

Derek must have looked wounded, because Delaney quickly added, "She was happy about the baby, but she was stressed, that's all." Summer pictured her elbowing Josie. Delaney continued, "I'm sure it's so much better now that you've got the nursing job and everything."

"The nursing job that keeps me away from the house most of the time," Derek said.

He sounded so sad. Summer wanted to hop out from behind the juniper bush and hug him.

"But it puts food on the table," Josie said, her brusque tone and accent reminding Summer of Josie's mother, impatient with Josie's self-pity when she got an F on her math test. "Pull yourself up by the bootstraps and fix it, *mija*. This is no time to feel sorry for yourself."

"This isn't your fault, Derek," Josie said.

Doesn't she know how much he hates when people say that? He thinks that's code for, This is totally your fault.

Delaney went on talking about Luke's heart and Willow's reappearance. Summer had to rescue her husband. He didn't need to experience even more stress, especially not on her behalf. She took a deep breath and emerged from behind the bush, doing her best to make it seem like she hadn't been eavesdropping.

Josie, Delaney and Derek froze.

"Oh, good," Summer said. "I caught you guys. I just wanted to say good-bye, and thank you."

She pulled both girls into a hug, and whispered, "I'm fine. Stop worrying."

"You're not fine," Josie said. She extricated herself from Summer's embrace so she could look her in the eye. "You're doing too much. You're heading straight for disaster."

Delaney elbowed Josie, just as Summer had pictured her doing a moment ago.

"Not straight for disaster," Delaney said. "You're just overdoing it. We don't want you to get sick."

"How do you know I'm overdoing it? I just got home from the hospital. All I've done is nurse and change diapers, and I think maybe I had a couple of sword fights."

"Before that," Josie said. "Scrubbing floors? Vacuuming nonstop? Scraping the grout with your fingernails? Don't you think we noticed you were acting out of character?"

Summer decided to latch onto that one: "So, cleaning my house is out of character?"

Why did I ever mention the grout? Why?

Josie and Delaney traded exasperated looks.

"Of course not," Delaney said. Summer could tell she was trying to be soothing, which only served to make her angrier.

"That's exactly what you're saying," she said. "Me cleaning the floors is out of character."

"Summer. Snap out of it! *This* is out of character," Josie said.

Derek stood a few feet away, his stance wide and his arms crossed. He had backed up a couple of steps.

"Well, that's what you're saying," Summer mumbled.

"Look," Josie said. Summer cringed and she saw Delaney cringe, too. Whenever Josie said, "Look," it meant she was about to get serious. Very serious. "You aren't being reasonable. I've—both of us have—always been blown away by how much you take on. You parent four kids. Now five. You work. You play with The Sweets. You have sex with your husband on a regular basis."

Derek flung his arms up and stalked back into the house.

"But when is enough, enough? You can't do it all. You may think you are superhuman, and you may have us thinking it too, sometimes, but you're not. You've just given birth. Your son is about to have heart surgery. Open. Heart. Surgery. You can't do this alone. Okay? Let us help you."

"I know I'm not superhuman!" Summer said. "Obviously. I know that. And I'll accept help from you guys! I just don't want help from that—that—woman! I don't want her here!"

She made a conscious effort to bring her voice down an octave and a couple dozen decibels.

"Willow ruined my childhood. She was a terrible mother. She left me in the grocery store when I was ten years old, for God's sake. She never loved me, never wanted me, never cared about me. Of all the people in the world, she is the one I least want spending time around my children. My children. Whom I love. Why can't you understand that?"

Josie and Delaney inched closer to one another, and Delaney spoke next. "We can. But people can change, can't they?"

"No!" Summer yelled. "They can't! Haven't you heard her, criticizing my decision to have lots of kids, criticizing my messy house, criticizing my choice in friends? Haven't you seen her, waltzing around with her glass of bourbon and an imaginary cigarette? Ridiculous! She hasn't changed. At. All. And I hate her. I hate her!"

She was so enraged she didn't notice the twin looks of horror on her friends' faces until she stopped shouting. They were both looking at a point over her shoulder. Naturally. Summer spun around and came face to face with Willow.

CHAPTER THIRTEEN

"You never did understand me," Willow said.

For the first time since Willow showed up on the doorstep, Summer really looked at her mother. She noticed lines in Willow's skin. Parentheses around her mouth. Crow's feet at the corners of her eyes. Long tracks across her forehead. The bones in her hands and shoulders stood out. And up close, her smile didn't look as self-assured as Summer always thought it did. Willow wasn't as confident of her role here as she pretended to be.

So Willow isn't the only one who isn't paying close attention to the people around her.

"Shut up, Winter," Summer said.

When Willow gave her a quizzical look, Summer said, "Never mind. Okay, I'll play. What do you mean, I never understood you?"

"We're going to go," Josie said from behind Summer.

"Yes, good idea," Delaney said. "Love you, Summer. We'll see you later."

Willow sighed dramatically. Summer embraced her friends, then turned back to her mom.

"See?" she said. "Even now, you have to point out that my friends are stealing your spotlight. But this isn't about you, Willow. It's about me. These are *my* friends. This is *my* moment. I just gave birth to *my* child. This is *my* life."

"I understand better than you think I do," Willow said.

"Well, why don't you tell me about it?"

Willow nodded. "When I was seventeen, I had it all." Despite the tension from a moment ago, her voice sounded dreamy. "I had parents who loved me and a man who was the moon to my sun. He worshipped me. Dennis. That's your dad's name."

A strange sensation overcame Summer. Willow had never mentioned Summer's dad's name. In fact, it wasn't until Summer was twelve and took sex education that she realized she even had a father.

Willow's eyes misted over. She blinked, and when she made eye contact with Summer again, her face had hardened. "Then I got pregnant."

"And your life was ruined. The end."

"Summer. Just hear me out. Okay?"

"Sorry."

"Then I got pregnant. I was overjoyed," Willow said. She smiled at the memory. "I mean, beyond belief. I'd always wanted to be a mother. Now I would have everything I ever wanted. Unfortunately, a pregnancy, especially one that happened before I was married, was not part of my parents' plan for me. To their credit, they only wanted the best for me. They didn't believe having a child out of wedlock was it. They approached Dennis, and they told him that he was to marry me or disappear. They'd rather have me raising a child on my own, the sad victim of a careless boy, than living in sin, raising a child with someone I wasn't married to. Can you believe that?"

Summer tilted her head, considering.

Before she could answer, Willow said, "Rhetorical question. Anyway. He disappeared. Not because he didn't want to marry me, but because he wanted to marry me in his own time, on his own terms. He didn't want anyone, especially my hoity toity parents, telling him what to do. And he knew I'd be unhappy if they disowned me. He knew, at that time, that it was impossible for me to walk away from them. We were close, believe it or not."

Summer could barely believe it. She'd never met Willow's parents. Willow said they were dead, and of course, Summer believed her. Why wouldn't she?

"At first, I didn't realize my parents had banned him from seeing me. I thought he didn't want you, and as a result, he didn't want me, either. I was heartbroken. I resented you. But a few months after you were born, Dennis came back. He sneaked into my parents' house. He climbed right up the trellis to my bedroom window. You can imagine the fright he gave me." She laughed. "Of course, I let him in, and he couldn't wait to see you, to touch your tiny hands, feel your soft white hair. My heart practically burst at the sight of it."

Summer couldn't picture cynical, jaded Willow with a practically bursting heart. But she could suspend her disbelief long enough to hear the rest of the story.

"My parents heard my window open. They heard Dennis's feet hitting the floor. After that one moment of pure bliss, wide open love, my dad thundered up the stairs. He threw Dennis out before we even had a chance to talk. I locked myself in the bedroom with you for days after that. The darkness was all-consuming."

She paused, shuddered, and took out a cigarette. "You were such a good baby. So quiet. So easygoing. I almost felt as if you didn't need me. You'd be fine with anyone. You wouldn't nurse. Stubborn little shit. Still, you were obviously thriving. You were fat and dimpled as a little piggy."

Just like now, Winter murmured in Summer's ear.

"I felt like you didn't need me," Willow said again. She paused, then, and raised an eyebrow. "Just like now."

Summer knew she should respond, should say something, but all she could think of was, I did need you. I needed you as a child and you let me down. So I made sure I didn't need you. And now you're on your own, just like I was. She remained silent, and Willow went on.

"So I started drinking. I started stealing Daddy's bourbon out of the cabinet. Mom started riding him for drinking too much. But it was me." A wry smile formed on her lips. "I got some small satisfaction out of that, I'll tell you. Drinking softened all the hard edges I came into contact with. It softened the hurt of Dennis leaving us. It softened the rejection I experienced when I believed you didn't need me. I drank bourbon at every meal, and soon enough, I drank it *for* every meal."

Summer had often wondered when Willow started drinking. She seemed so health-conscious otherwise, buying organic food, refusing Summer the sugary cereal in which her schoolmates found prizes, and lecturing Girl Scouts who sold their trans-fat-filled cookies at the grocery store. Although a small amount of sympathy crept in, Summer brushed it off.

"You can probably guess what happened next," Willow said.

When Summer shrugged, Willow said, "Your father came back. Dennis came back to the house one night when I was drunk. I could hear what he was saying, but my mind wouldn't take it in. He tried to tell me Daddy had sent him away, Daddy had threatened to have him blacklisted in town if he didn't leave us alone. My own father promised Dennis he'd never have a job in Juniper if we saw his face again. And because I was staying with my parents at that time, there was no way Dennis could contact us. But I wouldn't hear it. I blocked him out. I was drunk. I raged at him."

"So you knew your mom and dad sent him away, but you stayed angry at him," Summer said.

Willow nodded slowly and ran her tongue over her front teeth.

"I was angry at him for not standing up to them," she admitted. "I felt so grown up at the time. I assumed he felt that way, too. But Daddy scared the shit out of him. And I was angry at Daddy for that. So I moved out. And I kept drinking."

"And you kept drinking and drinking," Summer said.

Willow only nodded.

"Have you stopped drinking?"

Willow shifted her weight onto one foot and put a hand on her hip. "Mostly."

"Mostly?"

Willow shrugged one shoulder. "I have a few drinks a night."

"I don't want you drinking around my kids."

"Do you drink around your kids? Your friends keep mentioning your penchant for wine, so I'm sure you do."

"Not like you did," Summer said.

"Fine," Willow said.

"And no smoking in the house," Summer said.

Then, a sudden realization dawned on her. "What did you do with the baby?"

"I left her with Luke."

Groaning, Summer walked back inside to find her baby and relieve her six-year-old of babysitting duty.

. . .

LACK OF SLEEP and general overwhelm made the next several days fly by in a haze. In general, Olivia seemed content, but she did show her redhead temper if she didn't get to eat immediately upon requesting it through a sign language of fist-chewing. Willow toed the line, not helping so much as being another adult body in the house … but not messing anything up, either.

Luke's pre-surgery appointment was fast-approaching and Summer found herself increasingly anxious. She checked on him multiple times every night. She found herself checking on the other kids, too: putting a hand on Hannah's back as she slept to make sure she was breathing, or tucking the covers snugly around Sarah's neck like she hadn't done in years. She adjusted and readjusted the water glass on Nate's nightstand so he could reach it as easily as possible. She continued to overcook the chicken to ensure she killed any possible traces of salmonella.

If she slept at all, it was during a rare moment she sat down on the couch, and she always startled awake with the feeling that something was wrong. She was exhausted. And grumpy.

Summer chose to begin working again just a week after Olivia's birth. When some of her clients protested, saying she should take it easy, she said, "I'm a graphic designer, not a marathon runner. I just sit at the computer and design." In the back of her mind, though, she was thinking she couldn't afford to take maternity leave. She told herself she'd just have to push through.

Nevertheless, the first time the three older kids were at summer camp and Willow was watching the two younger ones, she sat down to work and found she couldn't concentrate. It was the first time Willow had watched Hannah and Olivia on her own, and Summer had to fight the urge to get up and peek on them, to make sure Willow hadn't put Olivia down for a nap on on her stomach and wasn't giving Hannah sips of bourbon to get her to sleep.

Summer decided she'd work on the logo design for Josie's big project, The Carla M. Garcia Community Center. Inspired by a student whose parents both worked after school, Josie had applied for (and been awarded) a grant to open an after-school program for kids.

They'd go there to do homework and eat healthy snacks, but more importantly, they'd have support and someone to talk to. In fact, Josie had asked Delaney to make a weekly appearance as the counselor-in-chief, putting to use her psychology degree.

It was a brilliant idea. Josie was so passionate about it, and Summer was honored to design the logo and the signage. But at the moment, Summer wasn't feeling passionate about anything other than sleep. So instead of working, she logged onto FriendZoo, where Winter helped her direct some of her frustration toward innocent bystanders who should probably remove her from their friend lists.

One acquaintance had posted a selfie from a basketball game the night before. Just like she had before Olivia was born, Summer imagined what she'd post in the comments: *Consider checking your teeth before you post next time. Also possibly make a dental appointment. Two words: Plaque issues.*

Instead, she typed, *Great smile.*

Another friend posted a meme that said, "My kids are my heart and soul, and they alway's will be. 'Share' if you agree."

This time, Summer did post a comment: *If your kids are your heart and soul, you'd better teach them proper apostrophe usage. Share if you agree.*

She got a good chuckle out of that. Until her phone dinged. Not once, but twice.

Josie: *WTF, Summer? Get off of FriendZoo now, before you wind up in the zoo. Or something. I don't know. Just get off.*

Delaney: *What are you thinking, woman? Do I have to confiscate your phone? (I'm practicing my parenting techniques. How did I do?)*

Summer sighed and rubbed her hand across her forehead.

She responded to Josie: *Okay, okay. But seriously. Alway's? Are you kidding me?*

And to Delaney: *You sound great. Very threatening. I'm getting off right now.*

Josie wrote back: *I know. I'm a teacher. You can't imagine how much it peeves me to see that. But get off. Now.*

Delaney wrote back: *Get off FriendZoo, or else.*

Summer responded to both of them: *Fine.*

Before signing off, Winter took control of her fingers on the keyboard. Some innocent soul who called Summer a friend had posted a picture of her terribly bratty child posing for the camera wearing a stupid hat. The caption said, "Isn't she cute?" Winter typed: *She has your husband's nose.*

Then she signed off.

Her phone dinged.

Josie: *Just had to get one last jab in there, didn't you?*

Delaney: *Wow. My threats are not very scary. My future child is destined to be a pain in the ass.*

Summer didn't respond. Instead, she began work on her design for the community center logo, starting with a bright sun in the upper lefthand corner. She had asked Willow to watch Hannah and Olivia for two hours, which was the window of time between Olivia's feedings.

Right on cue, Olivia howled. Summer saved her work and stood up. Maybe her subconscious would work on the logo while she was distracted. She usually took a moment to switch from work mode to mommy mode, but when she heard Willow yell, that moment was gone.

"The little shit pooped on me!"

Summer stopped in her tracks, her heart racing and her breath coming fast.

"*That's* what you were yelling about?" she said.

"Yes! What did you think I was yelling about?"

"Icky!" Hannah said, covering her mouth with one hand and pointing at Willow's skirt with the other.

Willow stood up, leaving Olivia on the couch.

"Why are you panting like that?" Willow said.

"I thought something was wrong." Summer concentrated on bringing her breathing back to normal.

"Something *is* wrong! She stained my skirt. I love this skirt. This stuff doesn't come out, either."

Summer shook her head and took the baby off the couch. "You can't just leave the baby on the couch like that. She could roll off."

"How about, 'Sorry about your skirt, Mom'?"

"Oh, yes. Sorry about your skirt, *Willow*, because your skirt is so much more important than my daughter's skull remaining intact."

Summer eased down onto the couch and began to feed Olivia. She saw hazards to her children's health everywhere. What if Olivia rolled off the couch and landed on the remote control truck one of the boys left on the floor? Her tiny, fragile bones would be broken. What if Hannah tripped over the truck and hit her face on the corner of the coffee table? Stitches, for sure. Summer should get some of those foam pads immediately. The coffee table was really dusty. What if dust particles made Luke's incision infected after his surgery? She'd have to be much better about dusting and vacuuming and disinfecting.

"We need to go to the store," she said to Willow. "Right now."

"What? Why? You just went. We have food. Want me to heat something up?"

"Icky!" Hannah yelled again.

"It's not for food," Summer said. "I need to get some disinfectant spray and vacuum bags. And maybe one of those duster things with the replaceable heads. I think we need a steam mop for the kitchen floor."

"I don't understand why a clean house is suddenly so important to you," Willow said.

Before Summer could respond, Willow (for once, self-censoring) quickly added, "That didn't come out in the way I meant it to. I just meant, you're worrying me. The house is fine. You seem a little … obsessive."

"You wouldn't understand," Summer said.

"Probably not," Willow agreed, her tone softer and more acquiescent than Summer thought she'd ever heard it.

Okay, Summer thought. *If Willow's going to be here, I should probably at least make an effort. What if we just had a normal conversation?*

"So, have you ever tried contacting Dennis again?" she said.

For a moment, Willow didn't answer. She stared straight ahead at the wall, and Summer thought she might have gotten too personal. Then Willow spoke.

"I haven't," she said. "I was so cruel to him the last time we talked, I've always been afraid he'd reject me."

Summer nodded. She could empathize. She still hadn't recovered from the first time Willow had rejected her. Summer was little, just six. A bad dream woke her up. Something about a monster truck. She'd seen one parked in front of the high school earlier that day, and it had terrified her. Its tires were taller than she was. Willow could have driven their junky car underneath it. The school's electronic marquee had advertised a monster truck show, and Willow explained to Summer that during a monster truck show, the big truck would smash a bunch of cars.

Willow demonstrated with her hands, and the thought of the destruction it would cause gave Summer terrible anxiety. What if the truck tipped over and the driver was smashed right along with the cars? What if the driver lost control of the truck and it smashed the people in the audience?

When Summer asked why people called it a monster truck, Willow had laughed. "It's like a big monster, with a mind of its own, and it's bent on widespread destruction." Even at age six, Summer knew what destruction meant.

So the nightmare consisted of a monster truck roaring up the driveway of their trailer and smashing the entire house to the ground, with Summer and Willow inside it.

She woke up screaming, and ran into Willow's bedroom. The bed was empty, and in her irrational six-year-old mind, Summer was terrified that the monster truck had already gotten her mother. Destroyed her.

Panicking then, she ran into the living room. Willow sat on the couch, a glass in one hand, a cigarette in the other. Summer flew to her side, desperate for her mother's embrace, for proof that she was alive and whole and hadn't been smashed by a monster truck.

Instead of holding her, though, Willow blocked her from climbing up onto the couch. Instead of setting down one of her vices, she'd turned her body so Summer bumped up against her forearm rather than curling onto her lap.

"Back to bed, young lady," she said, seemingly oblivious to the fact that Summer was traumatized and in need of comfort. "You shouldn't be up at this time, no, ma'am."

Her voice sounded almost gleeful. Summer recognized the cadence and the tone immediately: this was the beyond-conversation Willow.

She tried one, "But, Mama," but when their eyes met, she knew it was a lost cause. The lights were on but nobody was home.

So Summer put her head down and walked slowly back to her

bedroom, where she curled up under the bed, just in case. She fought sleep all night long.

Now, Summer looked over at her mother. Willow rejected her years ago, just as Dennis rejected Willow. But now Willow had come back. Was it possible that Dennis could come around, too?

"You never know what might happen," Summer said. "He could come around, especially after all this time."

"That may be true," Willow said. "It may be."

"I'm going to go for a walk," she said after a few quiet moments. "You've given me a lot to think about."

Summer nodded, but Willow remained standing there behind the couch, deep in thought. In that moment, Summer felt a tiny stab of pity for Willow, for the fact that she'd spent her whole life alone after being rejected by her high school boyfriend.

Well, not alone, exactly, Winter chimed in. *She had you.*

People always said forgiveness isn't a gift to the forgiven. Rather, it's peace for the forgiver. But Summer wondered how a person actually did it. How did you genuinely forgive someone who had caused you so much hurt? And more importantly, someone who didn't even realize she'd caused that pain?

Summer and Willow sighed at the same time.

Willow shook her head. "Sorry, lost in thought. I'm off."

Summer didn't remind her to change her skirt.

CHAPTER FOURTEEN

"I can't believe it's been a whole week since we saw Miss Olivia," Josie said as she breezed into Summer's house the following Thursday, her arms loaded down with bags. She dropped the bags on the kitchen table. "Give me that baby right away."

Delaney came in a minute later carrying a bakery box. "Let Happy Hour commence!"

"Speaking of Happy Hour, I notice Willow is absent this afternoon," Josie said. "Where is she?"

"She said she had errands," Summer said. She had visions of Willow in the bourbon section at the liquor store, squinting at labels. The now-familiar pressure in her torso began to build, taking up the space meant for her lungs.

"I think she dislikes us," Josie said.

"Doubt it," Summer said. "You're part of the reason I let her stay here. Let's change the subject. Delaney, how's the house hunt going?"

"I have big news," Delaney said.

"Aunt Dee brought us donuts!" Nate, following his donut radar, made the announcement and the kids stampeded to the kitchen.

"Contrary to popular belief, that is not the big news," Delaney said after handing Hannah a pink sprinkle donut.

Summer winced as Hannah immediately started dropping crumbs onto the carpet.

Delaney noticed, too, rolled her eyes at Summer's reaction. "I'll vacuum."

Summer immediately felt guilty. "No, it's not that. It's just—" *It's just that I feel like Sisyphus, rolling that gigantic boulder up the hill, only for it to roll back down again.* "Tell us your big news."

"Oh, yes. Okay. Our big news is that we're buying the house where your water broke. Jake and I both believe it's an omen that Olivia liked it so much she threatened to be born there."

Summer and Josie laughed.

"Does it fit all the criteria?" Josie wanted to know.

"Believe it or not."

Hannah climbed onto Summer's lap, and Summer sat quietly, listening to Delaney and Josie talk about the house, escrow, paint colors and nursery themes. She wanted to tell Delaney that nursery themes didn't matter, that healthy children were more important than curtains. If Delaney asked, she would just give one of her usual answers, the ones everyone thought were so deep, but were actually non-answers designed to keep anyone from getting mad at her. "Imagine each pair of curtains hanging in the nursery when you walk in. Which ones *feel* right?" Fortunately, Delaney didn't ask her opinion, likely because she was falling asleep on the couch.

Sometimes Summer wished she could go back to the time in her life just after she had Sarah, before everything felt so hectic and scary. Things were so simple, then. Not that she ever regretted the choices she and Derek had made together, but right now, she just felt so *tired.*

Although she was only half-listening, she noticed the girls' conversation had switched to The Carla M. Garcia Community Center. Summer had emailed Josie the initial round of logo designs the night before.

"Summer, those initial designs you sent me—they're perfect."

Summer could hear the emotion in Josie's voice and she smiled.

"I'm pretty much a genius," she said.

"You captured it! You captured the sense of fun and security I'm going for."

"Can I see?" Delaney said.

"I have it on my phone," Josie said. Summer felt herself drifting off to sleep, even as she heard Delaney *oohing* over the first option and asking to see the second.

When she woke up again, she heard the girls discussing Josie's upcoming anniversary. "After everything that happened over the past few months, I wanted to plan something special, just for the two of us."

Eyes closed, Summer nodded absently, thinking about Josie's recent flirtations with her secret ex-boyfriend, who also happened to be her boss. Summer and Delaney stepped in with The Marriage Intervention, helping Josie ditch the slimy ex-boyfriend and repair her marriage.

Josie ticked potential vacation spots off on her fingers and Delaney exclaimed about each one. San Diego, Denver, Zion.

"A vacation would be really nice," Summer said, as she pictured herself and Derek on some hot beach. He'd be wearing his swimming trunks, and she'd admire the muscles in his stomach and back. She'd be wearing a muumuu, obviously. He'd lay down next to her on a blanket, and breast milk would leak out of her boobs.

"Summer!" Josie's harsh voice interrupted her daydream. "Snap out of it, woman. Your baby is hungry and you've obviously left planet Earth."

Oh. Her breasts really were leaking. She took Olivia from Josie. "Sorry, guys. Just daydreaming about my own vacation. On a beach."

"Look, Summer," Josie said. "We're worried about you. You need a real, actual vacation."

"How can I take a vacation?" Summer said. "Please give me some advice, here. I have five children. One of them is a newborn and one of them is about to have major heart surgery. One of them is a preteen and the other two are probably developing psychological problems as we speak, because they're not getting enough attention."

A clock ticked, and Summer thought the sound might make her crazy. Her eyelid twitched.

Delaney and Josie looked at each other. While watching Summer carefully, Josie continued talking about vacation options. Spa versus skydiving, beach versus mountains, flying versus driving.

Summer closed her eyes, returning to her mental vacation. Beach, sand, waves, her husband. Peace and quiet. The sun on her skin. The coconut scent of the sunblock. Seagulls. Maybe she couldn't leave the house, or her life, right now, but she could certainly enjoy little trips to the beach in her mind. Maybe sometime in the near future a brilliant scientist would invent a way to experience a beach day from your couch, even as you were surrounded by dust and grimy children.

Willow's return to the house jarred Summer out of her meditative state. She blinked a couple of times, noticed a huge chunk of donut already ground into the carpet and saw Delaney elbow Josie. Willow looked breathless and excited, her lips pressed together as if she was trying to hold in a big secret. *What now?*

"I got a surprise for you," Willow said.

This is a first.

"Is it coconut-scented sunblock?" Summer asked.

Willow looked slightly perplexed. "No. It's a book. I saw it at the grocery store. I didn't even realize they sold books there, it's been so long since I actually stepped foot in one of those places."

She handed the gigantic hardcover to Summer.

"The Secret to Thinking Positive," Summer read aloud. "What is this?"

"Uh oh," Delaney said. "That is her deadly-calm mom voice."

Josie plucked the book out of her hand and turned it over to read the back: "Ten percent of life is what happens to you. Ninety percent is how you react to it."

Oh, perfect. A book is exactly what I need. Not a vacation, but a book.

"Deep," Summer said.

"I just thought, you know, with your recent attitude, this might help," Willow said.

"My attitude? You want to talk about my attitude? Why don't you take a look at my life. I don't need positive thinking. I need a damn holiday. Or a personal chef. A housecleaner. A designated laundry-washer and folder. Only, guess what? I can't have any of that. Instead, I get you. One more mouth to feed, one more set of clothes to wash, one more person to cater to."

"She's just trying to help, Summer," Delaney said, and Summer was horrified to see a tear leaking out of one of Delaney's eyes.

"Why are you crying?" she said.

"I don't know. It's just so ... so—I don't know, okay? I just *am!*"

"Oh, my God," Josie said. She rubbed a hand over her forehead. "The hormones in this place are just too much for me. I brought you a bunch of stuff."

Josie tossed the book onto the couch next to Summer and went into the kitchen, where she began looking through the bags she'd brought. Summer heard the fridge open and close.

"*I'm* not hormonal," Willow said, her voice too loud, which Summer knew meant her feelings were hurt. "I'm just fine."

She stood up and walked out of the room, her movements brisk. Summer could have sworn she saw her brush a tear out from under her eye.

"I don't think she really meant attitude," Delaney said, sniffling. "I think she meant, like, how you've been, you know, down, or whatever."

It was probably true. For the umpteenth time, guilt overtook Summer. "I'm sorry, Delaney. I really am. That was a really nice gesture Willow made. The first one she's made, ever, in my entire life. I just wasn't sure how to respond."

In her mind, Winter whispered, *It's a stupid gesture. Don't get me a book. Get me a personal assistant.*

Josie came back into the living room. "So I made you some lemon chicken. You can keep it in the fridge until you're ready to eat it, then cook it at three-fifty for an hour. Also, chili. Just heat it up. And I brought you chocolate."

She dug out an oversized chocolate bar, and handed it to Summer.

"Plus, I know you don't drink a lot when you're nursing, but I brought you this wine anyway. A glass a night. It'll be fine."

Summer could tell Josie was nervous. She was probably afraid Summer would bite her head off like she'd done to Delaney and Willow about the stupid book.

"This looks delicious," she said, admiring the chocolate, hoping her gratitude showed. "And of course I'll drink the wine."

"Magazines, too," Josie added. She held up a stack of them. "These are the ones I've read already, so I'm passing them on. Plus one I stole from the coffee shop and one I stole from the dentist's office."

"I thought Paul talked you out of stealing magazines," Delaney said.

"He thinks he did," Josie said.

"Perfect," Summer said. "A cop's wife, stealing magazines to give to her wine-drinking, nursing best friend who has five soon-to-be delinquent children."

Josie dropped the stack of magazines on the couch, on top of "The Secret To Thinking Positive."

"You know," she said, "I think it's time I make my exit. Are you coming, Delaney?"

Willow took Delaney and Josie's departure as a signal, and swept back into the living room.

"You need to get out." She said it with forced cheer, and Summer, still slightly stunned at Josie and Delaney having left, shook her head. "No, I'm fine."

"I think you and Derek should go on a date," Willow said. "I'll watch the kids. Just a short date."

When Summer didn't respond right away, Willow spluttered. "Just two hours between the little one's feedings. Dinner. A movie. Whatever."

"First of all, I'm not leaving my kids with you. Second of all, her name is Olivia. Third, just out of curiosity, why do you care?"

Willow sighed. "You're my daughter. That's why. It's what mothers do."

"You know what mothers do?"

"Summer. I raised you, didn't I? You turned out fine."

"Thanks. That's a real compliment."

Willow sighed again.

Very dramatic, Winter said in Summer's mind.

Go away, Summer thought. *I'm bordering on crazy as it is.*

The clock ticked. From somewhere in the back of the house, Summer heard the boys yelling, and Hannah squealing in response.

Summer could stand a night out with Derek. In fact, hadn't Josie and Delaney included date nights in their Motherhood Intervention rules? It didn't have to be anything fancy. Maybe they could just grab a quick ice cream or go for a walk. They wouldn't leave the kids alone with Willow for too long. What if they went after the kids' bedtime? Then Willow would just serve as a warm body at the house in case the smoke detectors went off. If one of the kids got up, she could probably convince him to go back to bed. But what if someone cut off a finger? What if Nate got into the matches?

Who am I kidding? I can't stay up past their bedtime. I'm barely awake now.

Was Willow capable of putting five kids to bed?

Absolutely not, Winter said.

Was it possible to punch your imaginary friend in the face?

Sarah could put herself to bed, and the boys could get completely ready on their own. They'd still expect to be tucked in by an adult, and they didn't know enough to realize Willow didn't really qualify as an adult. Summer sniggered at that thought. Willow cocked an eyebrow at her.

Hannah required lots of help. Olivia could just lay in her bassinet or the baby swing while Willow dealt with everyone else. So it was really just two people Willow had to take care of, and one of them couldn't even move of her own volition at this point.

"Fine," Summer said. "You win."

"What?"

"Actually," Summer said with a cackle, "You lose. Derek and I will go out tonight. We'll just go for an hour or so, like you said. Maybe we'll grab dessert or something. I think you can handle it."

Summer didn't miss the self-satisfied smile Willow hid as she walked into the kitchen. "I can handle it."

Delaney and Josie would be pleased, too. They'd congratulate her on taking time for herself and her marriage.

Horror-movie scenes of her children in Willow's care flashed through Summer's mind: Luke and Nate cut up and bloody from using real kitchen knives to sword fight. Hannah facedown in the bathtub, drowned with one arm down the drain and the other chubby fist clutching the water pony she so loved. Sarah's hair on fire, her face burned thanks to curling iron instructions from Willow. Olivia's tiny body in the trash can.

Oh, my. I really am losing it.

She had to stay home. If she valued her children's survival, she would stay home.

She had to go. She couldn't stay home every night for the rest of her life, listening to the ticking of the clock.

Josie and Delaney would be so proud. They'd think she was feeling less anxious. That she was able to let go a little. Relax. Have fun. Summer nodded to herself.

Fake it 'til you make it. I can do this.

Willow opened the fridge, and Summer heard her say, "I hope you two enjoy yourselves."

SUMMER AND DEREK decided on Hot Diggity Dog's, the drive-up restaurant they'd frequented as teenagers. On the way there, Summer picked at a loose piece of skin on her cuticle while simultaneously chewing her lip. She checked her phone every five seconds to see if Willow had called or texted to report an emergency. She couldn't stop thinking about Luke, about his tiny chest being cut wide open on a cold operating table in a cold room. She kept quiet about it, though, because she was supposed to be relaxing.

"Nothing like a little nostalgia," Derek said, oblivious to the runaway train in Summer's mind. He pulled the car into the corner spot.

With no little effort, Summer brought her train to a grinding halt and switched gears. She could do this. "I love that we used to come here and make out."

"Those were seriously the days," Derek said. "I had the hottest girl in school in my backseat. On her back. In this very same corner spot."

Summer swatted him on the arm. "You never had me on my back in the backseat."

"Okay, not in this corner spot. But at the drive-in, I did. They were playing that classic movie … what was it?"

"You don't know because you were trying to get into my pants for the first half, and we were having sex the entire second half. Well, for the final three minutes."

"Ha. You don't know either, because you liked it. Like I said, those were the days. You know, we should bring the Econo Van next time."

They ordered fries and chocolate milkshakes, just as they would have years ago. They sat in silence while they waited, watching the teenagers who drove in, pumped up on freedom and hormones.

"Our girls will never be allowed to wear something like that." Summer pointed at a pair of girls in tube tops and skinny jeans, their eyeliner thick and their hair perfectly straight.

"I have news for you, Summer Gray. Those are the kinds of things girls hide under their parent-approved baggy sweatshirts."

"We're going to have to check them going out the door."

Derek nodded. "I can't believe we have three girls now. Good thing we have two boys to balance them out."

For now, Winter whispered.

A carhop on roller skates glided to a stop at Derek's window and Summer was forced to sit in silence while Derek paid.

"Do you think Luke's going to be okay?" Summer said when the carhop rolled away after an eternity.

Derek sighed. "I think so. I researched Dr. Karlsen and it looks like she's one of the best heart surgeons in the nation. She's really good at what she does."

"You researched her?"

Even though Summer knew exactly what she was doing—latching on to something insignificant and readying for an all-out fight—she couldn't stop herself. Anger is so much more satisfying than fear.

"I recognize the deadly mom voice," Derek said, catching on immediately.

"Why does everyone keep saying that?" Summer said.

Derek laughed. "Because you keep talking like that. What's wrong with me researching Dr. Karlsen?"

"I already researched her, that's what's wrong. I told you she's well-respected and she knows what she's doing. Why couldn't you *trust* me?" Her rational inner voice (not Winter, that mean bitch) told her to stop, to take a deep breath, to get off this track. But it felt so good to direct all these icky feelings of stress and anxiety at a particular person.

Derek put his hands up as if he were surrendering. "Independent research, that's all!"

"You don't trust me."

Ridiculous. Of course he trusts me.

"That's ridiculous," Derek said. "Of course I trust you."

"Then why would you research on your own?"

"I know where this is going," he said. "It's like a runaway train. If I hadn't researched, you'd say that I should have. But because I did, you're saying I don't trust you."

Summer sighed, more because she knew he was right than because he was irritating her.

"Don't get huffy with me," he said. "You know I'm right."

He handed her one of his fries, and she took it. "You're right. I know you're right. I'm just stressed."

"Eat a fry, drink your shake, and we'll be okay. We'll make it through this. Luke will be okay, too. He's strong. Okay? Stop picking at your cuticles. You'll be sorry tomorrow when they're all sore and bleeding."

They ate the rest of their fries and drank the rest of their shakes in silence, holding hands across the center console, just like they'd done since they were teenagers.

Delaney and Josie were right. Summer needed date nights with Derek. For herself and for their marriage. And maybe having Willow here wasn't so bad. It had been nice to get away, even if it was for an hour.

That was Summer's final thought as they pulled out of Hot Diggity Dog's ... before Summer knew what they'd find when they returned home.

"EVERYTHING LOOKS QUIET," Derek said when they parked in the driveway. "Maybe we could stay outside and neck for a while."

Summer laughed. "If only."

The house was completely silent, except for the ticking of that damn clock. Summer felt a twitch on the right side of her face. Insanity, setting in. Olivia slept soundly in her swing, her hands folded neatly on her stomach.

"Sure is quiet," Derek whispered. "Where's Willow?"

The effect was eerie: Olivia sleeping in her motionless swing, the house appearing otherwise empty.

"She probably defected. Took off."

"Give her a break," he said, irritation so evident in his voice she laughed.

"I was just kidding," Summer said, and Winter added, "Geez."

"Your mood tonight hasn't exactly been conducive to kidding around."

Summer shrugged. They peered over the back of the couch to see whether Willow was laying down. She wasn't. Summer walked into the kitchen to see if she was sitting at the table. She wasn't. A sense of unease formed in the pit of her stomach.

"I'll go peek in on the kids and make sure they're not actually having ice cream parties in their rooms," Derek said.

"Check the bathroom," Summer said, picturing Hannah with her arm down the drain.

Summer searched the kitchen floor and counter for bloody knives. Was it possible that Willow had gone to bed, too? She never went to sleep this early but maybe she was reading or something. "The Secret To Parenting Your Adult Daughter After Disappearing for Fifteen Years." Did that book exist?

Derek returned. "Kids are all tucked in and sleeping."

"Thank goodness for that. Maybe Willow's outside on the patio."

Derek nodded, and they walked together to the sliding glass door on the other side of the kitchen.

When they stepped outside, they saw her. Willow had, at one time, been sitting up at the patio table. Now, though, she was slumped over, her forehead on the glass tabletop, a cigarette still burning in her hand.

CHAPTER FIFTEEN

Derek, unaccustomed to seeing a parental figure passed out drunk, panicked immediately.

"Call nine-one-one," he said.

Summer huffed out an impatient breath and walked over to the table. She jerked the cigarette out of Willow's relaxed grip and ground it out in the plastic ash tray Willow had undoubtedly sneaked onto the premises after one of her trips to the dollar store.

"She's fine," Summer said. "We don't need an ambulance."

"Shouldn't you check her pulse, just to be sure? Don't roll your eyes at me, Summer! I mean, is she even breathing?"

The speed and cadence of Derek's voice snatched Summer right up and plunked her down as her twelve-year-old self, returning home from a field trip to the Grand Canyon. It was late, after ten p.m., and Willow hadn't come to pick Summer up when the bus dropped the kids off.

Someone else's parent—a mother who had been waiting responsibly in her car when the bus pulled into the school parking lot— offered to drive Summer home, and kept her eyes off the trailer when she stopped at the curb.

The porch lights were off. As Summer approached the front door, the responsible mother called through her rolled-down window, "Can you see, honey?"

Summer had turned around and waved, smiling as though she

were overcome with pure joy at the thought of returning home to her own irresponsible mother.

She fumbled to unlock the door and was surprised to find the inside of the house pitch dark, too. All the hiking had left her thirsty, and she walked towards the kitchen, flipping lights on as she went. As she passed the small, rickety dining table, which stood on its three metal legs at the edge of the living room, Summer startled. Someone was sitting there. Well, not sitting, exactly, but had been at some point. Now, the person's upper torso was limp on top of the orange Formica tabletop.

Summer felt torn, frozen with indecision. Should she run right back out of the house, chasing the responsible mother down the street? Or should she satiate her curiosity about who was sitting at the table? If she left now, she could probably get to a neighbor's house and call the police to report an intruder. But then she'd never know who had broken in. What if it was her father? Or one of Willow's friends? This person obviously wasn't dangerous at the moment. But why would anyone in their right mind be sitting at the table in the dark?

Fate made the decision for her. The headlights of a passing car illuminated the figure at the table.

Willow.

Motionless. Silent.

Dead.

Summer's mother was dead.

It was the only explanation.

Relief and anger flooded Summer's bloodstream in equal parts. She heard a roaring in her ears and thought for a moment she might pass out. Death was at least a good excuse—perhaps the only good excuse—for forgetting to pick Summer up. On the other hand, Willow drinking herself to death was a final declaration of her true priorities. She'd chosen booze over her daughter one final time.

Summer took a deep breath and ventured forward, one tiny step and then another. She'd have to call an ambulance. Shouldn't she check Willow's pulse, first? Make sure she wasn't breathing? She'd have to tell the nine-one-one dispatcher something.

She inched toward the table.

Then, Willow moaned. Summer's own voice echoed the sound, and she jumped.

Alive.

The rage that suddenly flowed through her body was so strong it threatened to consume her. She couldn't scream, she couldn't throw a tantrum, she couldn't break anything. So she stood there in silence and hated her mom and loved her and felt the deepest sense of despair. Is this what their life was coming to?

The next morning, Willow nursed a killer hangover, and for the first time ever, Summer refused to bring her water or aspirin or a bacon and cheese burrito.

Throughout the rest of her childhood, Summer daydreamed about Willow dying. She ran through what she'd do, who she'd call, where she'd live. All the possible scenarios had one thing in common: Willow's death never surprised her. She felt completely prepared, ready for whatever new life faced her.

After all, a life without Willow couldn't be any worse than one in which she played the all-important role of Summer's nemesis.

Reeling from the memory, Summer grabbed her husband's arm and pulled him back towards the sliding glass door that led into the kitchen.

"Let's go to bed," she said. "She'll be fine out here. I've seen this before."

"No, really, aren't you going to check her pulse or breathing?"

"You can."

When Derek put his fingers on Willow's wrist, her head rolled to the side so her face turned towards Summer. Her mouth hung open just slightly, and a tiny dribble of drool slid out one corner to pool on the table. She sucked in some air, and her head rolled back to where it had been.

"Well, she's alive," Derek said, speaking so quietly it was almost under his breath.

"I wasn't worried about it," Summer said. "I told you, I've seen this before."

Head down, Derek followed Summer through the door. She slid the deadbolt into place.

"Shouldn't we leave it unlocked?" Derek said.

"Nope. She knows better than to wake us up. And I don't want any intruders kidnapping our children."

When they laid down in bed a long while later, Summer said, "This won't happen again."

Whether Derek heard the ominous tone of her voice or had already fallen asleep, he didn't argue.

THE NEXT MORNING, Summer waited for Willow at her own kitchen table. When she heard the patio chair scrape the concrete, she unlocked the sliding glass door. She stood inside it with her hands on her hips.

Willow dragged herself toward the door, smoothing her skirt. She already held a lit cigarette, gingerly, as if she were afraid she'd burn herself with it as she made her way back to the house. Summer yanked the door open. Willow jumped, her bloodshot eyes and mouth forming three perfect O's on her pale face. Summer stifled a laugh and at once felt cruel.

"What are you doing out here so early?" Summer asked, playing innocent.

Willow mumbled something Summer couldn't understand, and tried to push her way into the house.

"You're not smoking that in here," Summer said.

Willow stopped and looked Summer in the eye for the first time.

"Stop me," she said.

Summer heard the challenge in her mother's voice, and stepped quickly back and shut the door between them. Willow dropped the cigarette on the ground and smashed it with the ball of her bare foot, then winced and cursed. Summer opened the door, and Willow walked past her without looking up. She almost collided with Derek, who was making his way into the kitchen, rubbing the sleep from his eyes. She excused herself and made a beeline for the bathroom.

"She made it through the night, I guess," he said.

"Unfortunately," Summer said.

They sat at the table sipping coffee for a few moments without speaking.

"I can't believe the kids are still sleeping," Derek said.

"I know," Summer said. "I'd die for an extra cup of coffee this morning."

Summer didn't get to hear Derek's answer, which she'd hoped was permission to bathe her bloodstream in caffeine, because Willow finally emerged from the bathroom and limped into the kitchen. She got a coffee mug out of the cabinet and poured herself a cup, inhaling the steam loudly.

"Rough night?" Summer said.

"Especially because you locked me out there," Willow said.

"I assumed you were in bed in the girls' room."

"Liar."

Summer shrugged. "Willow, you need to leave. I mean, leave the house for good. I can't have you around my kids if you're going to be drinking like this."

"I raised you just fine."

"Did you?" All of Winter's little soldiers stood at attention in Summer's brain, spears at the ready. "I seem to recall raising myself. And it doesn't matter anyway. I don't want you here."

Derek slinked out of the kitchen. A fresh wave of anger threatened to take Summer's breath away. How could he leave her at this moment? Why wasn't he supporting her in this? Why did he keep disappearing? Willow took his spot at the kitchen table.

"I didn't mean, 'Enjoy your coffee and then go,'" Summer said. "I meant, leave. Now."

In response, Willow slurped the coffee. Olivia wailed. Willow remained at the table with her hands cupped around her mug, her eyes focused on something deep within it. Summer sat down across from her, and spoke as calmly as possible, despite the little soldiers getting ready to charge.

"I gave you a chance," she said. "I tried. But it's not going to work out. You need to get out. Today. And don't come back."

Willow looked up and made eye contact with Summer. "I don't have anywhere else to go."

To Summer's absolute horror, Willow's face crumpled and she began to cry.

"You have to be kidding me," Summer said. "Where the hell were you before this? If you recall, I haven't seen you for fifteen years.

And obviously, you've been somewhere. Because you're still here. Drinking. Smoking. Acting stupid."

Willow sniffled. "So I'm not welcome in my own daughter's house?"

"I don't even consider myself your daughter."

"You don't understand," Willow said. "I can't leave. I just can't."

Summer shook her head. "No. *You* don't understand. I can't have you here."

"Can I stay just a little longer? Please? Just a few more weeks. That's all I'm asking."

Summer expected her to say something like, "I'm in grave danger," or, "the Mafia threatened my life," or, "I'm dying and I have only weeks to live. Days, actually." But she didn't. The clock ticked. Neither of them spoke. Winter's soldiers were waging a battle with Summer's reasonable side. In her effort not to be like Willow, she was, in fact, being like Willow—kicking her own flesh and blood out of her house. *But Willow is an enemy*, Winter's soldiers shouted. She'd made herself an enemy fifteen years ago, and became only more fierce during the course of her ongoing absence.

The right thing to do, Summer's reasonable side argued, was to let Willow stay. That's the opposite of what Willow would do. Letting her stay created a huge opportunity for Disaster (with a capital D) to strike.

But Summer had raised herself. And she'd raised herself to do the right thing.

"Fine," she said. "A few more weeks. But we're going to lay some ground rules. No drinking. At all. And no smoking on my property. And don't expect me to leave my kids with you again. What if one of them had woken up and found you passed out on the patio? Is that how you want them to see you?"

Willow shook her head, still staring into her coffee. "Of course not. Of course it isn't."

"You have three weeks. And then you're out. For good."

Winter's war-hungry soldiers stuck their spears into Summer's reasonable side even as her reasonable side declared victory.

CHAPTER SIXTEEN

The next Sunday, the day before Luke's surgery, Summer found herself in a state of near-hysteria. She couldn't believe it, but she was actually grateful for Willow's presence. It served as a good distraction when all the kids were home. Derek had taken an extra overnight shift in order to be off the next day for Luke's surgery, so Summer was on her own.

While she scrubbed every surface in the house with disinfectant wipes—the walls, the kitchen counters, the furniture, the door handles—Willow played board games with the older kids and, true to form, pointed out spots Summer missed. After an interminable afternoon and evening, Summer tucked the kids into bed while Willow went for a walk and a cigarette.

Once all five children were asleep, Summer sat on the couch and stared at the TV, which was turned off.

Tomorrow. The surgery is tomorrow.

Even though she'd fixated on the operation since she found out about it, tomorrow had sneaked up on her. It was already here. She'd been so busy cleaning and dusting and fretting and vacuuming that she hadn't done what was truly important: spend time with Luke. He didn't seem to notice. Time passed, and life remained the same for him. He went to camp, came home, played with his siblings, did homework, ate dinner and went to bed.

And what did Summer do? She cooked, cleaned, folded laundry, cleaned, fit in a little work here and there. Cleaned some more. Now, in the depths of her worry, she realized how little she actually interacted with her children every day.

Today she had. Today she'd kissed each one in turn, noticing Sarah's thick eyelashes, the tiny freckles across Nate's nose, the way the ends of Luke's white-blond hair curved to one side, Hannah's chubby little cheeks and Olivia's perfect crescent-shaped toes. But she noticed these things only because she was terrified she'd lose Luke tomorrow.

Why didn't she take the time, steal these small moments, to notice them every single day? Willow came back in and sat on the couch next to Summer. For once, she didn't come up with something she thought was clever to say.

An hour passed, the two of them sitting side by side without sharing a conversation.

Summer stood up. "I'm getting ready for bed."

She went into the bedroom to change clothes, but knew she was too restless to sleep. So instead of laying down, she went into the bedroom the boys shared and sat at the foot of Luke's bed. Although she'd always thought it was creepy when she heard about moms doing it, she watched him sleep—the steady rise and fall of his chest, the way his arm laid across his stomach, his fist curled loosely. He always slept on his back, with his right leg bent and his left leg straight, one arm across his stomach and the other above his head.

His mouth was slightly open, but he breathed through his nose, which resulted in a quiet, regular snore. More than anything, Summer wanted to pick him up and hold him, to rock him like she had when he was a baby. He'd loved to hear "Singin' in the Rain," and it had soothed him when he cried, which was often.

She scooted up towards his torso until she was sitting right next to him and scooped him into her arms. He curled his body into hers, resting his head on her chest. She whispered the lyrics to "Singin' in the Rain," all the while crying and wondering how mothers coped with the death of their children.

If Luke died tomorrow, her mind would still feel the imprint of all the precious things he'd done. The way he cocked his head just slightly to the right whenever he didn't understand what someone said. The way he overreacted to the smallest things, stomping off with a quivering lip when she said they didn't have any more oatmeal, only to return moments later in a ninja costume, swinging a sword. The way he found absolute joy in teaching Hannah to walk, holding her hands and stepping carefully backwards to lead her throughout the house.

Within a few moments, she found herself sobbing, soaking his hair with her tears. She put him back down, tucked the sheet up under his chin and laid down next to him, stroking his head and his arm. How could she possibly emerge from this a whole person? When a child dies, so does a part of his mother.

Eventually, the sobbing quieted, and Summer felt her body relax. She managed to doze off a couple of times, but she repeatedly jerked herself awake to check the clock. She saw one a.m., two a.m. and three a.m. come and go.

When she was awake, listening to him breathe, she planned Luke's funeral, mentally flicking through images of flowers she'd seen at the shop downtown. He hated pink. The Universe should have made more blue flowers. What would she say? Maybe someone else would speak so she wouldn't have to. What would the kids wear? She didn't think they owned any black outfits. What would it be like to go shopping for clothes for your youngest son's funeral?

At some point after three a.m., she drifted to sleep with her hand over Luke's heart. She breathed in time to his heartbeat, imagining she could fold his body back inside of hers, so he was perfectly protected and safe, breathing her breath, her heart beating life into his.

But when she woke up at six, he was still separate, his body making its own indentation on the superhero sheets. She blinked herself awake, laying there a moment longer before gently lifting herself off the bed to brew coffee.

All she could do now was fake strength and bravery, and somehow get through today.

Both Delaney and Josie texted her just after six, while she measured coffee grinds into the filter. Josie was asking how Summer was, and Delaney was asking if she was up yet. Summer heard a quiet knock on the door just a few moments later, and after getting Chuck to stop barking, she smiled when she opened it to the girls, holding a steaming to-go cup and bakery bags from Ground Up, her favorite coffee shop.

"Oh my God, you look like shit," Josie said. Delaney shot her a dirty look and she winced.

"Did you sleep at all?" Delaney asked.

Summer shook her head, and Josie thrust the coffee into her hand. "It's mostly decaf with a few shots of regular. Go shower. We'll get the kids ready."

Summer nodded. She felt like crying (yet again), this time with gratitude, but her body was completely parched from all the tears it had expelled last night. Instead, she took a long drink of coffee, swallowed it and said, "Thank you," on a big sigh.

She embraced the girls tightly before heading into the bedroom. Derek was sleeping. His overnight shift ended at four a.m., so he'd get a few hours' sleep this morning before heading to the hospital. Which meant they'd both be exhausted today.

Perfect. Well, at least we'll be together.

She imagined the shower rinsing off all the negativity she'd felt laying in Luke's bed last night, and emerged feeling somewhat refreshed and a little more ready to face the day.

SUMMER WOULD NEVER UNDERSTAND why nobody made hospitals more hospitable. She and Derek sat in a waiting room a few hours after leaving the house, adjusting and readjusting their positions in creaky chairs with worn out cushions.

Derek drifted off to sleep, and Summer felt a mixture of jealousy and irritation. How could he sleep at a time like this? And why couldn't she? Luke had been off the wall this morning, overly goofy, running around the house in his underwear with his shirt on his head like a headdress, putting on Summer's high heels once he got into his pants and entertaining everyone through breakfast with a crazy song and dance. In the car on the way to the hospital, though, he sat quietly in the backseat, staring out the window.

"Your brother and sister and I put together that special box for you, for after the surgery," Summer said at a red light, twisting around in her seat to talk to him.

He nodded.

For the millionth time, she ran through the morning's schedule with him: "We'll go into a room where they get you ready, and then we'll have to leave you with a nurse—"

"Mom. It's fine. I know. I'll see you ..." his eyes got big and he spoke in a spooky voice "on the other side."

Summer and Derek both laughed, and Summer felt immensely grateful and chastened that her little boy was the one making her laugh this morning. Luke had his pre-op nurses in stitches with his movie character impressions, and when Dr. Karlsen came into the room in her scrubs, he grinned like they were old friends.

The doctor had hugged Summer hard, and said, "We'll see you in a bit."

That was that. Now they waited. Summer brought a book to read, but found she couldn't concentrate on it. She read and reread the same paragraph several times before putting the book back in her purse and looking around at the landscape paintings and pastel wallpaper. It took every bit of mental strength she had not to imagine a giant saw cutting through Luke's sternum, or his heart being pumped by a giant, sci-fi-worthy machine.

A volunteer manned the desk in the waiting room, and every few minutes he'd answer the phone on his desk and then deliver a message or update to one of the families in the room. Every time the phone rang, Summer jumped.

Two hours after Luke's surgery started, the volunteer approached her and Derek. She swatted Derek's chest and he jerked awake.

"You're Luke's parents, right?"

Summer nodded and felt her throat constricting. The old man grinned at them, his face creasing in such a friendly way Summer wanted to hug him. He probably smelled like Old Spice.

Summer's memory flashed on a moment from her childhood when she had leaned into a man's chest. He was wearing a flannel shirt and he smelled like Old Spice, and she had hugged him.

"The surgery is over," the volunteer said. "It went well, just as expected. No complications. Dr. Karlsen will be out here to talk to you in a while. You won't be able to see your boy for another couple of hours. He's in recovery now."

Summer sagged in her chair, the feeling of relief so immense.

Derek grasped her hand. When the volunteer walked away, Derek spoke. "I'm so relieved."

His voice broke, and Summer felt tears sting her eyes. "Me, too," she said.

There, in the uncomfortable, creaky hospital waiting room chairs, they embraced, crying. Summer held onto Derek, burying her face in his neck, and thanked the universe, God, whoever had watched over Luke, for keeping him safe. Derek squeezed Summer's hand and settled back in his chair.

"Wow," he said. "I didn't realize how worried I was."

Summer had realized precisely how nervous she was, and the relief was exhilarating.

"I'm exhausted," Derek said. He closed his eyes.

"Me, too," Summer said. She followed his lead, and as her mind slowed down enough for her to relax into sleep, she wondered about the mysterious Old Spice man. He'd probably been the father of one of her friends, or a teacher maybe. Although teachers didn't really hug students, did they?

She leaned her head back on the chair and fell asleep.

Summer woke up when someone tapped her lightly on the shoulder. She hadn't even realized she'd fallen asleep.

"Mrs. Gray."

Dr. Karlsen stood in front of her, smiling. Summer noticed she looked tired, though. Lines etched in her forehead and between her eyebrows. At first, Summer panicked, thinking something was wrong. But her rational mind reminded her that this woman, a mother just like she was, had just spent several hours with Luke's life in her hands. Of course. She was probably exhausted. Summer shook Derek awake. He didn't startle this time, thank goodness.

"Dr. Karlsen, hi," Summer said. "I'm sorry. I didn't sleep much last night and when the volunteer told me everything went well, the exhaustion just overcame me."

Dr. Karlsen's smile widened. "Yes, everything went well. We replaced the valve and there were no complications. You can see him now. He'll still have a tube in his throat and he'll be sleeping. But hopefully seeing him will be reassuring."

A nurse led them back to Luke's post-op room. He looked so tiny in the hospital bed, especially with all the tubes and cords running to his body from various machines and drip bags. The sparkle he'd had in his eyes all morning was gone, since he was on heavy pain medications and the anesthetic was still wearing off. But he smiled when he saw his parents, and Summer's own heart beat a little faster. She rushed to the side of his bed and took his hand in both of hers.

"Hi, Momma," he said. His voice sounded scratchy.

Euphoria rushed through her body, making her want to sing or cry or laugh or all three. He'd survived. He'd woken up. He was okay.

CHAPTER SEVENTEEN

The euphoria didn't last long.

Anxiety set in almost immediately. Within moments, Summer worried about Luke getting a blood clot, being in pain or falling and cracking his sternum open. She worried about his incision becoming infected. She worried about him having an allergic reaction to one of the medications.

Although she and Derek had previously agreed that they'd alternate staying with Luke and going home to take care of the other kids, she insisted on staying at the hospital around the clock.

It was her duty to protect him, and she watched over him continuously, as if, with laser focus, she could keep him safe. She could stop anything dangerous from hurting him. For the millionth time, she straightened his covers and dusted the railings on the bed.

She'd talked Derek into bringing her breast pump so she could send milk home for Olivia, and disinfectant wipes so she could clean the room's hard surfaces at least twice a day. "To prevent infection," she told Derek, who looked at her with some level of suspicion before nodding very carefully as if she were a bomb he was afraid to set off.

At one point, Dr. Karlsen came to check on her patient and after declaring his recovery "perfect so far," she turned to Summer and said, "But I'm a little worried about this patient's mama. I think you need some recovery time."

Summer smiled, and a brief flash of clarity told her the smile was a bit too wide, a bit crazed, even.

"Get some rest, okay?" Dr. Karlsen said.

Summer nodded. Winter chimed in: *You're a maniac.*

The intense vigilance lasted five days and by the time the doctors released Luke, Summer's entire body vibrated from overstimulation and lack of sleep. As she drove Luke home from the hospital, she cringed every time she had to step on the brake pedal. He sat quietly in the back seat, his hospital-issue, heart-shaped pillow tucked between his body and the seatbelt.

"I can't wait to get home and play with Nate," he said. "But do you think I'll be able to play?"

"Dr. Karlsen said you need a few more days' rest, and you have to be pretty careful about what you do with your arms. I'm sure you could play some quiet games. Board games. Card games. Stuff like that. But, no sword fighting for now. We can do lots of movie nights."

She managed not to say anything about the dangers of him tripping over toys, bracing his fall with his arms and re-opening his sternum. She managed not to choke out her greatest fear that he would suddenly go into cardiac arrest while walking through the house.

See? I can do this. I can act normal. Everything is fine. Fine. Nothing to worry about.

She examined Luke's face in the rearview mirror. He looked tired, obviously. Dark smudges under his eyes and heavy eyelids told her he'd need a nap as soon as they got home. She had no idea how she'd keep the house quiet. She squeezed the steering wheel, still examining her son for signs of impending doom.

Summer's eyes returned to the road just as the traffic signal turned red. She knew she should stop. The light was red. But she also knew that if she slammed on the brakes, the seatbelt would cut into Luke's chest. He had the pillow, sure, but it was just a pillow. How much could it really help? If she kept going, another car would probably hit her in the intersection, t-boning her van and killing Luke instantly.

After glancing both directions, panicked, she floored it. She heard a screech and her head swung crazily back and forth looking for the source of the sound. She didn't see anything.

"Mom, why did you squeak like that?"

"Oh, thank goodness," Summer said. "I thought that was the sound of tires squealing. I thought someone was about to hit us."

"That's how Aunt Delaney met Uncle Jake, right, Mom? Someone hit the van? Uncle Jake was a Good Sam American."

Summer could barely speak, her heart was beating so fast. She pulled over.

"Why are you stopping? Did someone hit us? This is where Aunt Dee pulled over after that crash, you know. Every time we drive by it now, she calls it the scene of the crime. She says, 'Not the scene of the car accident, but the scene of me not asking Uncle Jake for his number.' Why is that a crime, Momma?"

Despite the stress she was experiencing at the moment, Summer laughed. The sound came out high and maniacal.

"Aunt Dee had these weird rules before she met Uncle Jake. She used to refuse to ask guys for their phone number."

The shift in focus calmed Summer down, and she was able to pull back onto the road without her hands shaking too badly. The remainder of the ten-minute drive home passed by in a rush of hazards Summer knew she was imagining but couldn't help seeing: a bus stopping along its normal route, a car full of teenagers exceeding the speed limit to pass her as she went five under, a bicyclist in the bike lane coming just a bit too close to her van.

They arrived home without incident. Summer turned the keys in the ignition and laid her head back against her headrest, closing her eyes and doing her yoga breathing. When she heard Luke unbuckling his seatbelt, though, her eyes flew open and her heart sped up again.

"Wait! Let me help you down!"

She could imagine it now: Luke unbuckling himself, pushing open the van door, and tumbling out onto the driveway. His balance was probably off since he hadn't walked anywhere aside from the hospital hallways in days.

"Mo-om," he said. "I'm fine. Stop worrying."

Still, to her relief, he remained seated until she opened his door and helped him down. When he was safely on his feet, she blew out the breath she'd been holding.

"I've been walking, for like, six years," he said, grinning up at her.

Inside the house, chaos reigned. Summer should have known. It always did. Only, she wasn't always worried about her little boy killing himself on a discarded baseball bat (what the heck was it doing in the house, anyway?) or slipping on a coloring book someone left on the floor.

Nate and Sarah were playing the dance-off video game, and Hannah ran wild circles around them, her arms in the air and her shrill voice calling out the song lyrics she could understand. Mostly "booty" and "shake it."

Even while she laughed, Summer saw Hannah as a tripping hazard. Luke managed to make it onto the couch without falling, and Summer felt like she could breathe. The sense of relief lasted only a few seconds before she felt panicked again.

She walked into the kitchen and saw dishes piled in the sink and all over the counter. Had no one done dishes while she was in the hospital with Luke? Bits of food stuck to the faucet, hardened on and undoubtedly growing massive amounts of bacteria. Resigned, Summer rolled up her sleeves and began scrubbing.

How had they been eating? There were no clean dishes to speak of. She checked the garbage can. Paper plates pushed its lid open, and a couple of them had even fallen out and were crammed between the garbage can and the wall.

Germs everywhere.

Summer felt like screaming at the kids, letting loose on them for playing the stupid dance-off video game when the house was a total disaster. The entire top of the dining room table was covered with laundry. Dirty or clean, it was hard to tell. But at least Derek had the couch cleared off for Luke like Summer asked him to.

She couldn't blame him for not keeping up with all the chores. If anyone understood how much work it was to cart kids back and forth from camp and help them with chores and feed them and brush their teeth and get them to bed, it was Summer.

But she could blame Willow. Willow had insisted on staying to help, and what was she doing? Where was she? Derek, she knew, was sleeping. When they found out Luke would be discharged, Derek and Summer had agreed he'd go back to work that night. She expected him to be asleep when she came home, but who was supervising the bigger kids?

Alarm bells began ringing in the back of Summer's mind. They were quiet at first, but increased in intensity as she realized she hadn't seen Willow or Olivia. Speaking of Olivia, had anyone been feeding her? Summer checked the freezer to see how many bags of breastmilk remained. There was one left, which meant someone had gone to the trouble of defrosting them.

"Willow!"

Summer abandoned the dishes and went in search of her baby.

Between hip shakes and arm movements, Sarah said, "She took Olivia for a walk."

"Great. Who's watching Hannah?"

"We are!" Nate said.

"The two small people who are so immersed in the dance-off game they don't even notice Hannah is standing on the dining room table?"

The kids froze and turned around to look at the dining room table. Of course, Hannah wasn't on top of it (she couldn't possibly fit with all the laundry), but Summer had made her point.

"You tricked us, Mom!" Sarah said.

Nate laughed. "She's right behind us!"

"But you didn't know that," Summer said. "You had no idea where she was."

Their expressions sobered instantly.

Summer felt her temper rising into what Derek called The Danger Zone, so she walked back into the kitchen where she scrubbed dishes so hard her arm cramped. A while later, Summer heard Willow's return before the door even opened. Olivia screamed in her stroller as if she'd been tortured. Willow, completely drained, judging by her weary posture and the shuffle of her feet, pushed the stroller into the house and sighed with relief. "Oh, thank *gawd* you're here. This baby is hungry. I need a shower."

With that, she walked into the back of the house without even shutting the front door.

"Great," Summer said. She slammed the door and picked up the baby.

CHAPTER EIGHTEEN

"You know," said Josie, "The Motherhood Intervention still stands. You have to take some time for yourself."

Summer sat with Josie and Delaney on the couch in her living room. The girls had shown up after the kids' bedtime, rather mysteriously. They denied having been sent by Derek, but immediately started carrying laundry from the dining room table to the living room and, once it had all been transferred, began folding it and putting it in tidy stacks.

Summer gestured to the laundry. "You guys didn't even see the kitchen before I got ahold of those dishes. It's actually impossible to take time for myself."

Josie and Delaney exchanged meaningful looks. Summer huffed out a sigh.

"You guys. Seriously. I'm fine."

Liar. You're going crazy, Winter said in a singsongy voice.

"I knew, going into motherhood, that I'd have to make sacrifices."

"You do…" Josie said.

"But?" Summer said.

"But you also have to make time for yourself or else you really will go crazy," Delaney said. "I've seen what you've posted on FriendZoo lately."

"I'm just being honest! Susan Little's baby is horrendous looking. He looks like an alien rhino. And she keeps posting photos of him and talking about how cute he is. But he isn't! Come on. I know you're thinking it too."

Josie laughed, but quickly made a stern face when Delaney shot her a look.

"We are," Delaney said. "We are thinking it, too. But you just don't say it. Or type it. Whatever. I mean, you thought Nate looked like a little piggy when he was a baby. That was before social media got really big. But you did. And I dare anybody else to say so."

Fortunately, Nate had turned out to be a very good-looking child. But as an infant, he *had* looked like a piggy. At the time, Summer had prepared a response she could use if anyone ever said anything to her about it. She would have practically torn someone's face off.

Still, she tried to act nonchalant. She shrugged. "You're right. It was totally uncalled for."

"And besides that," Josie said, "it made you look like a real bitch."

Summer hung her head. "He's still ugly."

The girls didn't answer. They continued folding clothes. After a time, Delaney said, "I didn't realize children generated this much laundry. I'm scared."

"It's so gradual you don't even notice," Summer said. "Until it's covering your entire dining room table. Or all the flat surfaces in your living room."

"When are you having babies, Josie?" Delaney wanted to know.

Josie shrugged. "Well, seeing as how our marriage just got off the rocks, it may be a while. Although the anniversary trip we're planning may turn into a romantic baby-making trip. I ain't getting any younger."

"That would be very romantic," Summer said. "To conceive your first baby on a trip celebrating your anniversary. I mean, one of my kids was conceived in the Rowdy's bathroom. Not romantic at all."

"But steamy," Delaney said.

Josie wrinkled her nose.

"Where was your baby conceived, Dee?" Summer asked.

"You don't want to know," Delaney said. "I picked out drapes for our new living room, by the way."

"Oh, no you don't," Josie said, setting the shirt she was folding on her lap. "Where was it? Tell us now."

Delaney looked at the floor. "Well, you know how sometimes that urge just strikes you?" she said.

"Ye-es," Summer and Josie said.

"Well, that happened," Delaney said.

"Okay," Summer said. "But where?"

"I'm not sure you want to know," Delaney said.

"Ohmygod," Josie said. "Now we really want to know. I mean, you can't say that and not tell us, Dee."

Summer found herself laughing, a genuine laugh that originated somewhere in her belly and bubbled up through her body. "Tell us," she said.

"I can't. It's private."

"Did she just say, 'It's private'?" Josie said.

Summer nodded, giggling, and placed a baby shirt on the stack closest to her. "She did."

"Nothing's private here, sister," Josie said. "Especially when you say it's private."

A deep red flush moved from Delaney's chest to her neck to her cheeks.

"Spill it," Summer said, trying for her best serious expression.

"Fine," Delaney said, and all three of them burst out laughing again. Delaney had overused the term, 'Fine,' during The Dating Intervention whenever Summer and Josie had talked her into doing something out of her comfort zone. After that, it became a running joke. Still, Delaney didn't dish. She kept folding. One of Nate's shirts, a pair of Luke's pants, one of Summer's tank tops. Josie and Summer waited.

"Right there," Delaney finally said.

"Right where?" Summer said.

"Where you're sitting."

"No! You had *sex* on my *couch*?" Summer said.

"Don't tell me *you've* never had sex on your couch!" Delaney said.

"We have, but it's *our* couch!"

Delaney shrugged. "We were watching the kids one night, and they'd gone to bed. We felt frisky."

"Geez," Summer said. "I'd think watching my kids would make you *not* want to reproduce."

Again, Delaney shrugged. "I don't know what to tell you. Your kids are charming. Jake thinks so, too. Ergo..." She gestured at her growing belly.

A realization dawned on Summer. She looked over at Josie, who was holding a shirt in front of her face ... and who hadn't spoken since Delaney made her confession.

"Josie?" she said. "You've been uncharacteristically quiet during this exchange. Is there something you wish to share?"

"No, hm-mm," Josie said.

In slow motion, Delaney and Summer put down the clothes they were folding. Josie continued folding hers, still in very slow motion. Suddenly, she laughed. The T-shirt she'd been holding in front of her face danced as her body shook. Delaney and Summer looked at each other. Delaney looked a bit puzzled, but Summer knew what had happened.

"Admit it," Summer said to Josie.

Josie dropped the shirt, and clutched her stomach as the laughter had her doubling over.

"We..." she began, and then stuck a fist in her mouth.

Delaney looked at Summer again, the realization hitting her. Then she began to laugh too.

"Say it!" Summer said.

Josie shook her head. She clasped her hands together in her lap and managed to squeak out, "Paul and I had sex on your couch, too."

All three of them howled with laughter.

"We should have put laughing on your list of Intervention Rules," Delaney said as they eventually wound down, gasping for air. "It produces endorphins."

Summer knew it was true. The good, old-fashioned giggle-fest had left Summer feeling better than she had in days. Weeks, even.

So it was no surprise Willow had to pull one of her stunts and ruin everything.

Without any warning, without any of the customary knocking or doorbell ringing, the front door flung open so fast it hit the wall. Willow—who'd gone for her now-customary walk-and-a-smoke after the kids went to bed—stood in the doorway, her hands on either side of the doorjamb, one leg slightly bent as if she were posing for a magazine ad photo shoot.

Summer groaned, and Delaney and Josie froze.

ON SUMMER'S TENTH BIRTHDAY, Willow offered to throw her her first-ever birthday party. "You're entering the double digits," she said. "And that is something to celebrate."

Summer made the invitations herself, carefully folding paper into cards, neatly printing "You're Invited" on the front of each one and then using a ruler to make lines on the inside where she filled in all the details in her best handwriting. She gave them out at school, barely able to contain her excitement at having a real birthday party with friends and cake.

Willow and Summer spent an entire week preparing. Together, they cleaned the house. They pulled weeds, making their postage stamp of a front yard tidy. It was the happiest week of Summer's life, the first time they'd worked together on something fun and productive.

On the day of the party they woke up early to bake the cake and hang streamers. Willow even surprised Summer with balloons she'd bought the night before and hidden in her closet. Summer tied two of them to the mailbox and the rest to the table where they put the finished cake. Summer was giddy with anticipation. Just before people were set to begin arriving, though, Willow disappeared. Summer had no idea where she'd gone, but was quickly distracted when the first guest knocked on the door. The house was cozy so Willow had limited the number of attendees to three.

Although Summer's sense of unease grew the longer Willow was gone, she went ahead and orchestrated the games they'd planned out: Pin the Tail on the Donkey, Twister, musical chairs.

In the middle of musical chairs, the front door opened. Summer and her friends had been struggling over the remaining chairs, giggling madly, but their laughter stopped the second they saw Willow, posed in the doorway, her hands on either side of the door-jamb and one leg slightly in front of the other. She wore a huge sunhat and a tight-fitting dress, and Summer had the briefest thought that she looked like she belonged in a magazine ad.

"What have we here?" Willow said in a syrupy sweet voice, and Summer quickly reevaluated her magazine ad idea. Willow belonged in a movie, playing the role of the villain. Someone turned off the music. Willow strutted forward, leaving the door open. It was a windy day, and the breeze rushed in, making the streamers flutter and the balloons dance.

"We were just playing musical chairs," Summer said quietly. "Where were you?"

"I just went on a little errand," Willow said.

For a flicker of a moment, Summer thought maybe Willow had gone to get her a birthday surprise. A gift. A bike, maybe. Or roller skates. Then she held up a paper bag, and Summer flinched. Her friends looked at each other, their eyes huge in their ten-year-old faces. Summer could hold up her façade, though, she thought. She could play this off.

"Want to do the cake now?" she said to Willow as her friends moved close to one another behind her. "I know we've both been looking forward to eating it."

"Yes," Willow said, dragging out the word. "I think the cake would go very well with my date to your little birthday party."

She cackled then, withdrawing the half-empty bottle from her bag.

"Get me a knife, sweetheart, and I'll start cutting."

"Aren't we going to sing?" one of Summer's friends asked, her voice echoing in the gaping silence Willow had created.

"Dear me," Willow said. "How could I forget?"

She swiveled around, and raised her arms as if she were a conductor. "And a one, a two, and a one, two, three," she said.

Summer's friends tried, but fear made their voices weak and watery. No one had lit the candles, she noticed, blinking back tears as she made a wish anyway.

I wish my mom would die.

The thought, as private as it was, horrified Summer. But it entered her mind unbidden. The song ended. Willow grasped a huge bread knife in her unsteady hand and as she leaned forward to cut the cake she lost her balance and smashed her entire fist down onto what had been such a lovely creation.

It seemed to Summer like the whole thing happened in slow

motion. Willow's hand touched the frosting and then broke through its pristine surface. The top of the cake itself gave way, and her forearm plunged deeply into it.

Summer and her friends gasped.

Willow seemed not to notice until her fist had reached down into the bottom layer, and then she stopped the motion abruptly and said, "Oh, my."

That was it, Summer thought. "Oh, my."

In her attempt to extricate herself from the mess, Willow toppled the other way, flinging the knife into the air before it clattered down onto the floor.

Summer's friends stood frozen, staring at the mess in the dining room. Summer fled. She hid, alone in her bedroom, until long after her friends' sober parents came to pick them up.

THE MODERN DAY Willow looked exactly the same as she had on Summer's tenth birthday. And she was just as drunk, too.

"Why, hello, girls," she said, stretching out the word, "girls" as if it were honey she was licking off a spoon.

"Hello," Delaney and Josie mumbled, the hilarity from a moment ago leaking out slowly like the helium in ten-year-old Summer's birthday balloons. They kept folding laundry.

"What are you three up to?" Willow said.

Josie held up the shirt she'd been holding over her face just a moment ago. "Um, folding laundry?"

Willow arched an eyebrow. "Is that so?"

Summer's instincts prickled.

"Are you drunk, Willow?" she said.

Willow came further into the house, leaving the door open behind her. "Of course not, honey. I've been drinking so long, I don't even get drunk anymore."

Summer groaned again. Delaney and Josie set down their laundry and stood up.

"You're not leaving me," Summer said, her voice coming out in a half-hiss, half-growl. "I need backup."

They looked at each other, then looked back at her and nodded. "Okay," Delaney said.

"Fine," Josie said.

"So, I see the three of you have tackled the domestic duties." Sarcasm oozed from Willow's mouth.

"How much have you had to drink?" Summer asked.

"Not nearly enough," Willow said.

Delaney tiptoed over to the front door and shut it, then returned to her spot and resumed folding laundry.

"I told you that you had to stop drinking if you were going to stay here," Summer said.

Willow lifted a shoulder and dropped it. So casually. "I just went out for a bit. I wasn't drinking here." On the word, "here," she pointed at the floor.

A laugh escaped Josie's mouth.

"You've got to move out," Summer said.

Now Willow laughed, a high cackle that pierced the air like so many tiny arrows.

"You can't force me to move out," Willow said.

Josie stood up. When Delaney didn't, Josie nudged her with her foot. Once the two of them were standing side by side, Josie said to Willow, "I'm going to have to ask you to leave now, Willow."

Willow managed to look surprised, although Summer thought it was probably an act.

"Young lady, I don't believe you have the authority to tell me whether I have to leave."

"Oh, but I do," Josie said. "I have more authority to kick you out than you have to be here. Especially in the state you're in."

"And what state is that?"

"I think we all know what state that is," Josie said. "Drunk off your pretty, skinny little ass. And I'm positive Summer told you to stop drinking while you're here."

Willow laughed again. "She did, did she? And how do you know?"

"She told us," Delaney said, apparently having found her voice.

"Well, little ladies," Willow said, "I have news for you. I'm not leaving. I'm sticking around."

No one spoke, except Winter, who said, *Crickets.*

"Why are you doing this?" Summer asked. Despite Willow being a waif by their standards, Summer could tell her friends had entered fight or flight and were getting ready to flee. They stood side by side, their hands nearly touching as if, at any moment, they'd have to help each other escape.

"Why am I doing what?" Willow said.

"Getting drunk off your ass, after I asked you not to."

"Oh, I don't know," Willow said.

"I was serious when I asked you not to drink," Summer said.

"You didn't ask me. You told me," Willow said. "You act like it's so easy,"

"It's a choice," Summer said. "I choose to get up every morning and feed my kids. I choose not to get drunk every night. I choose to stay healthy, for them, for my husband, for myself. It's a choice, Willow, and you're making the wrong one. You're fifty-two freakin' years old, and you're still making the wrong choice."

Willow sighed.

"Very dramatic," Summer said. "But you need to leave now."

"I won't," Willow said.

Josie sucked in a breath. Delaney grabbed her hand.

"This is my house," Summer said. "You're no longer welcome here."

"Was I ever?"

Summer shrugged. "I guess not, no."

"You need my help," Willow said, her eyes hardening and gathering sudden focus as she looked hard into Summer's. "You are barely holding it together. You are on the verge of breaking. You think you're so strong, you think you have it all figured out. But you're this close" (she held up her thumb and forefinger, squinting at the measurement) "to an involuntary stint in the loony bin."

Summer *was* close to breaking. The truth of Willow's words stung, but she wouldn't let her see it.

"You need to leave now," Summer said.

"You can't tell me what to do. I'm your mother."

"You haven't been my mother for fifteen years," Summer said.

Derek, of course, chose that moment to walk through the front door. He paused after closing it, taking in the scene with a mixture of fascination and horror.

"Hi, ladies," he said. When he was met with a steely silence, he said, "Long day at work. I'll just go shower."

Summer felt her temper rising yet again.

"I'll see you out," she said to Willow.

She moved toward her mother, planning to lead her out the front door, but Willow spun around to get out of Summer's grasp and shouted, "You can't make me leave! I am your mother!"

Summer gripped Willow's arm and marched her toward the front door. Derek emerged from the bedroom in sweatpants and a T-shirt. "Wait."

Summer froze, and Willow smiled. Summer could see the victorious, catlike glint in her eye. Derek flinched when Summer made eye contact with him.

"Wait," he repeated.

Summer arched an eyebrow and Willow crossed her arms. Summer could see Willow's head nodding slowly. She pursed her lips as if Derek were reiterating some point she had made previously.

"Um, I think this is our cue," Josie said.

Delaney scurried around as if she were looking for something, but Summer knew it was just misplaced energy.

"You can go," she said quietly. "Don't worry about me, Dee."

Delaney's entire body relaxed and she and Josie practically ran out the door.

"You can go, too, Willow," Summer said.

"I'll just go to bed," Willow said.

"That's not what I—" Summer said, but Derek raised a hand to cut her off.

Willow sauntered out of the living room and Summer was left facing her husband, anger boiling in her veins.

A rapid boil, Winter said.

"What was the meaning of that?" Summer said.

"She's your mother. You can't just kick her out," Derek said.

"Oh, but I can. It's not your choice, not really. And she's not my mother." When Derek didn't respond, Summer added, "Since when do you get to decide everything that happens in this house?"

Now he held up both hands, surrendering. She knew he didn't want to fight. He was the non-confrontational one, the one who walked away. Nevertheless, at the moment, Summer felt like being the aggressor.

"Why do you really want her to stay here, Derek?"

She didn't even bother keeping her voice calm. She could hear it escalating just above the normal range and for once she didn't rein it in. *Why should you?* said Winter, who was now her ally, apparently. When Derek didn't answer, Summer stomped her foot. Because of the tension, she almost laughed at herself, at how much she resembled a toddler with the foot stomping, but she managed not to.

After a tick of silence, Derek said, "Let's not talk about this right now. We're both tired. Can we revisit in the morning?"

"Always the peacemaker," Summer said. "I want to talk about it now."

Derek adjusted his stance, shifted his weight and shook his head. "Tomorrow."

Typically, she'd agree. Typically, she'd nod. She'd follow him to bed, they'd kiss goodnight, and they'd go to sleep. In the morning, they'd be refreshed, ready to discuss whatever sticky subject had come up the night before.

But not tonight.

"No," Summer said. "Let's get this resolved tonight."

Derek raised both eyebrows. "You're kidding, right?"

"Nope. Why, Derek? Why do you want her to stay?"

"I want it for you. She's your mom."

"Are you kidding?"

"No. I'm not. I don't think you should turn her away. I don't think you should give up on this chance to heal your relationship."

"What are you, some kind of hippie?" Summer said. "It's my choice."

"I think you guys should reconcile," he said.

"Oh, do you, now?" Summer said. Her voice was so calm it scared her.

"I want this for you," Derek said.

"Do you really want this for me? Or do you want her here because you feel guilty that you're having to work so much and you can't help me?"

Although he'd been looking at the floor, he made brief eye contact with her and she knew she'd struck a chord. But he denied it, shaking his head again.

"If that's it, I appreciate it," Summer said, "but let's hire a nanny or something. It doesn't have to be her."

Derek sighed. "We can't afford to hire a nanny. And she's your mother."

"I think we have two different ideas of what the word 'mother' means," Summer said. "Your mother is the epitome of a good mother. She bakes. She hugs you. She brings our kids presents. Because of that, you don't understand that mothers can screw up your life just as well as they gave it to you."

"You need to give her a chance," Derek said.

"I did give her a chance. I've given her lots of chances. And she keeps screwing me."

"But you haven't seen her in fifteen years."

"I don't care!" Summer said. Derek flinched again. She knew her voice was too loud, and she didn't want to wake the kids. "I don't care," she hissed. "I don't care if I ever see her again."

"Let's talk about this tomorrow," Derek said again. "We should go to bed."

"Ugh," Summer growled. "I don't want to go to bed. I want you to go in there and tell Willow she has to leave."

"I don't want her to leave, Summer. Okay?"

Summer inhaled, ready to fire back at him. But he stopped her, his palm facing her like a stop sign.

"You're right on the edge. You're *this close* to losing it. I'm afraid I'm going to come home one night and you're going to have lit the house on fire because you forgot about some bacon on the stove, or you're going to have forgotten one of the kids at camp or totally skipped feeding them all day."

Summer's mouth dropped open. "Is that really what you think of me?" She was powerless to stop the shrieking. "Is that what you think of the woman you married? That I would catch our house on fire and forget to care for our children? Have any of them ever missed a single meal? Have I ever left one of them at the grocery store? I am so sorry that I failed to live up to your expectations."

"It's not that, Summer, I—"

"Don't placate me. You think I've lost it. You think I'm crazy. Incapable."

"It's not that. It's..." his voice trailed off. "I'm working. You're alone with them a lot. And you're working, too. You can't do it all. You just can't. And that's okay. It's okay to admit you need help."

"But not from her! I don't need help from that woman! And you can't make me!"

This time, she couldn't help but laugh.

Suddenly, they were both laughing. She fell into his arms, and they giggled and howled and held each other as they wept with laughter.

"You can't make me," became a joke the year Sarah turned four. A stubborn, spirited little girl, her parents had often had to coax her into taking baths, eating dinner, getting dressed, getting in the car.

Neither of them wanted to yell at her or spank her or threaten her with terrible consequences at every turn, so they started negotiating with her. Every time, they'd get so close, and she'd say, "You can't make me."

It was exhausting. But it was funny.

It was funny then and it was funny now.

"This conversation isn't over. She's not staying," Summer said as they wiped tears from their eyes.

"I think I can change your mind." Derek rubbed her back and let his hand roam down and cup her bottom. Summer swatted it away.

"Not tonight, you can't. I'm tired."

CHAPTER NINETEEN

"Summer."

Not even trying for pretenses, Summer dropped her head onto the kitchen table as Willow approached. "What."

"I'm really sorry," Willow said.

This is new.

"For what."

"Would you look at me when I'm talking to you?"

"No, thanks."

Summer had gotten up early to steal some alone time before anyone demanded her attention. Six a.m. had just ticked by and although she'd been awake for thirty minutes, Summer felt like it was too early to have to interact with Willow.

"Look. I'm sorry. Okay? I drank too much last night."

"You drank too much on lots of nights. What made last night so special you want to apologize for it? Why don't you apologize for drinking too much over the course of my entire childhood?"

"I'm sorry, Summer. I am. The day before yesterday, I—"

Summer cut her off. "'I finally got away from your madhouse, Summer, and couldn't resist a couple of nips from the bottle, but don't worry, I waited until after the kids were in bed to get completely sloshed.'"

"Don't mock me, young lady," Willow said.

"Oh, such a parental tone. You are ridiculous. I told you I don't want you drinking around me or my kids. You say it's so important to you to rebuild our relationship and to connect with your grandchildren. Yet you completely neglect my request to tone it down with the drinking. It's the one request I make. The single thing I ask for. I don't ask you to help with the kids, with dishes, or laundry, or all of those things you promised when you begged me to stay here. All I ask is that you don't get drunk off your ass. Then, last night, you waltz in here, drunk off your ass. Just like you did the day you ruined my tenth birthday. What the hell were you thinking?"

Willow slid into the seat across from Summer. "I did ruin that birthday party, didn't I?"

It was the first time Willow had ever admitted to ruining anything, and Summer felt her defenses go up. Willow must have an ulterior motive.

Still, Summer nodded. "You did."

After a pause, Willow said, "We were talking about your father the other day. Dennis?"

"Yes, we were," Summer said.

"It got me to thinking," Willow said. "Thinking about him and how much I loved him. Thinking about how much you're like him, and how much he'd enjoy seeing you and your children."

"Would he?"

Willow shrugged one shoulder, and scraped at something Summer couldn't see on the glass tabletop. Summer cringed. Probably more of that yellow film. "Well, I thought he would," she said.

"What do you mean?"

Now, Willow ran her palms over the surface of the table. "It doesn't matter. What matters is that you're right. I was disrespectful of the single request you made, and I owe you an apology."

A straight apology seemed weird coming from Willow.

There has to be something more to this. She wants something. Sympathy, probably.

A realization dawned on Summer. Willow'd just said, "I thought he did." What did that mean?

"Did you reach out to him?" Summer said.

"I told you. It doesn't matter."

"Oh, but it does," Summer said. "It matters because, for some reason, everybody except me thinks you should stay with us, even though you're a drunk and you're exposing my kids to your drunken idiocy. For some reason, everybody thinks I need your help. You don't even know how to help! For some reason, I'm the only one who sees through your façade. And I don't want you here. So tell me, is this apology supposed to mean something? Is it supposed to fix something? Because let me tell you, it doesn't undo all the wrongs you did. You showing up here, after all this time, pretending to be a mother figure to me, is bullshit. So where did last night's little escapade come from? It matters. It matters to me."

"Fine," Willow said. "I reached out to Dennis. Like I said, I thought he'd enjoy seeing you and your kids. I've been searching for him for a few days now. I actually found him. Summer, he lives just a few miles away. It took me a couple of days to work up the courage to go and see him. He works at the high school."

Myriad emotions took root inside of Summer. Meeting her father, now, as an adult, would be at once amazing and totally strange. Did she even want to get to know him? Well, of course she did. What was he like? Also, of course she didn't. He hadn't bothered getting to know her before, so why should she waste a single breath on him now?

So deeply immersed in her own thoughts, Summer forgot Willow had been talking about Dennis. She was startled when Willow spoke again.

"I wasn't sure whether I should call him," she said. "So instead, I took the bus to the school and waited for him to come out. I did that one day, stood on the curb and waited. I watched him come out. But I was too scared to approach him. So I walked away. Got back on the bus."

"The next day, I gathered all my courage and walked onto campus. I sat on a bench in the quad and waited for the bell to ring. When it did, I stood up. I stood there as he walked across the campus lawn. But still, I couldn't talk to him."

Despite her best efforts to remain emotionally distant from the situation, Summer found herself feeling nervous as Willow drew a deep breath to finish her story.

"He didn't notice you?" Summer said. Willow shook her head and Summer said, "So then what?"

"I went back. The third day. Yesterday."

So that's why she was inebriated yesterday. Something went wrong.

Willow continued: "I told myself, 'You're going to talk to him today. That's it. Just walk up and talk to him.' So I put on my best skirt. The one without the baby poop stains. I went back to that same bench. When the bell rang, I went right up to his classroom door. He was in there. Leaning over his desk, explaining something to a student. Even from the doorway, I could see the muscles in his arms. He was always exceptionally fit."

Summer rolled her eyes.

"What?" Willow said. "He was. Anyway. He looked up when he saw me, and our eyes met. I know, it sounds cliché, right?"

Summer nodded, shrugged one shoulder.

"So," Willow went on. "I'd always been expecting this romantic reunion, you know? I don't know why. But throughout my entire life, I always believed Dennis was the only one who could see me for who I really was. That's why I never dated anyone else long-term. No one really understood me like he did. So I assumed he'd forgive me for staying with my parents. But when I saw him yesterday, and he looked up at me, I could tell right away there would be no romance. His eyes hardened, like he was recognizing me as a criminal from one of those grainy bank robbery photos. You know? On the news? Or a sex offender on one of those posters: 'A sex offender has reported living in this neighborhood.'"

Summer nodded. She could picture it perfectly. "So there was no romantic reunion?" she said.

"No." Willow shook her head, looking down at her hands, which were busy knotting themselves together at her waist. "I saw that look on his face and I took off."

Went straight to the liquor store and binged on bourbon, Winter said to Summer.

"Went straight to the liquor store," Willow said.

Summer jumped. How had Willow known what Winter was saying?

"So you never even talked to him," Summer said.

"Never even talked to him," Willow said.

For a moment, they stood there, each lost in her own thoughts. Summer wondered what Dennis had really been thinking. She wondered if he'd have given Willow a chance. And she was surprised Willow hadn't pushed him in to talking to her. The sound of a bedroom door opening in the back of the house startled her out of her thoughts. For the second time in as many minutes, she jumped.

If Willow were one of her children, Summer thought, she'd come up with something reassuring to say before going to greet the kids and make breakfast. But she didn't. She didn't have to, and she didn't want to. If it took Willow this long to learn her life lessons, then so be it. The beauty of being grown up was that Summer didn't have to be emotionally tied to her any more.

For the next few days, Summer found herself thinking about her father. She didn't blame him for being angry with Willow. Willow was the type of person who sucked people in like a black hole, even as they scrambled for freedom, and then spit them out on the other side when she was done, with no apparent concern about how they'd fare in outer space.

Summer had been spit out. She'd experienced the feeling of free-falling through the universe, arms and legs scrambling for some kind of hold, but never quite getting one, until she was completely removed from Willow's orbit.

But didn't her father want to know how she'd turned out? Didn't he ever wonder about her, worry about her, wish he'd been able to meet her? He should have rushed up to Willow and asked about Summer. Why hadn't he done so years ago? What if his look hadn't been one of distaste, but one of surprise? Willow had probably caught Dennis off guard. Summer could understand the whirlwind of emotions that Willow Carson brought along with her.

Meanwhile, Luke continued to heal perfectly. Almost too well for Summer's own comfort, as he wanted nothing more than to resume typical activities like running and jumping and three-legged races with his brother. Nevertheless, Summer hovered over him, checking his forehead for fever several times per day, examining his incision for redness, hissing through her teeth if he lifted his arms above his shoulders. Waiting for the other shoe to drop. Every time she fussed over him, he said, "Mo-om," and she tousled his hair or leaned down to kiss him on the top of his head.

So when Josie and Delaney arrived the following week for Happy Hour, Summer found herself distracted, her mind flitting between Dennis and Luke. The girls brought Summer a bottle of Chardonnay, and Josie had opened it and poured two glasses while Delaney, a wine glass full of water in hand, set out some cheese and crackers and green olives.

They settled in the living room, Josie on the floor and Summer and Delaney on the couch.

"Is it going any better?" Josie asked, motioning with her chin toward Sarah's room, where Willow had said she was going to lay down (although Summer figured she was probably listening with her ear to the door).

"A little," Summer said. "I mean, she's not the biggest help with the chores, but she is helping keep the kids occupied. The baby grosses her out, but she'll spend time with the other four. Enough about that. I still can't believe you guys both had sex on my couch."

Just like that, they were laughing again. The merriment worked like a balm, soothing Summer's frazzled nerves.

"I don't know what was so romantic about it," Josie squealed. "We'd just gotten the kids to bed. I thought he'd be exhausted, you know? He'd just done battle with the boys, and I'd just gotten the girls to bed, and we sat down on the couch and before we knew it, we were kissing. And, you know, one thing led to another."

Summer dropped her head into her hand and groaned.

Delaney howled. She leaned back on the couch and slapped her knee. "It was almost the same with us," she said. "I know you think your kids are great birth control, Summer, but they're actually great kids. They're lots of fun."

Summer snorted, almost spitting out the sip of wine she'd just taken.

"In fact," Delaney said, growing solemn, "it was the whole putting them to bed routine that I think got us in the mood for having kids. There's just something so sweet and special about four squeaky clean, freshly bathed kids in jammies, and reading to them, putting them in bed, and then sitting in a quiet house that's just breathing with these sweet little souls."

"It's actually a turn-on," Josie said.

Summer barked out a laugh, and the three of them dissolved into giggles again. Several minutes passed before they managed to stop, and they sat in relative quiet sipping wine.

A few moments later, when Derek came through the front door, they began laughing again, and Delaney patted the spot on the couch between her and Summer. Derek shook his head, said, "I think I'll hang out in the bedroom," and bent over the back of the couch to give Summer a quick kiss. Josie whistled at that, and Summer could have sworn Derek picked up his pace. Even as he walked out of sight, though, she took notice of the shape of his backside. She licked her lips, and Delaney swatted her on the leg.

Time with the girls had left Summer feeling calm, centered, and happy.

Oh, and don't forget horny, Winter whispered.

As Summer rinsed the wine glasses and snack plates, she thought about how long it had been since she and Derek had been intimate. They'd had lots of intimate moments. Stolen whispers, hushed conversations, silent discussions through eye contact.

But when was the last time they had actually touched one another in a sexual way? So long ago Summer couldn't even remember. When she was pregnant with Sarah, they'd been so pleased with themselves for maintaining their sex life throughout the pregnancy, and reinstating it at precisely the six-week mark after she gave birth. Actually, Summer thought with a snort, they'd been pretty smug about it.

During the second pregnancy, they felt a little more tired. But because they'd been so smug about the first, they kept up almost the same pace they had before. Luke had come along, and they'd excused their mediocre sex life, saying they had two other children to tend to. During Hannah's pregnancy, they dropped the pretense. Keeping up a prolific sex life was hard work! And they were so tired.

So when Summer became pregnant with Olivia, they practically stopped all together.

Now, after listening to Josie's juicy recount of sex with Paul, and Delaney's almost-wistful description of a house filled with children, Summer wanted to rekindle the fire.

Derek was asleep already, but she doubted he'd mind if she woke him up for some attention of this nature. In their bedroom, she sneaked past him and went into the bathroom, where she showered and shaved and rubbed vanilla-scented lotion onto her smooth skin. It was his favorite, and she knew he wouldn't miss that detail.

Although it was getting late and she knew Olivia would be up to eat soon, Summer slipped between the sheets and curled her body against Derek's. In his sleep, he pulled her arm around his waist and held her hand.

She smiled against the back of his neck and began running her hand from his knee to his hip and back again.

"Are you wearing vanilla lotion?" he asked, his voice still thick with sleep.

"Mm-hmm," she said.

Although she couldn't see or hear it, she knew he was smiling.

"Feeling a bit frisky, are you?" he said.

Still giddy, she chuckled. He grabbed her hand and brought it around to the front. He was already hard, which Summer found exhilarating. She stroked him, not gently, and he sighed. He turned around to face her, and she could feel the urgency beneath his kiss. Derek put one hand on her waist and ran it up to her breast. Summer felt an immediate pulling in her lower stomach.

"It's been so long," Derek said, his voice almost a growl.

"Too long," Summer said, kissing him again.

As their bodies moved together, Summer found herself revolving around a set point she'd been unable to find in recent weeks. Her friends had brought it into focus, and her husband had provided the grounding.

"When can we actually do it again?" Derek asked, his mouth against hers.

"Just a few more weeks," Summer said.

"I can still make you a very, very happy woman," Derek said.

Summer laughed. "I am a happy woman."

"Just wait," he said. "You don't know what happiness is."

They kissed again, and Summer sighed. "Yes, I do," she said. "This is it."

After Derek made her a very, very happy woman, and she made him a very, very happy man, they lay in the dark on the bed, side by side, holding hands.

"What got into you?" Derek wanted to know.

"The girls just reminded me how much I miss this," she said. "And it was a lot."

Derek laughed and squeezed her hand. "You should have them over for Happy Hour more often."

CHAPTER TWENTY

THE NEXT MORNING, SUMMER AWOKE REFRESHED AND REVITALIZED, THE buzzing anxiety turned so far down she barely noticed it. She attributed this new zen feeling to the makeout session she and Derek had enjoyed the night before. Her body felt relaxed and pliable, and her mind felt as if someone had poured a vat of cool water over it. Or Chardonnay. Yes, definitely Chardonnay.

Still in bed, she stretched, the luxury of a moment alone making her lazy, tempting her to stay between the sheets all day.

Derek walked in with a cup of coffee, and she brought herself up to sitting.

"That looks delicious. You really know which buttons to push."

"I proved that last night, didn't I?"

She smiled and took the coffee cup from him. He sat down next to her.

"And," he said, "I have a few days off, now. I can push those buttons again."

He kissed her, and she shivered.

"Want me to keep the kids busy for a couple of hours so you can get your work done?" he said. "That beer label thing?"

Summer sighed as reality came through, rinsing her system clean of the fake Chardonnay buzz she'd felt just a moment ago. Because summer was nearly over, summer camp was closed. Summer usually loved having the kids home for an extra day, but Derek had just reminded her about how overwhelmed she felt with everything she had to do.

"I do need to get it done," she said. "But I'd much rather stay in bed."

Derek leaned forward, kissed her on the temple and stood up. "I'll hold down the fort for a bit. That was the whole reason I took night shift—so I could give you a few hours in the morning."

"But it's your day off," she said in a whiny voice.

"Get outta bed, you lazy wench."

Summer chuckled. An hour later, she'd finalized the first draft of the beer label for Juniper's microbrewery, and she had to admit, it looked pretty festive. She'd put in an English garden background and added masculinity by putting a rusty old truck in the foreground. They said they wanted to appeal to men and women, so hopefully this would do the trick.

Derek said he'd give her another hour, so Summer decided to go for a walk. It was something she hadn't done in years. The crisp morning air felt invigorating and the sun felt warm on her skin. The good mood that had greeted her upon waking stuck with her as she strolled along, admiring the spring flowers and the newly planted vegetable gardens.

Summer had to admit—only to herself, of course—that she'd been overwhelmed lately. Beyond overwhelmed. But the worst was over. Olivia's birth went smoothly. She was healthy. Luke's surgery was seamless, and he was healing. Derek was gone a lot, but at least he had a full-time job. When he'd first gotten laid off (around the same time they'd found out she was pregnant), she was stressed about money. Now things were fine, financially.

Her two best friends were moving along with their lives. Delaney, about to be a mother herself, seemed happy. And Josie, whose marriage had been on the rocks just a couple of months ago, was working hard to repair her relationship.

Willow's reappearance, however unexpected it was, may be a blessing in disguise. Summer couldn't quite see what the blessing might be, but she figured it was hidden somewhere. It just may take a while for her to dig it out.

Life was all about give and take.

Lately, Summer felt like life was sucking her dry, taking and taking and taking. Forcing her to give repeatedly, until she had nothing left.

It seemed now like things were turning around, and life was giving her something.

Tizzy, the orange tabby cat belonging to Summer's neighbor, Sharon Rimrock, emerged from Sharon's front yard and wound himself around Summer's ankles. He purred when she bent down to scratch his neck. This was a perfect example of life giving her this one special moment.

"I'll take it," she said.

As Summer walked back to the house, she found herself reliving some of her rare positive childhood memories. Maybe the encounter with Tizzy had reminded her. After positively destroying Summer's tenth birthday, Willow had gotten her a kitten. Summer now knew Willow felt guilty, and was compelled to make things right.

The day after the catastrophic party, Summer walked in the front door after school. Willow was waiting, ready to present the kitten with a flourish. He was mostly black, with a tiny white patch on the left side of his face, and Willow had tied a baby blue ribbon around his neck. When she held him up, as if he were a peace offering as well as a gift, Summer immediately noticed his eyes. They were huge, almost too big for his little face, and bright green. Summer squealed and Willow grinned back, pressing the kitten into Summer hands.

"For me?" Summer said.

"Yes," Willow said. "For you. A late birthday present. The shelter wasn't open yesterday, so I had to run over there today. I wanted to surprise you."

Even now, twenty-four years later, Summer could clearly recall wondering whether there was some catch. Maybe Willow would yank the kitten out of her arms and say, "Just kidding," with a nasty laugh. Or maybe someone else would come over to reclaim the kitten Willow had stolen. Even worse, Willow would probably let the cat out to be devoured by the hungry coyotes that yipped in the open lot behind their house every night during the spring and summer.

"What should I name you, little guy?" Summer said to the kitten.

For once, Willow didn't have a suggestion. Summer named him

Rocky. It seemed like a good, steadfast name. For the next several years, Summer waited for disaster to strike. She waited for Willow to insist on giving Rocky away. She waited for Rocky to escape from the house and disappear. She waited for Willow to refuse to buy cat food.

To Summer's astonishment, though, Rocky lived. He curled up on her lap while she studied, stretched out next to her while she slept and wound himself around her ankles while she cooked dinner. When Summer met Derek and moved into her apartment, Rocky went with her. And when they got married, he moved into their house, a fixture in her life until he died of old age.

Now that her mind was on this positive track, Summer thought about Willow taking her for a shopping spree after declaring her an "official teenager" when she turned thirteen. Thinking back on it, Summer wondered where she'd come up with the extra money, or if she always had it and just kept it for herself. They spent all day at the mall, loading their arms with clothes to try on, enjoying little fashion shows in the fitting rooms of various stores and stopping midday for cinnamon rolls and lemonade.

They walked down the mall, Summer's stride perfectly in time with her mother's. At one point, she looked over at Willow, and Willow looked at her. They grinned at each other and kept walking.

It was one of the happiest days in Summer's life.

Shortly after Summer's fifteenth birthday, Willow decided to teach Summer how to drive. Their car, a tiny Volkswagen Golf, had a manual transmission, and Summer was a slow learner. One weekend, Willow took her to the high school parking lot and had her practice starting from a stop, shifting into second gear and then shifting into third.

Every time Summer let her foot off the clutch, the car would jerk, chugging forward like an amusement park ride. She concentrated so hard, but she just couldn't get the car moving forward. After fifteen minutes of herky-jerky driving, inching forward, the tip of Summer's tongue between her teeth, her knuckles white on the steering wheel and her quads cramping from effort, Willow began to laugh.

When she did, Summer experienced a relief so profound she wanted to cry. She'd spent the entire lesson worrying that Willow would become angry and aggressive as she sipped on the flask she'd brought. But when she laughed, Summer laughed too, so hard tears leaked out of her eyes and her body went limp.

"Well, honey," Willow said, "you certainly didn't get your driving skills from me."

They traded places and laughed all the way home. So Summer's childhood played out against a background of fear and darkness. But there were highlights. Bright spots. It hadn't been all bad.

"Gratitude," Summer said aloud as she walked home. "I need to practice being grateful for what I had. For what I have."

Sometimes practicing gratitude was easier said than done, Summer knew. By the time she left home at nineteen, her relationship with Willow was so strained she had difficulty feeling grateful for anything. She felt like Willow had ruined her life, cast a shadow over so many potentially happy moments, wrung out every drop of joy.

At the time, it had been so easy to walk away, as saturated with indignation as Summer was. But on certain occasions, Summer longed for a mother. Not Willow, necessarily, because she'd never been a nurturing figure. But a mother she could reach out to, ask for advice, share successes with.

Derek proposed on a snowy night, in the center of the courthouse square. Crystallized flakes of snow glittered on the grass, and he walked her up the steps of the gazebo, led her to the bench, knelt down in front of her and promised to give her everything she needed, forever.

Afterward, they walked around the square, holding hands. Derek twisted the ring on her finger over and over again, both of them relishing the feeling of this solid proof that they'd spend the rest of their lives together. She went to bed that night wishing she felt the giddy happiness he deserved, but Willow's absence from her life dampened it. She wanted to want to call Willow. But she didn't. Instead, she wished she had someone to call. She'd called Delaney and Josie right away, but it wasn't the same.

That feeling of loss cast a shadow over her wedding day, despite Summer's best efforts not to let it.

When she'd found out she was pregnant with Sarah, she experienced a moment of longing so strong it threatened to overwhelm the elation she felt. She wanted, more than anything, to call her mom, to tell her she'd be giving birth to the next generation in nine months' time.

Of course, Derek's mom, Julie, had been overjoyed. Beyond overjoyed. She hugged Summer and Derek repeatedly, and insisted on hosting a celebratory dinner for them. She threw an extravagant baby shower and helped Summer create her birth plan. She massaged Summer's back during labor, cried at the sound of Sarah's first, newborn wail. All of those things had been wonderful. But still, Summer longed for her own mother.

Throughout her adult life, Summer sought ways to find inner peace and happiness. She took innumerable online personal development courses and turned to yoga as a vehicle for enlightenment. During one of the lectures she attended, she learned that every person in her life served a purpose. From every interaction, she could learn a lesson.

By reframing her relationship with Willow in this way, she began to understand that Willow's presence had taught her self-reliance and self-preservation. Willow's neglect had taught her to find contentment within herself rather than seeking it in other people.

For that, she knew she should be grateful. As she walked up the walkway to her present-day house, Summer thought she should focus on that aspect of their relationship.

She knew she should. But thinking about Willow still caused her to feel just a hint of loss. Despite her best efforts, her most yoga-like thought processes, she still felt like she had missed out.

"Gratitude," she said aloud, for the second time, as she opened the front door and stepped into the home she and Derek had filled with children and love. "Focus on what you're grateful for."

CHAPTER TWENTY-ONE

SUMMER'S NEWFOUND GRATITUDE LASTED FOR APPROXIMATELY FORTY-seven minutes. She walked into the living room with a smile on her face, ready to embrace all the little twists and turns that comprised her life.

With a lingering kiss, she sent Derek off to do the grocery shopping. When Nate dumped the entire contents of his cereal bowl on the floor, creating a puddle of milk and cereal that extended across the kitchen floor, Summer merely smiled and handed him a towel, despite his foot-stomping. Then, Sarah burst into tears because Summer hadn't yet washed her brand new light blue T-shirt and she wanted to wear it *today*. Where normally, Summer would have told her to find something else to wear and do her own laundry from now on, today she smiled serenely and offered to spot clean it.

Nothing could bring her down. Her happiness was independent of what everyone in her family did and said. Her happiness came from within.

Hannah slipped in Nate's spilled milk even while he was cleaning up the other side of the gargantuan lake, and hit her head on one of the dining chairs. Summer scooped her up and held her, making sure her daughter could feel her sympathy. Maybe even overdoing it a little. But Derek had pointed out once that she didn't show enough sympathy, that her "pick yourself up and dust yourself off" attitude came across as cold. Now that Willow's parenting was fresh in her mind, she knew where she got it. But she would not allow anything or anyone to ruin her serenity.

Someone let Chuck in, and the puppy came charging through the house, skidding to a sloppy stop in Nate's cereal mess, doing his best to lap it up. Everyone in the house braced for Summer's reaction.

If she were being honest, she almost lost her serenity at that moment, when Chuck's huge feet splashed milk and bits of cereal onto the wall. That stuff stuck like crazy. The serenity, which felt like a soft, cozy blanket, began lifting up at the edges, like a beach towel on a windy day.

But instead of blowing up, she smiled brightly and said (through gritted teeth, but who noticed?), "Aw, look at Chuck drinking the spilled milk. That's what dogs are for."

Of course, Willow was the one who broke her at that forty-seven minute mark. Later Summer would think, *It all comes back to Willow.*

But she wasn't sure whether that was Winter talking, or herself. Their voices had become so intertwined recently.

After Nate got his spilled cereal cleaned up and Summer managed to calm Hannah and Sarah down, Willow waltzed into the kitchen.

"What a ruckus," she said, looking down her nose as if she were the High Queen and all the rest of them were her underlings. "I couldn't keep sleeping with all the noise."

Even Sarah guffawed at that. "What did you think you were getting into, staying here with five children?" she said to her grandmother. "We never sleep past seven."

"Is there any coffee?" Willow asked. Sarah rolled her eyes and Summer laughed.

"It's long gone," she said to her mother. "I only made a tiny bit and I finished it off hours ago. But you can make more."

"Could you make it? I wanted to shower before I leave the house. I'm feeling a bit rushed."

Nothing like a little entitlement, Winter whispered. In her mind, Summer told Winter to shut up and stop sabotaging her serenity.

"I don't have time," Summer said. "I'm dealing with a few fiascos, here."

"Looks to me like you're just standing there. Anyway, no problem. I'll make it if you don't want to go out of your way."

Gratitude. Gratitude. Gratitude.

"Great," Summer said. "I'm going to get the kids dressed. Luke has his follow-up appointment this morning."

Willow nodded and went about making the coffee, exaggerating several yawns and rubbing her eyes. Still, Summer maintained her sense of calm.

"Have you had your follow-up appointment?" Willow asked.

Summer should have known by the renewed alertness in Willow's voice that Willow was taking the conversation down a different path. But her focus on gratitude gave her the false sense that Willow actually cared about her. It blinded her to the cut that was coming.

"Yeah, I had it at the two-week mark," she said. "Everything looked good."

"Everything?"

"Yeah, why?"

"Well, I mean, I'm glad you're healing well and everything, but what I mean to say is, did the doctor mention anything about your weight loss? Or lack thereof? I mean, shouldn't you be losing all that baby weight by now?"

Summer's mouth dropped open. She froze where she stood at the entrance to the hallway, Hannah on her hip. She wanted so badly to remain in her new, positive place. Pressing her lips together, she turned around and walked toward the bedrooms, reminding herself that her happiness was independent of everyone else's happiness.

Still, part of her, a tiny part, felt a mixture of anger and sadness. What right did Willow believe she had to criticize Summer even as they were working toward amends? And would she ever, *ever* just love Summer for who she was, *how* she was? Isn't that what mothers were supposed to do?

She sighed as she pulled an outfit for Hannah from the dresser.

It didn't occur to her at that moment to wonder about Willow's plans for the day, or the reason she might be feeling rushed.

The rest of the morning went relatively smoothly, with only one Hannah meltdown at the doctor's office, coinciding perfectly with the timing of Olivia needing an entire outfit change. Dr. Karlsen gave Luke a clean bill of health. He'd have to maintain a reduced activity level to give his incision more time to heal, but he was making nice progress.

Summer knew she should be rejoicing. She was happy, definitely, but Willow's earlier behavior cast a new shadow over the inner peace she was working so hard to enjoy. It wasn't just that Willow had said something about her weight; it was more that Willow thought it was okay to say something about her weight, that in being critical she believed she was being supportive and loving.

Willow left the house after taking a long shower and pouring all the coffee into her giant travel mug. She didn't come back all day, and Summer enjoyed not having her around. Between board games and dance parties, Summer kept the laundry moving through the washer and dryer and the dishes moving through the dishwasher. She managed to get all the kids bathed, which felt like a major accomplishment.

Throughout the day, she planned a romantic evening for Derek. She stopped by the store to buy massage oil, and managed to deflect the kids' questions about what it was and what she'd use it for. She scrounged up some candles and hid them in the closet to sneak into the bedroom when Derek woke up.

"Maximize the romance," she said to herself as she dug out a silky, all-strings negligee and hung it in the front of the closet so she could access it quickly later.

By the time Derek got up to eat dinner, she was feeling quite frisky. Throughout dinner she gave him little hints, rubbing his leg with her toes (at which point Luke yelled, "What are you *doing*, Mom?") and raising her eyebrows in a way she thought was suggestive (Sarah asked, over and over, "Mom? Are you okay? Do you have something in your eye?").

As they went through the bedtime routine, helping kids into pajamas, flossing and brushing teeth and reading stories, Summer brushed her body up against Derek's and grabbed his butt.

"Love pat," Hannah said.

"Nothing is sacred," Summer said to Derek at one point.

Finally, finally, they were alone. She went into the bedroom to change and when she emerged, Derek was holding up a glass of wine. His eyes widened, and he whistled through his teeth. He handed her the glass and ran a hand down her bare arm.

"To sacred romance," he said, winking at her. She grinned back at him. "Cheers."

The candlelight gave the bedroom a soft glow. Summer set her wine glass next to the candles on the dresser, and Derek put his beer next to it. He drew her close, his hands on her hips and his mouth on hers. They kissed slow and deep, like they hadn't done in months, or maybe even years.

"Should I shut the door?" Derek said quietly when Summer began unbuttoning his jeans.

She smiled and went to do it herself, grinning wickedly as she turned the lock. She wrapped her arms around his neck again, and his hands moved from her waist to her breasts. A breathy sigh escaped her lips, and she finished unbuttoning his jeans. He pulled them off and led her to the bed.

"I love this outfit," he said. "It's sexy. Or as Nate would say, super-duper sexy."

"I hope Nate wouldn't use the word, 'sexy,'" Summer said, her lips on Derek's.

They both laughed. "He would say 'super-duper,' though," Derek said.

"Stop talking and give me some super-duper lovin'," Summer said.

Derek quirked an eyebrow at her and used one arm to flip Summer onto her back. She squealed, and he grabbed both of her hands and held them out to her sides while moving his mouth from her lips to her chin, and down her neck to her collarbone.

She felt goosebumps rise on her skin, and said quietly, "Yep, this is what I meant by super-duper."

He laughed again, and found her nipple with his mouth through the thin fabric of her lingerie. When he let go of her hands, she ran her fingers through his hair and then pulled him up to kiss her again. Arching against him, she managed to pull his underwear down over his hips, and he kicked it onto the floor. He pulled his shirt off over his head and with a bit more urgency, yanked her string thong to the side. He cupped her gently, moving his fingers so slowly she almost cried out. When she reached down, she found that he was ready, and she smiled against his lips.

They both froze when someone knocked on the door.

"Shit," Derek said.

"Shit," Summer said.

"Knock, knock," said the voice on the other side of the door.

Derek and Summer looked at each other, and they both shrugged.

"Who is it?" Summer said.

"No! You're supposed to say, 'Who's there?'"

Luke. Why was he knocking on the door right now?

"Who's there?" Derek said.

"Trick or treat!" Luke yelled.

"Just a minute bud," Derek said.

"Trick or treat!"

"It's bedtime," Derek said, as he scrambled to find his underwear and shirt.

Summer laughed, but she, too, got up and got a bathrobe.

"I'm dressed up like a ghost right now," Luke said.

"It's not even Halloween," Summer called. "Wrong season."

"Trick or treat!"

Derek answered the door, and when Summer saw Luke's face, her stomach dropped. His eyes were red and only half-open, and his cheeks were rosy as if he'd been outside playing on a summer day.

Only, he hadn't.

She knew the moment Derek laid a hand on his forehead that she was right and her greatest fear was coming true: Luke had a fever.

CHAPTER TWENTY-TWO

"You're burning up, buddy," Derek said.

"I do feel kind of sweaty," Luke said. "But I thought it's just because I was dressed up like a ghost."

"Let's get you into some shorts," Derek said, leading him back to the boys' bedroom.

Alone for the time being, Summer felt the floor tilt beneath her. Her mind started running a million miles per hour. Infection. It was one of her worst-case-scenario nightmares and now it was coming true. She'd taken him to the doctor this morning, and neither Dr. Karlsen nor the nurse had seen even a hint of infection. In fact, his temperature had been below ninety-eight point six.

How had this happened? Her memory flashed images of her hands bleeding from scrubbing the counters so hard, her knees red from scouring the floor. She vacuumed for so long her ears rang. She had cleaned up every single source of contamination.

Except …

At that moment, Chuck came trotting into the bedroom.

"You!"

They'd have to get rid of the dog. The kids loved the germ-infested little beast, but he'd have to go. All those hairs. Luke probably had one stuck in his incision. It was probably covered in bacteria. And Summer would have to vacuum and disinfect the entire house. Again. Having made the decision, Summer hurried into the boys' room, where Derek was helping Luke change.

"Aren't we supposed to take him to the ER?" she asked, her voice coming out panicked even though she meant to conceal her fear.

Derek nodded. "I haven't taken his temperature yet but I'm sure it's at least a hundred and two. That's pretty high. Ghost or no ghost."

Luke giggled. "Da-ad."

Derek shrugged. "What? It is. Nobody should have a temperature this high after surgery, buddy. No big deal, though. That's what they made medicine for. We'll get you fixed up."

Summer could see the wheels turning in Luke's head as he figured out what this all meant. Derek must have noticed, too, because he put an arm around Luke's shoulders. "Seriously, bud. No biggie. Why don't you go grab some books and stuff to bring with you?"

Luke nodded and headed for the living room.

Not for the first time, Summer wished she could be a child again so someone could reassure her. Derek would try, but she could also see the tiny vertical line between his eyebrows, a sure sign he was worried, too.

Luke returned with a bag full of books and Derek said, "Shall we go?"

Wait. Why did Derek think he was taking Luke? Shouldn't Summer be the one to take him? She wanted to be with him. If she was with him, she could make sure the nurses and doctors at the ER did everything correctly.

"Why are *you* taking him?" she said, her voice coming out low and growly.

Derek jumped as if her words had stung him.

"I just assumed I would, since—"

"I need to be with him—"

Her voice cracked.

"Summer." He put his hands on her shoulders. "You know how it is at the ER. We could be there for hours. I thought you'd want to stay with Olivia. We used up all the frozen breastmilk and we don't want to bring her into the hospital and expose her to those sick people."

Summer took a deep breath and felt herself stepping away from the cliff that was anxiety. Derek was right, of course. She nodded. "Okay. I'll stay here. Hold down the fort."

She cupped Luke's face in her hands and kissed him on the forehead. Yikes, he was hot.

"Okay, buddy," Derek said. "Let's hit it."

As they walked out the front door, Summer bit her lip to keep from crying.

Somehow, fifteen years after Summer had taken the privileges and duties of motherhood away from Willow, Willow's mothering instincts kicked in. Her timing couldn't be worse. Just as Summer put the teapot on the stove to boil, Willow walked into the kitchen, rubbing her eyes. "What's going on?"

"Why are you up at this time of night?" Summer said.

"I don't know. You were being quiet, but I sensed you were awake. Instinct." She tapped her temple.

Summer snorted. "Luke woke up with a high fever. Derek's taking him to the hospital." She got a mug out of the cupboard and didn't offer Willow one.

"Can't you just give him some ibuprofen or something?"

Willow missed Summer's reaction—an annoyed sigh and rolled eyes—because Summer's head was in the pantry. Summer chose a teabag and turned around, but didn't make eye contact.

"No," she said. "He just had surgery, Willow. We can't risk an infection. He could just have a virus, but we won't know until a doctor examines him."

"Hm. Well, why aren't you going back to bed?"

"You would ask that," Summer said. "I'm worried, that's why. I know I won't be able to sleep until Derek calls with an update and I know Luke's okay."

She tore open the teabag's wrapper and put the bag into the mug, her movements sharp and jerky.

"Well, I'll sit up with you."

Summer didn't answer.

"I'll just get myself some tea," Willow said. She retrieved a mug for herself and set it on the counter next to Summer's before digging her own teabag out of the pantry. The teapot whistled. Summer poured water into the mugs and carried hers to the kitchen table.

Willow followed.

Summer inhaled the steam from her peach tea, and Willow tapped her fingers on the tabletop. Willow began to talk.

"I went to see your father again," she said.

"So that's where you went yesterday?" Summer said.

"I kept waiting for you to ask."

"Well, it's none of my business, is it?"

Willow raised a shoulder. "I guess it is."

"Hmm."

Summer knew she should ask how it went. But she didn't really care right now. So she stared into her tea and waited. Willow would tell her eventually.

"I was nervous," Willow said, and Summer braced herself for the long story, in which Willow's feelings would undoubtedly play the starring role. "I walked up to the school just as the final bell rang."

As Willow went on to describe the way her fingers tingled with nerves, and the way she'd worn certain shoes to ensure her calf muscles stood out, Summer's mind wandered to Derek and Luke. They would have made it to the hospital by now. She could picture Derek sitting on a chair in the triage area, snapping impatient answers at whichever unfortunate soul had the job of inputting Luke's details. Any minute he would send her a text message asking for some critical piece of information like Luke's blood type or the insurance policy number or Summer's star sign. She checked her phone again. No text.

Luke was probably sitting on the chair next to Derek, his knees pulled up under his chin, his eyes big as he took in all the activity. Summer hoped he wasn't traumatized by anything in the ER. Hopefully they'd get him into a room quickly.

"So I decided, 'This is it, Willow,'" Willow was saying. "And I marched right into his classroom."

Summer brought her mind back to the kitchen. Willow had marched right into Dennis's classroom?

"So what happened?"

He looked surprised, for sure," Willow said. "And not as angry as he did the other day. Not as happy as I expected, either." She took a sip of her tea. "He looks exactly the same. He's aged well."

She would talk about his looks rather than the actual conversation, Winter said.

Willow continued: "He has some graying around the temples, but it's actually quite sexy. I never would have thought I'd like that. And his chest hair sticks out above the top of his collar. Again, I found it surprisingly sexy."

"Obviously," Summer said. She heard the wry tone of her own voice and wondered if Willow did, too. She must have because she switched gears.

"Anyway," she said. "He said my name. 'Willow?' Like a question. Like he wasn't sure. I said, 'Hi, Dennis.' He didn't smile, exactly, but something changed in his eyes. He asked about you, Summer. He said, 'How is our daughter? I suppose she's all grown up by now.'"

Knowing Willow, she was probably hurt that he'd asked about Summer first.

"Initially, it annoyed me that he asked about you, first."

Summer was about to respond, rapid fire, and say that showed he was a good guy, but Willow held up a hand to stop her. "I know," she said. "I came to my senses. The fact that he asked about you first shows that he's a good guy."

Summer nodded, drank some tea, checked her phone. No messages.

"Then what?"

"So I told him all about you. I told him how you're married to a nurse—a man nurse, of course—and how you just had your fifth child. I told him how you work as a graphic designer and how you have his eyebrows. Well, his old eyebrows. Not his new ones. His new ones are kind of bushy."

Summer surprised herself by laughing. So Willow had given Summer's father the demographics. But she probably hadn't told him anything about Summer's personality or tastes. Willow probably didn't even know. She probably hadn't bothered noticing that Summer abhorred the texture of shrimp and that she took cream but not sugar in her coffee. She probably hadn't noticed that Summer valued honesty above everything else, and that she was a steadfast friend and a patient mother.

"I told him you're kind of a hippie," Willow said. "What with your yoga and inner peace and all that."

When Summer raised her eyebrows, Willow laughed. "But don't worry. I told him you don't burn incense or wear tie-dye." She laughed. "He said you sound like a really good person."

Winter said, *She probably took credit for the way you turned out, but we all know that's a lie.*

"I told him I couldn't take credit for how well you turned out," Willow said. "I mean, I can't, can I?"

Here, Winter was stunned into silence.

"Since when did you become so introspective?" Summer said.

"Oh, Summer. I've always been. I just don't like thinking or talking about it. If you were me, would you like looking in the mirror?" Before Summer could answer, Willow added, "And I don't mean the actual mirror. I mean the proverbial one."

"Probably not," Summer admitted. She was surprised that Willow didn't look hurt by the admission. "So what else did you talk about?"

"Well, I asked him what he's been up to, which, of course, we know is teaching, and he asked me what I've been up to, which, of course, is drinking, mostly. Just kidding. I just told him, 'A little of this and a little of that.' Gotta keep the mystery going, right?"

"I guess so," Summer said. "So how did you leave it?"

"We exchanged numbers. The real shit of it is, he's single. Divorced, actually. I couldn't decide whether I liked that or not. I always fantasized that when I saw him again, he'd tell me he waited for me. Pined away, you know? But it turns out, he got married shortly after we, um, broke things off."

Willow answered the next question before Summer could ask it. "You have a brother. Well, a half-brother."

Millions of questions came to Summer's mind then. To hide her surprise and all the thoughts racing around like balls in a pinball machine, she looked down at the table. How old was this brother? (A few years younger than her, probably.) Had she ever met him? (Most likely she had. Such was small-town life. He'd probably stood in front of her in line for coffee, or held the door for her at the bank.)

It felt strange to think she may have crossed paths with him and not even known it. Weren't they cosmically connected somehow? Wouldn't her soul recognize his?

She looked up to see Willow watching her expectantly.

She shrugged. "That's nice."

Willow didn't answer. Summer continued to feel antsy and helpless as she waited for Derek to text with a Luke update.

"Well, I'd better get to disinfecting," she said.

She stood up, retrieved the can of disinfectant spray from under the sink and began spraying surfaces—again.

"I guess I'll go back to bed," Willow said.

By the time Summer turned around, Willow was gone, her mug on the table, still full of tea.

Alone with her thoughts, Summer ran through that list of a household's most bacteria-infested places. She'd seen it in an article once. The kitchen sink, the bathroom, the door handles. She'd have to scrub those as well as spray them. *Scrub. Spray. Scrub. Spray. Scrub. Spray.* She started to feel a little dizzy, and figured it was just because she was inhaling aerosol. Derek and Luke had been gone two hours. Summer hadn't finished scrubbing or spraying, but she took a break to text Derek.

Any updates?

After a few minutes, he replied: *They've got us in a room. Gave him ibuprofen and acetaminophen to bring the fever down. He's still pretty hot. Waiting for a doctor.*

She went back to cleaning. Why wasn't Derek demanding that a doctor see Luke? He should be out in the corridor, waving his arms. He was just too nice. He'd wait until Luke's fever climbed even higher, because he didn't want to stress the nurses and doctors out or make them think he was a jerk. Luke was probably droopy-eyed and miserable next to him. Why wasn't he forcing them to examine him? He needed antibiotics.

Even though she knew she was being totally irrational, she texted Derek again: *Don't let them make you wait. Page the nurse. Tell them he needs the doctor right away.*

She could imagine him, sitting on one of those plastic chairs, holding the phone in his lap, reading the message and closing his eyes in exasperation. When he didn't respond, she knew he was biting his virtual tongue.

She kept cleaning.

JUST AFTER DAWN, Summer woke up on the couch, the spray can on the floor next to her, a wad of paper towels still clutched in her hand. She didn't even realize she'd fallen asleep, but her trusty alarm clock, Olivia, was now going off, ensuring she didn't miss the start of a new day.

Her phone. Where had she left it? Surely Derek had texted by now. She went to get Olivia and then carried her through the house, frantic, looking for her phone. Lack of sleep made her eyes dry and rough, and she blinked repeatedly to moisten them. As she hunted for her phone, Olivia's cries became more insistent, and Summer bounced her, making *shhh* noises as she retraced her steps from the night before. Tea at the table with Willow. Scrubbing the kitchen sink. Wiping down door handles.

She found it under the sink in the kids' bathroom. That's right, she'd run out of paper towels and had looked there for a new roll.

5 Messages.

She scrolled frantically for a message from Derek, and found it at the bottom of the list, received just after four a.m.: *The doctor just examined him. Obviously he has an infection of some kind. They're starting IV antibiotics, and they'll run tests to see what's going on. They think he'll be fine, once we get the infection cleared up. I texted Josie and Delaney to see if they could help you in the morning.*

"I don't need help," she said to no one. Her voice sounded grumpy and pouty in the ringing silence.

Olivia wailed. Summer went into the living room to feed her and read the remaining messages.

The first was from Josie, who had copied Delaney. She'd sent it just after six—so only about fifteen minutes ago: *We'll be over at 6:30. Why didn't you call us last night when Derek took Luke to the hospital?*

Delaney had responded just after that: *You need to learn to ask for help.*

Then Josie: *We know you're practically perfect. ;) But it's okay to lean on us. That's what we're here for.*

Delaney: *Preach it, sister.*

Summer smiled despite herself.

The girls came in like drill sergeants (well, drill sergeants with donuts). All the kids were up by six forty-five, and Delaney and Josie fed them and got them dressed while Summer showered. Willow continued sleeping.

"Your house is spic and span," Josie said when Summer returned to the kitchen, dressed in holey jeans and a raggedy T-shirt (because they were the only clean clothes she could find), her wet hair piled into a bun.

"When did you do all this cleaning?" Delaney asked.

Summer felt trapped when she heard the threatening tone in Delaney's voice. She glanced around at the kids, who stared at her with wide eyes. Then she looked at Josie, who was cutting a donut into tiny pieces for Hannah and alternately feeding her bites of scrambled egg, and then at Delaney, who was twisting Sarah's hair into a fancy braid.

Her friends stared back at her, their eyes piercing.

She sighed because she knew what was coming. "Last night."

"Last night, when? When you should have been sleeping?"

Summer shrugged and nodded, like it was no big deal.

"Woman. How can you take care of all these people if you won't take care of you?" Josie said.

She had a point. "I couldn't sleep," Summer said.

"Look," Delaney said. "We can't stay here all day. I've got a full schedule at the clinic and Josie's got an in-service training thing at school. We've already discussed what's going to happen. We're going to finish getting the kids ready. We're going to make them lunch and leave it in the fridge. You're going to leave for the hospital so you can be with Luke. And Willow is going to babysit."

Summer felt her head shaking before Delaney even finished her last sentence.

"It's only for a couple of hours," Josie said. "You have to be with Luke, and you need Derek there for support."

"She's still sleeping!" When she realized her voice sounded screechy, she took a deep breath and repeated herself.

"I'll wake her up," Sarah said. "And don't worry, Mom, I'll be here to help with Hannah and Olivia."

Summer nodded. She was outvoted.

"Fine," she said, and she didn't miss the smiles Josie and Delaney exchanged before they answered, "Fine."

A few minutes later, Willow entered the kitchen looking groggy, her hair sticking up in the back and her eyes only half-open.

"So you're going to stay with the kids," Delaney said in the same bossy tone she'd used on Summer a moment ago. "It's just for a couple of hours. And then either Summer or Derek will come back to relieve you."

"I have things to do," Willow said, quickly adding, "but I guess that's okay," when Josie shot her a look.

"Why don't you take them to the park or something?" Delaney said.

Summer cringed. The idea of Willow taking the kids out of the house sent her into a near-panic again.

"It'll be fine," Josie said. "The only one we really have to worry about is Hannah, right? And Sarah's going to keep a careful eye on her. Like a hawk."

Sarah smiled, but kept her eyes on Summer. "Like a hawk."

All the possible disaster scenarios went through her mind. As Delaney and Josie made sandwiches, Summer rattled off instructions for the kids: "Nate, don't run in the parking lot. Sarah, hold Hannah's hand when you get out of the car and don't let her climb on that one ladder thing where she always gets stuck. Make sure Willow doesn't leave Olivia's car seat at the park with Olivia in it. Check before you come home that you have your siblings. Both of them. Do a head count. Nate, don't hang upside down on that green bar. It's slippery and I don't want you getting a head injury or breaking your neck. I've told you that a million times. Sarah, don't let him talk to strangers. Well, kid strangers are okay. Be polite. Make sure Hannah says 'excuse me' when she's pushing past people to go on the slide. Make sure she sits down on the slide. Make sure Willow feeds Olivia. There's breastmilk in the fridge."

"I thought we were out," Sarah said, and Summer's throat tightened. Sarah was growing up into such a responsible girl.

"I pumped last night," Summer said before giving her a kiss on the forehead.

Sarah nodded dutifully and when Summer took a breath to

continue, Josie held up a hand. "They'll be fine, Mama." Then she rubbed her forehead. *"Dios mío."*

Again, Summer felt the first stirrings of panic: a tight feeling in her chest and the increasing of her heart rate. Delaney must have noticed the symptoms.

"Deep breaths," she said, and then she and Josie herded Summer out the front door.

CHAPTER TWENTY-THREE

Because Derek had taken the backup car and Willow would
need the van to take the kids to the park—*and lose them,* Winter whispered—Josie drove Summer to the hospital. Thanks to Josie's
company, Summer made it all the way there without having a meltdown. The sliding doors whooshed open as Summer approached,
but instead of walking in, Summer sat down on one of the benches
outside. She dropped her head into her hands, but didn't cry.

For the first time in years, she wanted to run away from her life.
She loved her children. She loved Derek. And she loved Josie and
Delaney. But right now, it all felt like too much. She couldn't bear it.

What if she got on a train and rode it east, all the way to Florida?
She could start over, alone, and live a stress-free life as a graphic
designer on the beach. Or what if she hopped on a plane and went
north, to Canada? No one would think to look for her there.

Derek was a catch. She was sure that if she disappeared, he could
snag a new wife. Although it was unlikely any woman would walk
into a marriage with a guy who had five children and a recently
disappeared wife. He'd be alone and lonely forever.

But if she was in Florida or Canada, maybe she would stop
caring, eventually.

What would he tell the kids?

"Sorry, guys. Your mom had a major meltdown. It's not you, it's
her. Nevertheless, she's not coming back."

She imagined their faces. Sarah would be so stoic. She would try to understand, the little adult she was.

Oh, God. I'm ruining her. She is a little adult.

Nate would become angry, kicking at the carpet, throwing toys at the wall. Luke would cry, his elfin face distorting. Hannah would wander the house, repeating, "Mama?" over and over again until one of her older siblings (Luke, probably) told her to be quiet. Olivia would never know the difference.

Her tiny baby wouldn't even know her, which might actually be a positive.

And she'd be sitting in some coffee shop drinking caffeinated lattes, her laptop to keep her company. When was the last time she'd had a caffeinated latte? Some good-looking young man would approach her, strike up a conversation about the weather, and then ask for her number. She'd say, "Oh, I couldn't, I'm marr—" but then she'd look at her bare ring finger and laugh before he entered her digits into his phone.

The vision of her new life was becoming so real that for a moment Summer could hear the hiss of an espresso machine. In that one fraction of a second, she experienced a yearning so deep she wanted to cry. When she realized the sound actually came from the hospital doors opening, she chided herself for getting carried away.

At that moment, a handsome, muscly man with a nice glaze of stubble across his chin walked out of the hospital. What would it be like to start all over with a man? She always thought she'd dread it. How awkward, having someone other than her husband see her naked.

But at this moment, she imagined the sexy hospital guy, not knowing she had children, viewing her body as if it were brand new, not wrecked by years of pregnancy and nursing. At this, she laughed. Her breasts hung like pancakes off her torso, and the skin around her middle was loose, like an elephant's. Dead giveaways. Okay, so in her fantasy runaway life she wouldn't have a boyfriend. Maybe she could just do booty calls with Derek. Or maybe she wouldn't even need sex. They made such effective toys these days.

Her imagination brought her back to the coffee shop. She'd sit there, all day, without anywhere else to go or anyone else for whom to be responsible. No book orders to fill out or spirit days to find outfits for. No evening soccer practices or reading twenty minutes per night. Most importantly, no bone-deep worry about little tiny people whom she couldn't keep safe on her own. No watching every rise and fall of a chest, petrified, waiting for it to stop. No imagining finding one of her children's dead bodies in bed one morning, stone cold.

Just Summer.

She leaned her head back against the bench and sighed. Her eyes closed, she could feel the edges of sleep sliding over her.

She shook herself. "Get up, woman," she said aloud, then opened her eyes and looked around to make sure no one had heard her. She was alone. She stood up, steeled herself, and walked through the doors to the hospital to join her son and her husband ... and her real life.

Despite having been up all night, Luke looked much better than he had the last time Summer saw him. The red spots on his cheeks had gone back down to a healthy rosy color, and his eyes looked clear. He grinned when he saw her, and all her visions of living a solitary life, drinking caffeine and flirting with single men, slipped away.

"Mom! I got to eat Jell-O for breakfast! All that red dye and sugar, first thing in the morning!"

Summer did a mock groan, and they both laughed. She sat on the edge of the bed and leaned forward to hug him.

"You feel normal," she said.

"I'm totally not normal. This illness has made me a machine. I'm a machine, mom. I'll be showing you my superpowers soon."

"I can't wait. Where's Dad?"

"He went downstairs to get coffee. He'll be right back."

"How are you feeling? Besides super, of course."

"I feel way better," Luke said. He wrinkled his nose. "Except for this, like, super feeling. It's tingly."

A nurse pushed the curtain back and came into the room, all smiles. "You've got a superhero for a son," she said to Summer.

Summer tousled his hair. "He just told me."

"I'm Tammy." She reached down and gently pinched Luke's toe under the sheet. "I'll be taking care of this guy today. I've got to take him for some scans, just to make sure everything's okay with his ticker. You can come along, or you can wait here."

Summer looked at Luke. "I'm fine, Mom, if you want to wait here for Dad."

Summer nodded and Tammy helped Luke into a wheelchair and wheeled him away. Summer sat down on one of the mauve chairs near the bed and Derek returned almost right away.

"You look surprised to see me," she said.

"I didn't think you'd leave the kids with your mom." He bent down to kiss her.

"Willow," she said.

"I didn't think you'd leave the kids with Willow."

"Josie and Delaney made me."

"They'll be fine," he said.

"I've heard that before," Summer said.

"Aren't we missing someone?" Derek said.

"Tammy took him up for scans. I was just waiting for you to get back. Let's go meet them."

Summer and Derek were the only two in the elevator. For the first time in her life, Summer felt claustrophobic, and struggled to inhale the warm, thick air. A few yoga breaths seemed to help, but her heart still raced. She tried for a change of focus.

"Derek?"

"Hmm?"

She took the time to really look at him, and she noticed his red, puffy eyes and the way his hair stuck up at odd angles. She leaned toward him and kissed him on the cheek, which was just as scruffy (and sexy) as the cheek belonging to the guy who'd emerged from the hospital a few moments ago.

"Do you ever imagine just leaving this life? Like, going to Florida or something and sitting in a coffee shop?"

Derek laughed. "Not anymore. I did when I was younger, though, when we first had Sarah and she cried all the time. I thought, 'I could learn how to surf. I could drink coffee on the beach. Every day.'"

Summer smiled. "But not lately?"

"No, not lately. I think I've settled into my role as husband and father pretty well, don't you?"

"Yes! I wasn't talking about you, really. I was thinking about myself."

"Is this one of those, 'It's not you, it's me' conversations? Because if it is, those are always a lie."

She laughed. "No! It's not."

"Do you ever wish you could leave this life?" he said.

She didn't want to admit it. He'd feel bad. He'd feel guilty, like he wasn't providing well enough, or taking good enough care of her. The elevator stopped with a jerk, and the doors slid open before she had a chance to answer.

"It's to the right," she said.

Luke's scans came back normal. The doctors weren't sure whether he'd gotten an infection or some kind of bacterial illness, but the antibiotics would kill it off. They wanted to keep him for one more night, and Luke seemed perfectly content, so Summer took the car and headed home to be with the other kids.

Derek had instructed her to stop for a caffeinated latte ("The kids will be fine for an extra half-hour," he said, "and a little caffeine won't hurt Olivia. You don't do it all the time."), so she did.

At Ground Up, she immersed herself back into that imaginary life. Although she automatically sought a table with a bunch of chairs, she felt giddy when she realized she didn't need one. Instead, she chose a luxurious arm chair in the corner of the coffee shop, away from everything else.

In that dimly lit corner, she sipped her coffee and visualized the beach. She could hear the ocean's waves coming up onto the shore, and seagulls calling as they circled above. The breeze smelled salty and felt heavenly on her skin.

How long could she sit at the beach? Hours, probably. Days, maybe. She could sleep on this imaginary beach, feeling the heat of the sun move over her face as it arced through the sky.

"Excuse me, ma'am. Are you okay?"

Summer blinked, bringing herself back to reality, almost surprised to find herself still in Juniper. The woman who'd brought her out of her daydream was a young mother, balancing a little boy on her hip, a to-go cup in one hand and a bakery bag in the other. Her son, who was probably about one-and-a-half, repeatedly banged a set of plastic keys on the lid of the cup.

"I'm fine, thanks," Summer said. "Just taking a little break from reality."

The baby let out a holler and nearly smacked his mother's coffee cup out of her hand. She winced.

"This is just the beginning, sweetheart," Summer said. "I have five of them at home."

Her tone said, "You're doomed," even though she usually tried to sound upbeat when she spoke to young mothers who still thought motherhood was full of promise.

"Wow," the woman said. "I don't know how you do it. You must have your hands full."

"Yep. I do."

The woman's face seemed to say it was no wonder Summer needed a break from reality. Her voice said, "Well, have a nice day."

"Thanks," Summer said. "You too."

The break was over.

Summer, feeling somewhat refreshed, decided she'd better head home. As she drove, she relished the sense of calm her visualization had given her.

THE HOUSE WAS EMPTY. The clock was ticking. Not even the dog greeted her. Summer could hear her heart pounding in her ears. She could feel it in her fingertips. She could even see it, tiny black lines pulsing across her vision. She'd been gone for hours. Willow should have the kids home by now. It was past lunch time. Well past lunch time.

Where were they?

"Willow?"

No answer.

She walked through the house, checking the bedrooms, the closets, the bathrooms. She opened shower curtains, checked under desk chairs. Maybe the kids were playing hide and seek. They always thought that was so funny.

"Sarah?"

Sarah wouldn't be hiding. She was too old, far too mature, for that.

Maybe they were outside.

Summer sensed her legs moving too fast, although she could barely feel anything below her knees. Just as she reached the sliding glass door, she pitched forward, her upper body having caught up just as her legs slowed down to stop.

Her palms smacked the door. It stung, but it pulled her out of her panicked state long enough for her to unlock the door and then realize that if she were unlocking the door, no one was outside.

Still, she scanned the backyard, then scoured it.

Nothing.

Where was her family?

Willow had probably lost Hannah. That was the only possible explanation. Otherwise, why hadn't she come back? She had probably forced Sarah and Nate to search the park, just as Summer was now searching the house. Hannah, undoubtedly, was walking right into the street, across that stupid little sidewalk that was supposed to serve as a divider between the playground and the parking lot.

Not all the cars had backup cameras or even sensors. Come to think of it, Hannah was probably dead. Run over. Laying on the asphalt.

Summer could only hope she had just run off.

"Oh, my God," she said.

Her feet tingled. Her hands tingled. Her entire body shook. Summer had passed out only once during her entire life. She had gone with Summer and Delaney to an amusement park and Josie, had talked them into riding the biggest roller coaster in the world.

They stood at the turnstile, waiting to go into the serpentine line. Summer was terrified. Her hands tingled, her feet tingled, her heart raced.

"This is a one-time opportunity," Josie had said, her big brown eyes boring into Summer's, her hand tight on Summer's wrist. Delaney was on the fence and Summer was the deciding factor. The pressure. Summer could barely stand it. Both Josie and Delaney stared at her.

She took a deep breath, clenched her fists, and nodded. "Okay," she said. "Okay."

They got in line. They inched forward, toward the platform and away from it. Summer became increasingly scared, and increasingly shaky.

It was their turn. Summer stepped onto the platform. She walked toward the empty seat, Josie in front of her and Delaney behind her. She looked at the harness, a huge black metal monstrosity that would go over her shoulders and hold her in place, and her breath came even faster.

One more step, and she felt a split second of overwhelming dizziness.

I'm passing out, she thought.

She woke up to a view of the sky, its edges impeded by the faces of Delaney, Josie and the ride operator, a kid with a huge blond afro. All three of them peered down at her as she blinked herself back into consciousness. She had the strange sensation that someone else was breathing for her. Her lungs inhaled and exhaled on their own, machine-like.

They didn't ride the roller coaster that day, and Josie later admitted it wasn't the biggest one in the world. She'd only said it was to inspire the girls to ride it with her.

Present-day Summer felt the warning signs.

Not only were her hands and feet tingling, but she also sensed the whole world spinning around her. A different version of herself perched up near the ceiling, watching the entire scene unfold, watching her run frantically around the empty house. She wondered if that version of herself found this mildly amusing.

"Nate!"

Sarah might not hide, but Nate certainly would. Although, her mind reminded her, he wouldn't be here alone.

No one was here.

Hannah wandering into the parking lot wasn't the worst of it. What if some child molester—the guy who drove the ice cream truck —what if he had Sarah in his greasy clutches? The experts said you weren't really supposed to teach your kids stranger danger anymore, that it's usually someone who knows them.

Had Summer taught Sarah the right things? Would Sarah know not to follow him away from the playground even if he offered her free ice cream or said he had lost his puppy or kitten?

And what about Nate? Summer scoured her memory for the conversations she should have had with them. Nothing.

She stood in the middle of the living room, the whole house now spinning around her as if it were a globe and she were the axis.

The edges of her vision went black. She noticed too late that she was standing right next to the coffee table.

She passed out, her last thought before her head hit the corner of the coffee table with a horrible thunk, *Now how will I help them? My children are doomed and it's all my fault.*

CHAPTER TWENTY-FOUR

When she woke up, there was none of that cliché, quiet hospital-machine beeping that usually accompanies the scenes where someone wakes up from being passed out. None of that peace and quiet. Summer first noticed her lungs breathing for her just as they had on the roller coaster platform. *In, out. In, out.* Her eyes blinked involuntarily. *Close-open. Close-open.*

All of this was happening in an unbearably loud place. When her eyes were open, her eyeballs roved from one side to the other as she tried to figure out where she was. An ambulance. She noticed the silver bedrails on either side of her, and the oxygen mask tight against the bridge of her nose and down around her chin. She could hear the roar of the engine and the sound of the road whizzing by beneath them.

Shit. They found me on the living room floor and called the freakin' ambulance.

Someone was talking loudly, prodding at her at the same time. Someone else spoke quietly. She felt the prick of an IV going into her arm, and the quiet talker leaned toward her. Derek. Of course. Why hadn't she recognized his voice?

"You're awake. Thank goodness."

Hearing him soothed her, but only momentarily.

Panic took hold again immediately. "Wait. Who's with Luke?"

Derek sighed. Even now, she could see frustration walking across his features before he put on a mask of calm. "Josie."

Now Summer sighed, but with relief. It lasted only a second before panic seized her in its wicked grip.

"The kids?" she said, the way her voice sounded muffled through the oxygen mask giving her a sense of otherworldliness.

"They're fine. They got back from the park and found you on the living room floor. You've got a nasty gash on your head. A big bump, too. You look like Hannah."

Summer smiled at this. Hannah walked around with a perpetual bump on one side of her forehead. She felt the smile fade as horror set in. That dark, overwhelming fear when she couldn't find the kids. She passed out. And her kids, whom she was trying so hard to protect, found their mother on the floor. Bleeding and unconscious.

She groaned.

"Are you okay? What's wrong? Does something hurt?"

"The kids. I can't believe they found me like this."

Now hysteria washed over her, bringing with it the urge to weep. She wished she could rewind and remain calm, stop the tide of panic that had swallowed her up so completely.

"So what happened?" Derek asked. He reached down and held her hand.

"I—I don't know. After the hospital, I stopped to get a coffee, like you said to, and I came home and no one was there. You know how strange it is to come home to an empty house. I expected Willow to have the kids back by then. You know she's not very responsible. So all I could think about was Hannah wandering off or running into the parking lot and getting run over or Sarah or Nate getting molested by that creepy ice cream truck guy."

The words came tumbling out fast, and the loud talker said in an intense voice that made Summer cringe, "Classic panic attack, man."

Summer had a half-second's warning before she passed out again.

THIS TIME, she woke up in the quiet hospital. Talking to Derek and finding out the kids were safe must have given her subconscious a little break from worrying, because she felt calm. Strangely calm. A kind of calm she hadn't felt in months.

She must be on drugs.

And she liked it.

She felt like she was drifting, maybe laying on a raft in a swimming pool, the sun sparkling off the water next to her.

"You're awake," Derek said.

Summer turned her head and saw he was sitting in a chair right next to her bed. She giggled. "Well, hello, Captain Obvious."

He smiled, but it didn't erase the worry from his face.

"You're really dehydrated."

Even in her floaty state, she could hear the accusatory tone in his voice.

"How do you know?" she asked.

"They drew blood and took urine."

"Why do you sound grumpy?"

He inhaled through his nose and exhaled through his teeth. This wasn't good. He only did that when he was really angry, like the time she had backed their first car, brand new, into a light pole in the grocery store parking lot. They'd just run out to get some ice cream. It should have been a fun trip. And it was, until she backed up without looking, and clunked the car into the pole. Derek inhaled through his nose and exhaled through his teeth, exactly as he'd done now. They returned home with a quart of ice cream, a broken tail-light, a completely mutilated bumper and Derek's grudge looming, ominous between them.

It wouldn't have been that big of a deal, except they'd just bought the car. It was their first purchase as a couple, and Derek was so proud of it. They had lived on a tight budget for an entire year just to save up enough cash for a down payment.

Although it had been kind of adventurous and romantic to eat ramen noodles several times each week and forego date nights and cable TV, Derek was looking forward to living it up in the months following the car purchase. He wanted his wife to be able to drive around in a nice-looking car, not a jalopy. He wanted to be able to provide his wife with the finer things, like a steak dinner once in a while.

But it would cost a thousand dollars to fix the car.

"Why are you angry?" she asked now. The drugs that were giving her that glorious floating feeling made her sound flippant. She noticed, but couldn't quite adjust to serious.

"This isn't the time to discuss it. You're on drugs."

"I do feel verrrry relaxed." She could hear the slight slur in her voice, and it made her giggle.

"What's funny?"

His phone chirped and saved her from having to answer.

"Josie's coming over."

Although Summer immediately thought, *Ooh, Happy Hour with drugs*, she somehow managed to refrain from saying it out loud. That probably wouldn't sit well with Derek.

Speaking of Derek, where was he? Without saying good-bye, he was gone. Had she fallen asleep?

After just a beat of empty silence, Summer could hear Josie's heels in the hallway outside her room. *Click, clack, click, clack.*

"I hear you coming," she said loudly.

When Josie did walk into the room, her eyes were smiling. Her mouth was set, though.

"Hey," she said.

"Why so serious?" Summer said.

Josie sighed. "Luke's doing great. They're going to release him soon. Maybe tonight, probably tomorrow."

"That's good news, right?"

"If his mama's there to take care of him, it is."

"Why wouldn't she be?" Summer asked.

Josie looked around, exaggerating the movements as she focused first on the monitor, then on the IV bag, then on the hospital bed. She grabbed the sleeve of Summer's hospital gown between her thumb and forefinger. Summer wondered, vaguely, where her clothes were, but before she had a chance to try to form a memory of where they'd gone, Josie began speaking.

"Um, I don't know, Summer. Maybe because ... She's. In. The. Hospital."

Right.

"I'm fine. They're going to discharge me today, too. Just a misunderstanding."

"A misunderstanding?"

Summer nodded. Surely it was.

"A misunderstanding?" Josie said again. Summer swallowed. Josie kept talking. "You're dangerously dehydrated. Your blood sugar is really low. I mean, really low. You're losing weight and not just baby weight. You're really, really sick."

I am?

Summer knew she'd been stressed out. She knew she'd skipped a few meals and forgotten her water bottle several times. Well, okay. Maybe lots of times. She knew these were all big no-nos, especially because she was breastfeeding. But she'd made enough milk so she thought she was fine. Not that she'd been feeling well. She'd been weak and tired and at least a little dizzy, pretty much nonstop.

"I'm sorry," Summer said to Josie, but then realized she didn't know why she was apologizing.

"Don't apologize to me, *amiga*," Josie said. "Apologize to Derek. Poor guy looks like he's been wrung out."

"Why does he get all the sympathy?"

Josie sat on Summer's bed next to her, stretching her legs out alongside Summer's. She took Summer's hand in hers and leaned her head on Summer's shoulder.

"He doesn't. I feel bad for you both. I think you're just plain exhausted. And having Willow here doesn't help one bit. You lost it when she was late getting home from the park, didn't you?"

Summer swallowed the lump that formed in her throat and nodded. Josie squeezed her hand.

"I'm sorry," Josie said. "Delaney and I, and Derek, too. We all thought she'd be a big help for you. But she seems to be more of a stressor."

Summer laughed, and it sounded harsh, even to her. "Yeah, right. She's never been a big help to me."

"No?"

"No."

"Are you okay?" Josie asked.

"I don't know," Summer said. "It's just … it's just so much. It's always something, you know? As if giving birth to our fifth child just as my estranged mother showed up on our doorstep wasn't enough, then Luke had to get the heart surgery. And as if those three things weren't enough, my estranged mother tells me I have a long-lost brother, and—"

Josie put a hand up to stop her. "You have a brother?"

"Half-brother. Yeah. Somewhere in Juniper, I think."

"Wow. It's almost too much to take in," Josie said.

"You're telling me, sister," Summer said.

"Are you going to meet him?"

Summer shook her head. "I don't know. I mean, I'd kind of like to, but I just don't know. I guess I'll have to think about it. I'll probably secretly hate him since he grew up with the dad I never met, and a nicer mom than I did."

"You don't know she was nicer than Willow."

"Ha. How could she not be."

Josie laughed. "None of this sounds like the Summer I know."

"I haven't been feeling like myself lately."

"No kidding," Josie said. "So tell me how it came to this."

She gestured at their surroundings.

"Well, you kind of already know," Summer said.

"Tell me anyway."

Reliving those moments sounded about as fun as getting her fingernails pulled out with pliers, Summer thought. She spoke quietly, in the hopes of preventing anyone other than Josie from hearing how crazy she felt this morning. "I think it really started about a week ago," Summer said. "I know I haven't been eating or drinking enough. It was exacerbated when Luke woke up with a fever and Derek took him to the hospital. I stayed up almost all night, cleaning. Then, today, I came here to visit with Luke. When I was leaving, Derek suggested I stop for a coffee. So I did." She left out the parts about fantasizing that she was able to start a whole new life, possibly with a boyfriend but most likely without. "When I got home, I expected Willow to be back from the park already."

Josie nodded. "It was after lunchtime and you thought Hannah would need a nap."

"Yes. You totally get me."

"I do. But Willow probably doesn't even realize Hannah takes a nap."

"Right. But I wasn't thinking logically."

"Right."

Summer described the rest of the experience in detail, from the tingling hands and feet to the racing heart and the frantic search for her children in the empty house.

"Silence is probably very unnerving to you," Josie said.

Summer laughed. "It is!"

"Sounds like a good, old-fashioned panic attack," Josie said.

"Now that I'm talking about it from a new state of mind" (she motioned at the IV through which someone had administered anti-anxiety medication) "I can see that."

"And it was probably compounded by the fact that you haven't been taking care of yourself. Dehydrated? Low blood sugar? That's not like you."

Summer had been waiting for this. Actually, this was the reason she had been dreading this conversation. A tiny seed of self-loathing had been planted in her mind hours ago, the moment she realized she was in an ambulance. She never let herself get sick. She always took care of herself, even while she took care of everyone else. She chided mothers who said they didn't have time for eating snacks or going to yoga class. And now here she was, completely depleted. Worse than that, she was completely depleted and now couldn't take care of anyone.

"I'm a hypocrite," she said.

Josie squeezed her hand. "Kind of."

THE DOCTORS DECIDED to keep Summer overnight. She told Derek and the girls she didn't need company, and spent the entire after-noon and evening enjoying the feeling a brain saturated in chemicals gave her.

At nine the following morning, someone said, "Knock, knock," and pulled the curtain open. The woman was obviously some kind of counselor or social worker. Instead of a white coat and stetho-scope, she wore khaki pants and a light blue blouse with a name tag (Cassie) pinned to the front pocket. Trendy glasses made her hazel eyes look owlish on her tiny face.

Summer couldn't help it: she said, "Oh, great. Now I get a psych evaluation from someone half my age."

Not really your style, Winter said. Summer knew it wasn't her style, but she didn't care. She almost always worked so hard to make everyone comfortable. Typically, she would have greeted this new interruption with a bright smile. Not today. Yes, she was still on some kind of drugs. But also, she already knew she'd messed up. She didn't need a professional to tell her she'd broken.

"I'm Cassie," the woman said, "the hospital's social worker."

"Great," Summer said.

Cassie laughed, and undeterred, pulled a chair up alongside the hospital bed. "You're Summer," she said.

"Look, Cassie," Summer said. "I'm fine. I don't need a social worker. I had a breakdown, but I'm okay. I've had a lot going on."

"It's standard practice for the doctors to order a quick evaluation with a social worker for patients who have had a panic attack," Cassie said. "So if you're okay, it should just take a few minutes. Let's just get it over with."

Summer knew this Cassie woman, who was obviously too young to have children of her own, wouldn't empathize with the stress and pressure she had been under for the past several months. But Summer could play this game.

"Fine," she said.

"Great." Cassie smiled, and Summer thought that smile was just a little too bright. "Why don't you tell me what happened. How you ended up here."

"I don't know if you know this, but I have no idea how I ended up here. I was home, and then I was here."

Cassie took off her glasses and leaned forward. Summer expected her to hoot, but her eyes did look a bit more proportionate now that they weren't behind those thick lenses.

"Look," Cassie said. "I've seen this more times than you may realize. I know that you know exactly what happened. It's your job to be a mother to your children and a wife to your husband. Right now, I'm guessing you feel inadequate. You want to jump back on the horse and forget this ever happened. But I'll tell you something. This happened because you're overstressed, overtired, and over-whelmed. It's my job to help you cope. And I take my job very seri-ously. So if we could just cut the crap, I'd really like that."

Hmm, Winter said. *Pretty respectable.*

Cassie spent an hour with Summer, and once she left, Summer

laid back against her pillow and closed her eyes. She wanted to relax, to give herself over to the drugs. She wondered if they'd send her home with an IV drip of these miraculous substances. If not, she could probably steal some.

Yes, the silence was foreign to her. But right now, she wanted to bathe in it.

Although she hadn't wanted to admit it, Cassie had some good insights and suggestions. Summer had gone ahead and told her pretty much everything, starting with Derek's job loss when she was first pregnant with Olivia, filling in the middle with Luke's heart surgery and the subsequent infection, and ending with Willow getting home late from the park. She alluded to her childhood, being raised by a drunk single mother, and to the recent discovery of a previously unknown half-brother. She frosted the entire story with the chastising she'd received from Josie, and the deep feelings of guilt she was experiencing now. When she was finished pouring her guts out, Cassie sat back in her chair, tapping her glasses against her lips.

"You've got a lot going on, Summer Gray," she said. Summer simply stared at her, and she smiled. "I probably would have had a breakdown, too."

"Thanks."

"It sounds like the issue with your mother is really compounding all the other, normal stressors." She put finger quotes on the "normal." "And even those normal stressors are a lot. I mean, pregnancy and childbirth are stressful on their own. A spouse's job loss? Stressful. A child's serious illness? Stressful. Throw in an unexpected appearance by your estranged mother and it's a recipe for a breakdown. You have nothing to be ashamed of."

"I feel like I do," Summer said. "I feel like I should be able to handle all of this. This is what I signed up for."

If she wasn't on drugs, she probably would have cried then.

"It's Life, with a capital L, right?" Cassie said. "But it's throwing a bunch of curveballs at you, all at once. Nobody should be expected to hit all of them."

"Well, when you put it that way."

They spent some time exploring ways Summer could decrease

her stress level, and Cassie recommended Summer seek longer-term counseling once she got out of the hospital.

Now, Summer imagined the silence as a sparkling, golden liquid, swirling all around the room, caressing her body and soothing her frazzled brain. Yes, she wanted to get better. She knew she needed to get back to her family, and to Life with a capital L. But it felt so good to just relax, to just be. Summer wondered how long she could remain in this state, laying quietly in a bed, absorbing the calm that surrounded her.

Not long, apparently.

Summer woke to the sound of someone trying, and failing, to be quiet as she tiptoed into the room.

"Delaney."

"Damn, I thought you were sleeping," Delaney said.

"You're not very sneaky."

"Sorry. I'm here to take you home."

Home is where the heart is. A house is built from boards and beams, a home is made from love and dreams. There is nothing like staying at home for real comfort.

For the past fifteen years, Summer had worked so hard at making a home for herself and her family.

That day Willow left ten-year-old Summer standing in the produce department at the grocery store, Officer Telluride had told her he'd take her home, as if she should be relieved. In reality, she dreaded the feeling of that place she called home, the feeling of quiet and fear and apprehension. She dreaded the constant longing she felt for something more, or maybe just something different.

Now she was thirty-four, walking back into the very same situation she'd sworn to change. She had everything she'd always wanted —a nice husband, a big family, a puppy—but she still longed for something different, and home was the very last place she wanted to be.

Nevertheless, she signed the discharge paperwork and climbed into a wheelchair so an orderly could wheel her down to the exit. Delaney seemed nervous the entire time, tapping a foot, examining her cuticles for hangnails, checking her phone for messages. Summer was relieved when they got into Delaney's car and she could call her out on it.

"Why are you so nervous?" Summer said, her tone sounding way more demanding than she meant it to.

"What? What do you mean?"

"What do you mean, 'What do you mean?'"

Delaney laughed, a high, airy sound that conveyed nerves more than amusement. Still, she didn't answer.

"Dee. Tell me what's going on."

Delaney backed out of the parking spot and drove toward the exit, giving the road a serious amount of attention.

"I just don't know how to handle this version of Summer. This isn't like you. You're not yourself. I feel like I'm on pins and needles. Eggshells. I'm really worried about you. I haven't been sleeping at all."

Guilt and anger, in equal parts, rushed into Summer's bloodstream.

"Oh," Summer said, sarcasm creeping into her tone. "I am so sorry. I am so sorry that while I've been dealing with Willow, five children, a heart surgery and a mental breakdown, you haven't been sleeping. I am so sorry *I* put *you* through that, Delaney. I just can't imagine what it's like."

They pulled out onto the main road and Delaney sighed, pretending to hit her head on the steering wheel. "That's not what I meant."

"I know." Summer felt like a jerk. Of course her recent stress had affected her best friends. "I'm sorry," she said. "I really am. Okay? I know what you meant. I was just being a bitch."

"You totally were."

"I hereby resolve to be nicer."

Delaney laughed. Then Summer laughed. They both laughed, tears leaking from the corners of their eyes, until they pulled into Summer's driveway. Before unbuckling her seatbelt, Summer took a deep breath. Life with a capital L was waiting, whether she was ready or not.

CHAPTER TWENTY-FIVE

The second she set foot in the house, Summer could tell Derek had given the kids a serious talking to. He'd probably spent all morning cleaning, too. She could see the lines in the carpet from the vacuum, and because they were wobbly and multi-directional, she knew what Nate's contribution had been.

Sarah, Luke and Nate sat side by side on the couch. Sarah had her feet tucked up under her and was reading, which wasn't out of the ordinary. Nate and Luke also had books in their laps, which was very out of the ordinary. Not surprisingly, Summer could see they were engaged in some kind of physical game, either thumb war or arm wrestling. She smiled.

Derek had strapped Hannah into her high chair and moved it into the living room. He'd given her a book, too, but she used it to beat on her tray as she squealed.

"Welcome home, Mom," the three big kids chorused.

"Home, Mama!" Hannah shouted.

Derek, carrying Olivia, came in from the bedroom. "Hi, Summer. Welcome home. Thanks for bringing her, Delaney."

"I risked my life," Delaney said, "but I'd do it again for you."

"Daddy made us promise to sit down and be quiet. He said we couldn't move from this spot."

"Luke! I also told you to pretend I didn't tell you that!"

Summer couldn't help but laugh at Derek's expression. Luke giggled.

"Mom, he said that if we can sit quietly for the first hour you're home, he'll feed us ice cream," Nate said, and Sarah answered, while still looking at her book, "And they'll never sit still again."

"It's so good to be home," Summer said. Then it dawned on her. "Where's Willow?"

The three big kids looked up from their books, and Summer sensed a secret afoot.

"She's packing," Derek said. "She felt responsible for your, um, fainting spell. She felt guilty she was so late bringing the kids back from the park."

"I told her it wasn't her fault," Sarah said. "You just had a lot going on and you weren't feeling like yourself."

For reasons Summer couldn't explain, even to herself, Sarah's words caused the panic to set in again. A cold sweat broke out on her forehead. *Breathe in, breathe out.* Willow's presence had definitely caused a lot of stress over the past several weeks. But she was Summer's mother. Even though Summer hadn't kicked her out, it felt like she had. Where would Willow go?

Where has she been all this time? Winter asked. *She's an adult. It's not your responsibility to figure that out for her.*

Of course, Willow, with her knack for breaking silence, clattered into the living room just then, teetering on impossibly high heels and dragging a huge duffel bag behind her.

Every head in the room swung towards her.

"All packed up and ready to go," she said.

Every head in the room swung back towards Summer. Everyone waited for her to speak.

"That's a big bag," she said.

Derek took a sudden interest in his shoes. Delaney shifted from one foot to another. The kids blinked.

"Well, I guess I'll hit the road," Willow said.

Decision time, Winter said.

Allowing Willow to stay was, undoubtedly, the right thing to do. She was family. Summer didn't believe in turning family away. Just because Willow had been a crappy mother didn't mean Summer had to be a crappy daughter. In fact, being a good daughter would stop the cycle. And more importantly, it would demonstrate her values to her children. And yet, having Willow here had been the final straw when it came to Summer's mental health break. Somehow, despite her promise that she was here to help, she managed to create additional work for Summer. Her presence compounded Summer's stress and made Summer nearly homicidal. Summer opened her mouth, then closed it again before any sound escaped.

Willow stood there with her bag. She looked around the room, from person to person. She blinked. "Well, I guess this is good-bye," she said.

She still didn't move. She was obviously waiting for something. She was waiting for Summer to stop her. Summer knew the right thing to do. And she always did the right thing. But wasn't doing the right thing exactly what had landed her in the hospital?

The entire family—her kids, her husband, her mother, and even Delaney—waited on her to make a decision.

Why did all the responsibility have to land on her shoulders? Couldn't Derek have just asked Willow to leave before Summer returned from the hospital? Why didn't he have the courage to do that? She always had to be the courageous one.

When Sarah was two and became dangerously dehydrated from a fever, Summer had to pin her arms down while the nurses at the hospital stuck an IV in her arm. Sarah thrashed and screamed as blood poured down the crook of her elbow, and Derek turned his back, supposedly afraid he'd act out a violent fantasy on the nurse if he watched.

When Nate was three and fell off the jungle gym at the park, his forearm was completely bent in the middle. Derek turned ghostly pale and covered his face with his hands while Summer commandeered Sarah and Luke into the car and drove them all to the hospital.

These situations arose constantly over the course of their marriage. And now this. Forcing her to choose. Forcing her to choose between her mother's happiness and her own sanity. In essence, forcing her to kick her own mother out of their house.

Well, guess what, world? I can do it. I've been courageous since I knew what it meant.

"Yes, I guess it is good-bye," Summer said to Willow.

Willow's face fell. Sarah's face fell. Nate's face crumpled. Luke looked wildly from Summer to Willow to Derek, unsure what to make of all this. They'd all been expecting her to say Willow could stay. In that split second following her announcement, Summer wavered. She wavered like the heat waves coming off asphalt on a summer day. Then she broke.

"Fine. You can stay."

In that instant, the house—and all those pairs of eyes blinking at her in surprise—became suffocating. She marched right out of the house then, in search of fresh air.

Just as the front door shut behind her, she heard Willow say on a sigh, "I just knew she'd come around."

Just like that, she was trapped. Again.

DR. STRASSER SMILED at Derek and Summer from behind the desk in his pristine office. "I would say it's nice to see you both again, but I wish we were meeting under better circumstances. Let's dive in."

Summer smiled. Dr. Strasser was like an old leather armchair. He was a fixture, one she always felt comfortable in. He'd been their counselor for years and had seen them through some rough patches, like the time they went without sex for four months because she was too embarrassed by the way she looked to get naked, and the time Derek had his own breakdown after she gave birth to Luke and he was afraid he couldn't support their growing family.

Derek nudged Summer, jarring her out of the past. Looking back on it, life seemed so much simpler back then.

"We're happy to see you, Dr. Strasser," she said.

He smiled.

"Tell me what's going on," he said, steepling his fingers in the way that had driven Josie crazy when she and Paul came in during The Marriage Intervention.

Summer was at a loss for words. Both Derek and Dr. Strasser looked at her, waiting. She could hear the clock ticking. It reminded her of the clock ticking at her house.

"Summer?" Derek said.

"I'm not sure where to begin," she said. She felt herself burst into tears. "My life is a wreck."

Dr. Strasser raised an eyebrow and handed a box of tissues to Derek, who held it out to Summer. Although she wanted to continue, to lay it all out there for Dr. Strasser, her body emitted nothing other than a high-pitched squealing sound.

Derek rubbed her forearm, and when she looked at him out of the corner of her eye, she could see him trying not to laugh. Unexpectedly, this brought on her own fit of laughter, in a note as high as the squealing, only this time, hysterical in nature. When she finally calmed down enough to look up at Dr. Strasser, she saw that his own eyes twinkled with sympathy. His mouth remained unsmiling.

"Sorry," she gasped. "So sorry. It's just that—well, it's just that this isn't like me. The crying, the squealing, the hysterics. The mental breakdown."

"I understand," Dr. Strasser said. "Why don't you tell me what's going on?"

"Right," Summer said.

When Dr. Strasser and Derek looked at her again, waiting, she shrugged and threw her hands up. "Fine. I'll give you the short version."

They sat in silence while she went through the list of stressors for what felt like the umpteenth time: Derek losing his job, another pregnancy, The Dating Intervention, The Marriage Intervention, Luke's heart problems, Willow knocking on the door.

She ended with, "I came home from the hospital and, Hallelujah! I thought my mom was leaving. But everyone guilt-tripped me into her letting stay."

At this, Derek sat up, his posture straight and his eyes wide with indignation. Summer held up a hand to stop him from protesting, and felt the anger growing inside her torso.

"So I let her stay. So she is still there. She is still flouncing around the house like some kind of beauty queen, acting like she's a big help, but actually just causing me more work every time she gets a smear of baby poop on an article of clothing. It's too much. It's just too much."

"Ah."

Dr. Strasser's response only served to anger Summer further. That's all he had to say, after she'd poured out the past year of her tragic life?

She knew better than to say anything to Dr. Strasser about his disproportionate reaction, so she turned on Derek. "Did you have something you wanted to add?"

He dropped his head into his hands.

"If I may?" Dr. Strasser said.

"Please do," Summer said.

Dr. Strasser leaned back in his chair. "It certainly seems like you've had a lot going on."

This is what you're paying him sixty bucks an hour for? Winter said.

The normal Summer would have nodded, eager to hear what else he had to say. But the Summer who had been born of exhaustion and overwhelm during the past several months, who thrived on anger and anxiety, mimicked Dr. Strasser's body language and sat back in her own chair.

"First of all," Dr. Strasser said, "I think you need to find something, an activity of some kind, that relaxes you. You need some stress relief. I know you enjoy yoga, and I'd say it's time to get back to that."

Derek looked smug, and Summer refrained from elbowing him.

"Second of all, you need support."

Again, Derek sat up straight, prepared to respond. Summer knew what he was going to say, though, and she beat him to it. "I have to admit, I have a hard time accepting support."

Derek looked smug. Again.

"She does," he said. "I do everything she asks of me."

"But sometimes I don't want to have to ask! And now you've guilted me into letting Willow stay with us." She shrugged a shoulder. "Freeloading disguised as help."

"I didn't guilt you into it, I—"

"You should have had her out of there before I even got home from the hospital. But you don't want to be the bad guy."

Holding up both of his hands, Dr. Strasser said, "Hold on, now. Let's bring this conversation back under control. Summer, I'm hearing you say that you don't want to have to ask Derek for help. You want him to step forward and help you. Is that correct?"

Summer nodded.

"I'm not a mindreader," Derek said quietly. "I seriously do everything I can for her." He turned his attention to Summer. "And don't you think I've been stressed out too?"

"Of course you're not a mindreader," Dr. Strasser said. "And it's completely natural that you've been stressed out, too. I think we need to examine how the two of you can support each other in the ways you need to be supported."

At that moment, a fresh wave of guilt washed over Summer. Of course Derek was stressed out, too. She'd been thinking only of herself.

And, to be fair, Winter said, *of all your children.*

Summer nodded at Winter, and Derek looked at her quizzically.

"Next," Dr. Strasser said, "we need to explore your relationship with your mother. I can understand you wanting your own space. However, I am sensing that you carry quite a bit of anger around that relationship. If you can work on resolving some of that, it may be possible to rebuild."

Summer heard herself say, "Hmph," and she almost laughed again.

Wow, you really are losing it, Winter said.

"Last, you need to take responsibility for your decisions," Dr. Strasser said to Summer. "And if you don't like what's happening, you need to set boundaries."

Summer stared at him, and felt her eyebrows rising into her hairline with surprise.

"Well, it looks like we have our work cut out for us," Dr. Strasser said. "Shall we begin?"

CHAPTER TWENTY-SIX

"WILLOW. I NEED TO TALK TO YOU."

The kids, sprawled all over the couch with various body parts in their grandmother's lap, looked up from their movie to stare at Summer.

"Now?" Willow said.

"Yes, please," Summer said, even as she felt her teeth grinding together in frustration. *No, Willow, a year from now.*

Willow sighed as she detangled herself from the kids and hoisted herself off the couch. Summer gestured toward the kitchen. Derek sat down on the couch. All of a sudden, Summer felt nervous.

Again, her memory transported her deep into her past, to a time she interrupted a show Willow was watching because she needed to talk to her. It was before she met Josie and Delaney, so she was probably in sixth grade. Summer had just returned home from school, her lower lip busted wide open and swollen.

When school dismissed for the day, Summer and her classmates headed for the door. Summer reached it at the same time as Jenny Carmichael. Jenny Carmichael had probably never set foot inside a Goodwill, and her parents probably drove a Volvo; at least, that's what Summer always imagined. When they reached the door, Jenny looked Summer right in the eye and said something about Summer going home to her white trash drunk of a mother. Summer tried to punch her in the face. Jenny, of course, was more conniving than

Summer (wasn't everyone?), and dodged Summer's fist only to immediately swing her own, hitting Summer square in the kisser.

The impact surprised them both, and when Jenny saw the blood dripping down Summer's chin, she lifted a hand to her own mouth, her bright green eyes going comically round above it. Summer wasn't angry that Jenny Carmichael had called Willow names. It was true. Willow was a white trash drunk. Summer was angry that Jenny Carmichael chose to be intentionally cruel.

Summer could have gone to the nurse for an ice pack. She could tell from the amount of blood that she'd probably need stitches. Instead, she grabbed a wad of paper towels from the bathroom and ran all the way home, pressing them to her lip.

When she walked through the door, she anticipated at least a tiny bit of sympathy from Willow. Maybe some frozen peas slapped onto her face. Willow was fully immersed in a rerun of "I Love Lucy." She didn't turn around when Summer came through the front door, and Willow mumbled her typical greeting: "How was your day can you get me some aspirin."

Then, Summer made the terrible mistake of saying, "I need to talk to you." Willow turned her head, slow-motion. She became wide awake the second she saw Summer's face.

In the moments that followed, Summer wished so deeply that she'd handled the situation differently. But didn't all children seek their mothers' comfort when someone hurt them?

Not always, Summer realized. Not when it's the mother doing the hurting.

As a sixth-grader, Summer was terrified of Willow. So when Willow's face contorted into an angry grimace, Summer's first instinct was to run. But she had nowhere to go.

"Just what have you gotten yourself into, young lady?"

Summer pulled the wad of paper towels, now saturated with blood, away from her lip and felt the wound with the tip of a finger. It wasn't just a split lip. It was a wide gash.

"Great. That's going to need stitches," Willow said. "What the hell happened? What were you thinking? I can't afford stitches. I can barely afford to feed you."

She stood up, then, and moved toward Summer with a speed Summer had never witnessed. She looked wildly around the room, her eyes landing briefly on surface after surface, like a fly would do. Summer should have known what was coming, but Willow had never laid a hand on her.

She found what she was looking for, or at least something suitable: a shoe Summer had discarded the night before, next to the couch on the floor. Willow swooped forward and picked it up. A sixth sense had Summer covering her face with her arms.

Willow drew back as if she were going to throw the shoe, and she brought it forward, repeatedly, hitting Summer on the back of the head, the shoulders, and the back. Part of Summer (probably Winter) wanted to scream, to tell Willow exactly why she'd taken a swing at Jenny Carmichael. Jenny Carmichael with her perfectly straight brown hair and her perfectly sober mother and her perfectly shiny Volvo. As Willow continued to whack her with the shoe, Summer wanted to spit the words out, to tell Willow what people thought of her.

But she couldn't do it. She didn't want to say the words aloud any more than she wanted to hear them again. Because wasn't she a reflection of her mother?

So she didn't say anything. She remained silent and took the beating. She remained silent while Willow drove her to the hospital, their dented, rusted-out, pea-green Volkswagen Golf weaving all over the road. She remained silent while Willow signed her in. She barely flinched when the doctor gave her a shot to numb her lip, and didn't utter a word as he sewed in three stitches. She didn't have to be a reflection of her mother. She was classy. She was strong.

"AS YOU KNOW, Derek and I met with Dr. Strasser today."

Summer and Willow sat at the table on the back patio, Willow jiggling her leg impatiently.

"The head shrinker?" she said, her hateful tone coloring the space between them an acid green.

"No, Willow. The psychologist. He's a doctor. He went to school for eight years to learn how to help people fix themselves after experiencing crappy childhoods like mine."

She regretted it the moment she said it. Not because it wasn't true, but because she knew it would distract Willow from the conversation Summer actually wanted to have.

Willow's eyes snapped up to meet Summer's. "Did you ever go hungry?"

Summer shook her head. "Look, that's not what I want to talk about."

"But you said it."

"Because I'm frustrated."

"Why? Because I'm here to help you? Because I put my life on hold to stay with you?"

A million thoughts raced through Summer's mind. What life had Willow put on hold? What help was she actually providing? Who did she think she was kidding? Summer put her hands up as if she were surrendering.

"I need to set some boundaries with you."

Willow looked down at the tabletop. "Boundaries?" she said. Then, after a brief pause, she made eye contact with Summer, a malevolent smile on her face. She shrugged. "Sounds like head-shrinker language to me. Is that what the head shrinker told you to do?"

"If you're going to stay here, I need you to stop drinking. For real. I need you go to a twelve-step-program. I need you to come home on time when you're watching the kids. If you're going to stay here, I need you to contribute in a meaningful way. Cook, clean, do some laundry. Dishes. I need you to be nice to me."

"What about what I need?"

"What do you need? A roof over your head? Check. Food in your belly? Check. A place to sleep? Oh, okay. Check!"

The volume of Summer's voice had crescendoed to a yell. Willow stood up, and the legs of her chair scraped the concrete.

"I refuse to stay here to help you if you're going to put all these restrictions on me."

Summer felt herself shaking with rage.

"Restrictions?"

"For you to insinuate I have a drinking problem and demand that I go to a twelve-step program is ludicrous. I do not have a drinking problem." She scoffed, and then went on, "If you ask me to watch the kids, and I take them to the park, I'll come home when I want to.

If they're having fun, and I'm having fun, we'll stay at the damn park. They're not going to starve to death if they get their perfectly portioned afternoon snacks fifteen minutes later than usual. I do contribute in a meaningful way. Having their grandmother around is priceless for your children."

As Willow stood up and walked back into the house, Summer noticed the only item Willow hadn't addressed was "be nice to me."

At twelve years old, Summer had chosen silence. But now, she was an adult. She didn't have to be silent. She could have her say. So she listened to Willow's explanation of why she shouldn't have to help Summer in a meaningful way. Then she responded.

"Fine," she said. "I was trying to do the right thing by allowing you to stay here, but obviously, this situation isn't working out. You need to leave."

CHAPTER TWENTY-SEVEN

SUMMER ALWAYS BELIEVED NANNIES WERE EXCLUSIVELY FOR EXCLUSIVE parents. Parents with very few children and lots of extra money hired nannies to raise their kids while they played tennis and drank Old Fashioneds and chatted about the stock market and horse racing.

Derek was now suggesting (well, demanding, actually) that she hire a nanny. Or at least a mother's helper. The idea didn't thrill her. She wanted to raise her own kids. Nevertheless, she agreed to interview a few girls for the position. And because she knew she may have a tendency to be judgmental during the process, she asked Delaney and Josie to sit in on the interviews.

Summer looked at them now. Delaney, hands clasped together under her belly, her arms practically pinned to her sides, seemed nervous. Josie, of course, tapped a pen on her notepad, impatiently. This woman doesn't have time for wrong answers, the tapping said. Summer suppressed a laugh.

"Thanks again for doing this, guys," Summer said.

"Wouldn't miss it," Josie said, adding a quick, businesslike nod.

Delaney just smiled.

"Josie, you sound like a drill sergeant," Summer said. "You're going to intimidate them."

"If *I* intimidate them," Josie said, raising an eyebrow at Summer, "how do you think they're going to handle your children?"

"Just be nice, okay?" Summer said.

"You asked me to be here," Josie said.

Delaney laughed. "We'll do the good cop, bad cop thing. You be the moderator." Suddenly, she stood up quickly. "I printed out some lists of questions I found on the Internet."

Summer rolled her eyes. "I know what questions to ask."

The doorbell rang.

"Cross this one off the list," Josie said under breath. "She rings a doorbell when she knows you have two kids under two. Never ring the doorbell."

Now questioning her decision to ask the girls to join her, Summer got up to answer the door. The girl who blinked back at her from the other side looked about fourteen. Summer panicked and almost shut the door in her face. She reminded herself that her perception of age was a direct function of her own age. And she was getting old.

When Summer led her to the couch, the girl introduced herself as Moonbeam, and Summer laughed out loud.

"Really? Moonbeam?" Josie said.

Without breaking the rhythm, the girl answered, "My mom gave birth to me in a moonbeam on a hot fall night. So she named me Moonbeam."

"Is this for real?" Josie whispered, way too loudly.

The girl nodded, shrugged one shoulder. "She was kind of a hippie."

"Next," Josie said.

Moonbeam blanched, and Summer said quickly, "She's joking. Anyway, we have a few questions for you. First of all, what experience do you have watching children?"

"I think the more important questions are, can you do laundry, will you do dishes, and do you know how to get ketchup out of the carpet?" Josie said.

"That's not on my list," Delaney said.

Summer held up her hands, and grimaced at Moonbeam, hoping the expression conveyed some kind of apology.

"Um, well, I—" Moonbeam began.

"Summer? Can I talk to you in the bedroom?" Josie again.

Summer dropped her forehead to her palm, but stood up and followed Josie to the bedroom.

"This girl's not a good fit. You can't say 'Um, well, I' if you're watching five kids. You need someone with more spunk."

"You didn't even give her a chance!" Incredulous, Summer threw up her hands.

"You ain't got time for this," Josie said.

Summer laughed, despite herself.

The next applicant, an androgynous individual named Terry, turned the tables on Josie and interviewed Summer.

"How do you deal with discipline?" Terry wanted to know. "What activities do you do with your children?"

("I just try to keep them alive, basically," Summer answered.)

"What should I know about health and safety in your house?"

"Just keep 'em alive," Summer said.

"What role do you see me playing in terms of your family?" Terry said.

"Just keeping my kids alive while my husband and I are working or on a date."

"What, exactly, will my duties be?"

"Just keep 'em alive," Josie, Delaney and Summer said.

By the time Terry left, Summer felt exhausted.

She didn't want to ask or answer these questions. She just wanted someone to help with the kids for a few hours each day. Then, they struck gold. Someone knocked four times on the door, and Josie smiled. "I like that. A nice, brisk knock. This one means business."

The woman on the other side of the door was mid-twenties, with glasses, dark eyes and a big smile. "You must be Veronica," Summer said. "Come on in."

"Wow, it's like the Spanish Inquisition in here," she said when she sat down across from Summer, Delaney and Josie. Delaney and Josie elbowed Summer. Veronica did seem promising.

"Look," Veronica said. "I want to be up front. I don't have kids, and I don't plan on having kids. I'm not a mommy type. If you're looking for soft and mushy, you're not looking for me."

"Do you even like kids?" Delaney asked.

"Oh, I love kids," Veronica said. "And I'm great with them. But I'm more of a quirky aunt type than a nurturing mommy type. I just wanted to put that out there. I won't take their nonsense, I won't coddle them and I'll make them do their chores and homework. But when all of that's done, we'll have a lot of fun. I play a mean game of poker, and I'll kill them at chess."

Summer nodded. She knew everything she needed to know.

"You're hired."

"I NEVER THOUGHT I'd say this," Delaney said, "but it feels like we haven't been here in forever."

Rowdy's was hopping this Thursday night, packed with college kids starting their weekend and professionals in loose ties wishing it were Friday.

Benjamin had delivered their drinks—a vodka cranberry for Josie, a water (with a side of green olives) for Delaney and a glass of white wine for Summer—and grinned down at them.

"Ladies! It's been forever. I'm so happy to see you all together, out on the town again! It feels like I haven't seen you in ages."

"We were just saying that," all three girls said.

When Benjamin walked away, Josie said to Delaney, "I never thought you'd spend more than a few days away from here, either. I'm so glad we forced you to get a real job."

"Bartending is a real job," Delaney said. "It provides a service. A critical one, I might add. And I was good at it."

"Maybe so, but you were wasting your life after years of vet school," Josie reminded her.

"Speaking of real jobs," Delaney said, characteristically changing the subject, "nannying is a real job. How do you like Veronica?"

"Ohmygosh, I think I love her," Summer said, stretching her arms over her head luxuriously. "I mean, she hung out at the house earlier this week while I was working, and I could hear her out there with the kids, threatening to cut Luke's head off with a sword if he didn't finish his homework by the time her phone timer went off. Classic! She's great."

"So this is the first time you've actually left her with all five kids, right?" Josie said.

"Yeah," Summer said. "And I feel good about it. I mean, Derek is there, sleeping, but she can handle it."

Summer couldn't believe how good it felt to get out of the house and not worry about the kids. Veronica seemed sensible, practical and funny. And the kids really liked her.

A sense of peace was settling over her. She was glad she could say the same about Delaney, who was currently in the middle of describing the paint colors she and Jake had chosen for the living room ("the base is kind of like a creamy butter yellow," she was saying). This was normal. Talking about jobs and paint colors.

Josie had just updated them on the Carla M. Garcia Community Center, which was set to open in a couple of weeks.

It felt so good. Summer could sit here at Rowdy's forever. Well, she thought, as the college kids at the bar jumped off their stools, cheering, shouting, doing high fives, maybe not forever. But for a long evening, anyway.

"Where'd you go, Summer?" Josie asked, reaching across the table to squeeze Summer's wrist.

Summer smiled, and knew it was a bit dreamy. "I was just thinking about how much I'm enjoying this," she said.

"Good," Josie said. "It's about time."

Yes, Summer thought, *it is*.

After two hours of chatting and watching the college kids do tequila-shot competitions, Delaney begged Summer and Josie to visit her new house and help her choose paint colors. The three of them stood in the living room, in the same spot where Summer's water broke just a few weeks before.

"So here it is," Delaney said. "The scene of the crime." She lifted her arms out to the side, palms up. "But from now on, I want you to think of it as my living room."

She produced a fan of paint chips from her purse.

"I think I have some Scotch tape in here somewhere."

She tore a few chips off the fan, each a slightly different shade of butter yellow, and taped them to the living room wall.

"Wait, let me guess," Josie said. "Melted butter, fresh butter, and curdled butter."

Delaney spun around to face them, looking exasperated.

"Has Jake been talking to you?"

"No! Why?" Josie looked innocent, but almost too innocent. Summer wondered whether she really had talked to Jake.

Delaney sighed. "He thinks all three yellows look so similar we'll be happy with whatever we choose."

"You will," Summer said. "They look pretty similar. I like the creamy butter one."

Delaney laughed. "That's not even an actual name."

"You know what's important, Dee?" Summer said. "It's not paint colors. It's what happens here—" she pointed at the floor—"and in there"—she pointed at the kitchen—"and over there." She pointed toward the bedroom. "It's not about what your house looks like. It's about the memories you create within the walls. It's not which color you choose, it's you and Jake painting the walls together. Trust me, six or seven years from now, you won't even notice the paint colors. You'll reminisce about the time—"

"Summer's water broke the first time we were all here together," Josie said.

Summer went on: "You'll think about bringing your new little baby home, which will happen in just a few weeks, and feeling like you don't quite know what to do. You'll set the carseat somewhere and take him or her out, and you'll sit on the couch and feel like your family is home. And that is what matters. So creamy butter, melted butter, churned butter, butter on toast, none of it matters. Okay? Don't stress over this. It's a small thing. Inconsequential. Pick one and move on."

Delaney burst into tears. "Oh, Summer. That was the most beautiful thing you've ever said to me," she said.

Josie groaned. "I can't take this hormonal storm right now. I just can't take it."

Summer returned home more relaxed than she had felt in months. Years, even. To her surprise and delight, Veronica had orchestrated showers and baths for all the older kids, and they were in pajamas, their hair wet and combed, their teeth brushed and books in hand, ready for bedtime reading.

"I told them that if they were all bathed by the time you got home, I'd buy them ice cream next time I came over," Veronica said, her expression apologetic but her eyes sparkling. "I swear I won't bribe them every time, but I figured you'd like having them clean. No offense, but that Nate's got stinky feet. He needed a good shower."

Luke and Sarah had a good chuckle at that, and Veronica winked at Nate. "Just kidding, buddy. They're not so bad. Luke's are way worse."

After she left, Summer read to the kids and began the process of tucking them all into bed. When it was Sarah's turn, she said, "Mom, can I ask you something? Where's grandma? I mean, Willow. Are we going to see her anymore?"

A tiny crack formed in the sense of calm and peace Summer felt just moments before. And instead of answering, "I sincerely hope not," like she wanted to, she said, "I'm not sure."

Usually, she'd ask why or what Sarah was thinking about, but not tonight. She kissed Sarah on the forehead and stood up to leave, but Sarah stopped her. "Mom?"

"Yeah?"

"I miss her."

On the inside, Summer cringed. She didn't know how it was possible that Sarah missed Willow. How could you miss something that sucked the life force out of you?

"I'm sorry, honey."

She left then, closed the bedroom door and leaned her back against it. As parents, she thought, we constantly question our decisions when it comes to our children. All we can do is hope we've made the right ones.

As Summer went into the kitchen to put the clean dishes away (Veronica had actually taken the initiative to start the dishwasher— Summer was in love), she thought about what Sarah said.

Of course Sarah could miss Willow. Willow was a different person to her granddaughter than she was to Summer. And Sarah, having all her basic needs met, didn't require as much from Willow as Summer had years ago. Her expectations were lower. Although, Summer thought, a child expecting her mother to give her an iota of love and attention didn't seem beyond the realm of normalcy. Still, Sarah's comment reminded Summer that growing up with Willow hadn't been all bad.

One summer, their little Arizona town got so much monsoon rain the streets filled with water. Willow obtained a kayak—by which means Summer had no idea—and paddled Summer up and down the street in it. At first, Summer was embarrassed by her mother's laughter, ringing out into the air like she was some sort of wild animal. But Willow's joy at doing something so exciting rubbed off on Summer, and she found herself smiling, waving at their neighbors as if she were in a parade.

Exhibiting an unusual amount of forethought, Willow packed them a picnic dinner and they ate it in the kayak. Even now, Summer could taste the mustard on the cold cheese sandwich, and feel her teeth crunching through the carrots Willow packed as a side.

One winter, a huge snowstorm blew through, blanketing the entire town in fluffy white powder, closing schools and businesses for two full days. Willow dug some cardboard boxes out of a Dumpster, flattened them into sleds, and pulled Summer through the snow for hours. They came home that evening and ate chicken soup from a can, a rare treat. They sat at the kitchen table, smiling at each other over their steaming mugs.

While Summer had always craved routine and normalcy, Willow seemed to thrive on excitement. Her best mothering capabilities emerged when an adventure cropped up.

In the kayak that summer day, she pointed out the different types of trees, their leaves shaking in the wind. "That's a willow tree, a weeping willow. That's where I got my name. My parents lived in a house with a huge, beautiful willow out front. And that's a dogwood. Isn't it pretty? They love our summers. Well, not days like today, but you know what I mean." She talked about architecture, pointing out the Victorian houses that lined the next street up and the Craftsman houses they floated past a few minutes later.

The sledding experience had brought up laws of physics, gravity, momentum.

During both days, Willow's eyes were bright and clear, and she seemed to enjoy Summer's presence rather than resent it.

Summer's phone, which she'd left somewhere in the living room, jarred her out of her walk down memory lane. As she rushed to answer it before it woke someone up, she reminded herself that even though Willow had some good qualities, Sarah was better off without the whirlwind of destruction that was her grandmother.

Summer didn't recognize the phone number on the Caller ID. It was a local number, a cell phone. Had Derek been in an accident on his way to work? Was this the hospital calling? Or a Good Samaritan on the side of the road? He'd been so exhausted lately, it was plausible he'd fallen asleep at the wheel.

The now-familiar sensation of panic began to claw its way into her body. Her heart pounded. Her breathing whooshed in and out of her mouth. Her hands shook. So when she answered and heard Willow's voice on the other end of the line, anger turned her blood to lava in her veins.

"What do you want?" she asked, powerless to stop the hatred from infusing her voice. "I told you not to bother me."

"You sound tired," Willow said.

"I'm pretty sure," Summer said, "that this is almost the exact same way our first conversation started, that day you showed up at my door. I don't take that as a compliment, in case you haven't noticed during the time we've spent together. Were you just calling to point out how rundown I seem, or did you have something to say?"

A few seconds of silence ticked by.

"Can we meet in person?"

Summer groaned, loudly.

"Do we have to?"

Willow laughed. "You sound exactly like you did when you were in elementary school. Whenever I'd wake you up to go to school, you'd groan and ask if you had to. It was so cute."

Summer didn't answer. She had always been so exhausted as a kid, because Willow never made her go to bed at a decent time. She'd drag Summer out to the store at ten p.m. to get cigarettes, or to the convenience store for a packet of corn chips. Because it was her reality, Summer never questioned it. She never wondered why other kids went to bed at eight or nine, while she fell asleep on the couch at eleven and woke up at midnight to put herself to bed. What the hell was Willow thinking?

Summer still hadn't responded, so Willow plowed ahead. "Anyway, can we meet? I can come over now."

Summer imagined her nice, quiet evening as a perfect, shiny bubble. Then she imagined it bursting, its walls falling to the floor like the shell of an egg. Her imagination added smoke rising from the carnage.

"How about tomorrow, instead? I'm kind of busy."

Busy being not *busy,* Winter said, *is not the same as being busy.*

"Fine," Willow said. "I'll see you tomorrow. Meet me at that coffee shop you like, that one with the bouncy horse. Say, nine o'clock? I have a surprise for you."

CHAPTER TWENTY-EIGHT

Surprises from Willow were rarely uplifting in any way.

At some point during Summer's childhood, Willow bought a wooden spoon with which she said she would paddle Summer's backside if she misbehaved. She drew a smiley face on it and announced it as a surprise, pulling it out from behind her back with a flourish.

A few years later, she brought home a broom she'd pulled out of a restaurant Dumpster. "Surprise! I got you a new broom! Not sure if it'll improve your housekeeping skills."

"I have a surprise for you," she said one day when Summer arrived home from school. She drew out the "you" in a way that put Summer on edge. By then she was savvy to Willow's idea of a good surprise. This time it was an iron she'd found at Goodwill.

Summer wondered what Willow had come up with this time. One of those automatic vacuums would be nice. But since she was an adult, Willow would probably buy her a lollipop … something she would have appreciated thirty years ago.

The instant she stepped through the doorway of Ground Up, Summer knew what Willow's surprise was. Willow sat with her side to the door, across the table from two men. Her posture confident and charismatic, Willow tilted her head back and laughed at something one of the men said.

Summer knew immediately who the men were: her father and half-brother.

She couldn't decide whether to be happy or angry.

She should be elated. She had always wanted to know her father, and now that she'd discovered she had a brother, it would be great to get to know him, too. Only … she wasn't really in the right space to welcome these strangers into her life. Yes, she'd made progress over the past few weeks, but she felt like she was being held together by a piece of thin, brittle thread. One slight breeze and she could easily break apart, crumble into tiny pieces and float away on the breeze.

There were so many ways this could go wrong. Her father might not want to know her. He might not like her. She might not like him. And her brother. Most likely, he had enjoyed a normal life with two parents who loved him, one of them the father she never knew. Resentment and jealousy bubbled up in her body.

The men—Summer's father and brother—reacted to Willow's dramatic gestures exactly as they should, smiling back, laughing, nodding.

Could Summer be part of this? Could she have this family? By the looks of it, she could. She could walk right in. They were primed and ready, sweetened up with Willow's own personal elixir. Knowing Willow, she had told them all about Summer. She had cleverly disguised criticism as description, casually mentioning Summer's insane number of children and weaving in her mental breakdown. But still, they waited here for her.

Did she even want this family?

There was the small talk and the pressure. Putting on family breakfasts, vacuuming the window blinds.

At this very moment, she decided, the answer was no. She had her own family, one she'd worked hard to build. One that didn't expect her to clean crumbs out of the sliding glass door track. One that didn't include Willow. So before Willow or either of the men could see her, she turned around and walked away.

"WE NEED to stop holding emergency Happy Hour meetings until after I have this baby," Delaney said. "It's not as fun when I can't have my Guinness."

Rowdy's was quiet tonight, a few patrons sprinkled amongst the hightop tables, chatting quietly—a big difference from the cheering, rambunctious crowd the girls usually saw.

"Sorry, Dee," Summer said. "I felt like I was in crisis."

"Wait, so, you just walked out?" Josie was incredulous.

Summer shrugged one shoulder. "What would you have done?"

"I don't know," Josie said. "I mean, they're your family. That's your father, your brother. Aren't you curious?"

"Yeah, I am," Summer said. "But is curiosity a reason to start a new relationship?"

"It was for me," Delaney said. "Jake made me really curious."

The girls laughed. "Somehow it's not the same," Josie said.

"Seriously, though, Summer," Delaney said. "Why didn't you want to meet them?"

Summer sighed. "I don't know. I mean, if I'm being honest with myself—"

"And we know you advocate that," Delaney said.

"Yes, I do," Summer said, elbowing Josie. "If I'm being honest with myself, I was, or am, annoyed with Willow for setting up a meeting without asking me first. I mean, even now she makes it all about herself. All hail Willow for bringing this family together. All hail Willow for surprising Summer with such a wonderful gift. I mean, she didn't even ask me if I wanted to meet them. She didn't even give me the option."

Both Josie and Delaney nodded.

"Have you talked to her?" Josie wanted to know.

"No," Summer said. "She keeps calling, but I haven't picked up."

"I won't say this a bunch of times," Josie said, "but keep in mind what I said before. I lost my mom before I was ready. I know you don't have the same relationship with Willow, but I don't want you to regret not investing in this relationship when you had the chance. You don't know when she might be gone."

Benjamin, always aware of precisely the right moment to deliver another round, set glasses on the table and winked at the girls as he walked away.

"Maybe you could at least just answer her call," Delaney said. "See what she has to say."

Delaney had a point. Summer could talk to Willow. Maybe she

had a perfectly good explanation for springing that meeting on Summer. And even if she didn't, at least Summer could give her a piece of her mind. All she had to do was wait. If past behavior was any indication of future behavior, Willow would call again at least one more time this evening.

The call came just a few moments later as Summer drove home from the emergency Happy Hour meeting.

"You answered," Willow said.

"Obviously."

"Don't take that tone with me."

"Willow. I need to tell you that I'm sorry I didn't come to the coffee meeting the other morning. But—"

"It was very rude of you," Willow said. "I went to all that trouble to arrange a meeting. With your father, whom you haven't seen in, well, in your entire life, really. And your brother. Your brother!"

It was exactly as Summer had expected. Willow truly believed she played the starring role in this production. She believed that by creating an opportunity for Summer to meet Dennis and his son, she was doing Summer a favor. She didn't possess the capacity to understand that Summer may not have wanted to meet them. And now she felt hurt and offended by Summer's lack of appreciation.

"Look, Willow," Summer said. "I *am* appreciative. I'm grateful you did something you thought would be good for me. But you were thinking about it from your point of view. You didn't even stop to think about what would be good for me."

She was so caught up in her diatribe that she almost missed the red light. She slammed on the brakes. The van's tires squealed. Willow was silent for so long, Summer thought she might have hung up. She looked at her phone and noticed the call timer was still ticking. So she waited.

"I just thought you'd like it, that's all," Willow said. Her voice sounded small and quiet. Unsure.

"I probably would like it," Summer said. "When I was fully prepared for it. I've been exhausted lately. Stressed out. The last thing I need is the pressure of trying to impress my long-lost father and secret brother."

"Impress them?" Willow said. "You've never tried to impress

anyone. Besides, they're your family. Why would you have to impress them?"

"You wouldn't understand. You're naturally charismatic. Adventure suits you. The unknown fuels you. But for me, the unknown, the new, the adventure, it all stresses me out. I know you don't understand. I know you can't empathize. But it's the truth. We're both adults now, but you still don't know me. You still don't realize that was way too much to spring on me right now. And for that, you should be sorry."

Summer wondered if the people in the car next to her noticed the passion with which she spoke. The light turned green, and Summer accelerated with way too much force.

CHAPTER TWENTY-NINE

Basically, Summer thought, Willow had ruined her childhood. Summer had no frame of reference until she met Derek's mom, Julie, so hadn't been particularly unhappy. She spent a lot of time disappointed, of course, but she figured Willow spoke the truth when she said Summer was just oversensitive and more needy than the average child. Most likely, all parents were like Willow.

Summer realized now that she'd been unconsciously feeding her anger for the past fifteen years. At first, it was like a baby bird, requiring just bits of food deposited into its open mouth. It grew, unbeknownst to Summer. Then Willow arrived, unlocking the anger, which was now a huge, swooping owl, seeking any wrongdoings it could get its talons on. If something scurried past, some memory or infraction, that owl dove right in, hungry for more.

During the week since Willow's failed surprise family reunion, Summer had realized there was a problem with anger, especially when it lurked in every crevice of her being. Anger is destructive. It permeates everything.

Summer found herself snapping at Derek and the kids and avoiding Delaney and Josie. Her design work was subpar.

Back on FriendZoo, she posted, in shouty caps, about posts with improper grammar use (*"WHY IS APOSTROPHE USE SO HARD TO UNDERSTAND?"*) and criticized the way people spent their time (*"IF YOU HAVE TIME TO TAKE THESE STUPID QUIZZES, YOUR*

STRONGEST QUALITY IS ACTUALLY TIME-WASTING, NOT KINDNESS!").

She hated shouty caps.

Her phone constantly buzzed with texts from Delaney and Josie, telling her to get off the computer before everyone unfriended her.

Not that I care if they do, she responded.

She could practically see them rolling their eyes. This anger was a welcome change from the constant anxiety and near-panic she'd experienced before her breakdown and the two days she now referred to as her blissful hospital staycation.

But she knew she had to let it go. The first step: identifying its cause. Well, that was easy. It was Willow. It was Willow and her terrible mothering, her complete lack of empathy or sympathy or common sense.

The self development books Summer read—and she read lots of them—said forgiveness was key. It was the vehicle to inner peace. "Forgiveness isn't for the person you're forgiving. It's for you."

"Understand that the person who hurt you was doing the best he or she could with what he or she had at the time," they said.

Was Willow just doing the best she knew how? Yes, maybe her best was terrible. But it was still her best. Summer didn't have to be bosom buddies with Willow, but the two of them could still have a peaceful relationship. Right?

Maybe.

But again, she thought, how do you forgive? Summer wondered. Especially when the person had no idea what she'd done or how much she'd hurt you?

That was the rub.

Dr. Strasser wanted to know how Willow's actions made Summer feel. Of course, "angry" escaped her lips first.

"Dig deeper," Dr. Strasser said. "I want to know how her actions made you feel then, as a child."

Because she'd spent so much time reliving her childhood recently, the emotions were right on the surface. "Lonely," she said. "Sad. And something else. Something important, but I can't really put a name to it."

Dr. Strasser simply tilted his head, waiting.

"Longing. A deep sense of longing. Like I wanted something more, but I could never have it."

Now, Dr. Strasser nodded. She couldn't tell if he was nodding because he suspected this all along, or because she was putting her feelings into words. She waited, unsure about what else to say. Anger, sadness and longing pretty much summed it up.

"What else?" Dr. Strasser said.

"I think I'm angry now because she waltzed back into my life like nothing ever happened. Like she wasn't a terrible mother. And she wants to be a part of this world I've worked so hard to construct. But not because she missed me or loves me. It's because she wants it for herself, so she can feel like a good mother."

"Your mother sounds like she has a touch of narcissism," he said.

"A touch?" Summer laughed.

"Well, I've never spoken with her," he said. "So I can't say for sure. But the best thing you can do for yourself is to move forward. Create what you want now, and live it. It's time to disconnect yourself from that part of your past and all the pain you associate with it."

"It's just so hard when she's here now."

"It can be. That's perfectly normal. If you want her to be a part of your children's lives, as you say you do, then you need to resolve your feelings about what happened before. You can't let her past actions control the way you feel and behave now. Forgiveness is about taking back your personal power."

When he put it that way, Summer felt like forgiveness was within reach. Maybe, just maybe, she could achieve it.

Of course, Willow wasn't going to make forgiveness easy on Summer. Why would she? She started sending Summer text messages several times each day:

I don't understand why you wouldn't want to meet your father.

I'd think after all these years you'd be curious.

And what about your brother? You always said you wanted a sibling.

My feelings are really hurt. I planned that meeting for YOU.

I can't believe you'd treat me this way after everything I've done for you.

"At least she's giving me the opportunity to practice maintaining inner calm," Summer said to Derek one night as they got into bed. "Gotta be grateful for that."

Derek pulled Summer's body toward his. "Keep this in mind: by being a crappy mother, Willow taught you how to be a good one. You can be grateful for that, too."

Summer nodded, and said, "I just wish I could be grateful for something positive she did."

"She gave you life. And without life, you wouldn't have gotten me."

Summer chuckled sleepily and turned to face him. She kissed him gently, and he ran a hand down her side.

"Can we stop all this talking, now, and just do it?" Derek asked.

Again, she laughed, and she let him pull her into a whole different state of being.

CHAPTER THIRTY

The experts said you didn't have to reconcile with someone in order to forgive her. Summer understood the concept on an academic level, but it felt so difficult to put into practice.

Forgiving Willow for past hurts was one thing. Let bygones be bygones. Let wounds heal, or at least cover them up. Summer struggled with the idea of what happened next. The kids would want to spend time with their grandmother and it would be unfair to them to keep her from them. It wasn't as if Willow treated them the same way she had treated Summer as a child. But she was the same person. Therefore, her mere presence had the potential to cause even more pain in the future. Summer had the capacity to steel herself against Willow's hurtful words and actions, but the kids didn't have years of practice at it.

Summer would have to forgive her mother over and over again.

Days turned into weeks, and Summer turned the conversation over and over in her mind. It was like kneading bread, and her brain became tired of the repetitive motions.

Luke's health was back to normal. He ran around the house as if his body hadn't been cut wide open just a month ago. In fact, he had more energy than ever. Whenever the constant running, jumping off couches and sword fighting started to grate on Summer's nerves, she reminded herself she should be grateful for the health of all her children.

Olivia was developing quite a personality, smiling every time someone made eye contact. Sarah was growing up so nicely, and she began to help with the cooking and cleaning. She read some of Summer's favorite books from childhood and they discussed "Where the Red Fern Grows" and "The Indian in the Cupboard." They baked brownies together, chatting about Sarah's friends at school and their plans for the impending holiday season. Even Nate started helping around the house, gathering laundry without being asked (or told) and corralling Hannah while Summer cooked dinner. He'd become quite adept at getting her to eat vegetables for a snack, by flying them into her mouth like pterodactyls while she sat in her high chair.

Derek had stopped walking on eggshells whenever he and Summer talked, and the ease with which they communicated felt refreshing. Summer felt easy and calm. As if everything was falling into place.

Yet, the fact that things were still unresolved with Willow niggled at the back of her mind.

Since the day Summer walked out of their house at nineteen years old, she felt perfectly content not to have Willow in her life. But then Willow came back. No, she still didn't act like the mother figure Summer always wished for. No, she wasn't helpful. She wasn't warm and fuzzy. She wasn't supportive. But she was family. She was Summer's mother.

Since Willow first showed up on the Grays' doorstep, she had been the one reaching out. She called again after Summer sent her away. She planned the surprise family reunion and sent innumerable follow-up texts.

Each time, Summer welcomed her in a completely unwelcoming way. Now, Summer decided, it was her turn to reach out. Because maybe she needed to seek forgiveness as well as give it.

Seek forgiveness for what? Winter asked. Summer could hear the sneer in her alter ego's voice.

Perhaps Willow's initial reappearance and continued communication were her own type of apology. And Summer stood immovable. She hadn't been willing to bend at all in acceptance of Willow's olive branch.

Monday morning, Veronica came over to watch the kids. Summer resolved to call Willow before noon. Between projects, she picked up the phone several times, looked at the screen, let her fingers hover over the keyboard and set her phone down again.

At eleven on the nose, she dialed Willow's number. Willow picked up after three rings, and Summer wondered if she was putting as much thought into the number of rings as Summer was. Three meant she hadn't been waiting. She hadn't jumped to answer it right away. But she hadn't let it ring too long, either.

"Summer."

"Hi, Mom."

Summer hadn't called Willow Mom (without prompting) since she was nineteen years old. They both chose not to say anything about it.

Willow spoke first. "I'm glad you called."

"I was wondering if you wanted to meet," Summer said.

Willow surprised Summer by saying, "I'd like that."

They seemed to be dancing on thin, fragile ice, each of them being careful not to create even the beginning of a crack. It felt a bit awkward, Summer thought, but it also felt vindicating to know Willow was treading lightly, thinking before speaking as she'd rarely done before. Although the conversation consisted primarily of small talk and scheduling, Summer could feel the subtle difference in Willow. She was gentler. Less pushy. Softer. The hard edges didn't poke through the phone line and impede Summer's sense of being.

After agreeing to meet at eight the next morning, they hung up and Summer experienced a sense of hopeful anticipation she'd given up on years ago where Willow was concerned. Summer wanted to like her mother. She wanted Willow to be at the top of her list when she had exciting news to share, or when she needed advice. Just because it hadn't been that way before, didn't mean it couldn't be that way now. They didn't have to be best friends, or even friends. But they could be mother and daughter again. In a different, healthy way.

Maybe things could get better. Maybe Willow could change.

TRUE TO HER WORD, Willow arrived at Summer's house just after eight the following morning. She smiled warmly, as if they'd been

BFFs for the past fifteen years rather than estranged mother and daughter.

"Hi, Summer," she said. She opened her arms.

Although leaning into Willow's embrace felt completely foreign and unnatural, Summer let Willow wrap her arms around her. Willow rubbed her back and then patted it a few times. After what felt like an eternity, Willow grabbed Summer's shoulders and held her at arm's length.

"It's such a treat to be here," she said.

Summer cocked her head to one side. "What do you mean? You've been here for weeks."

"But you've never invited me," she said. "Until now."

"I should have invited you earlier," Summer said. "Want some coffee?"

Willow stopped in the entryway. The offer surprised her. During the past several weeks, Summer had practically ignored Willow's presence. Instead of offering Willow coffee and a place to sit, Summer would carry on with her dish-washing or clothes-folding.

"So, what's the occasion?" Willow said. "What convinced you to invite me over?"

"I wanted to talk to you," Summer said.

"So, let's talk." Summer was surprised Willow's words didn't hold any sarcasm.

"Why don't we sit at the kitchen table?"

Willow sat, and Summer moved to the counter to fill the coffee pot with water and put fresh grounds in a filter. She sat back down as the coffeemaker gurgled.

"So?" Willow said. "What did you want to talk about?"

Summer looked out the window, and then back at Willow.

"Should we wait for the coffee?"

"Suits me fine," Willow said.

Neither of them had ever been good at small talk. Or sitting still, for that matter. Willow clasped her hands together so hard on the tabletop that her knuckles were white and Summer realized with a start that her mother was nervous. The coffeemaker sputtered and hissed, signaling the end of its cycle. Summer stood up and poured them each a cup.

"It's decaf," she said apologetically as she set Willow's on the table in front of her.

Willow shrugged and took a sip. "It's fine," she said. "Good, actually."

Summer sipped her coffee, contemplating the words she'd choose.

"So what's up?" Willow said.

Summer took a deep breath. *It's now or never*, Winter said.

"I wanted to apologize."

It was difficult, but Summer dragged her eyes away from the tiny bubbles floating at the top of her coffee and made eye contact with Willow.

Willow looked surprised. "For what?"

"For what?" Winter said. *Shit. If she doesn't know, why tell her?*

Summer felt an almost-laugh rising in her chest.

"For not being as … welcoming as I should have been, I guess," Summer said. "For not trusting you were here with good intentions. For all of it."

Willow nodded, almost as if she'd been expecting Summer to say something like this. Almost, Summer thought, the anger seeping in again, as if she thought she *deserved* an apology. Summer tamped the rising anger down.

"Thank you," she said. She, too, had been examining the contents of her cup, but she looked up at Summer then. "It means a lot."

Summer saw Willow's hand move away from her mug as if she wanted to reach out and touch her. But she stopped herself and wrapped her hands around the mug again. "I have to admit," she said. "I expected you to be happier to see me. I expected you to accept my help."

Summer nodded.

Not that you've been much help, Winter said. Summer pushed her voice away.

"I know," Summer said. "And I'm sorry. I'm just not used to it. I mean, Derek is a huge help, of course, and—"

"Obviously!" Winter said, cackling with crazed humor. "You couldn't have made all those babies on your own!"

Summer fought every urge she had to lash out at Willow.

"I just meant to say, I'm not used to your help. To having that extra set of hands. And I didn't know how to accept it graciously. So I'm sorry. I want to have a relationship with you."

Willow nodded again, less smug this time, and more like she was listening to what Summer had to say. At first, she didn't speak. Summer braced herself when Willow took a deep breath.

"Summer, I need to apologize, too."

If this was a conversation with one of the kids, Summer would pretend to clean her ears like she did when they said something off the wall.

"I went to a meeting," Willow said, staring into her coffee, her eyes unfocused as her mind saw something different. "An AA meeting. And they talked about making amends. I need to do that with you."

Summer froze. Make amends? Was that similar to apologizing? She should Google it.

"Wait, Willow. I think that's, like, Step Nine, isn't it? Have you done One through Eight?"

Willow laughed, a dry, harsh sound.

"Not yet, Summer. But I've been working on it. I read through some literature, and it struck me that I need to make amends with you. I need to apologize to you."

"For what?"

Yes, asking Willow what she was apologizing for was a test. Yes, she had her own list of things for which she thought Willow should make reparations. But she wondered what Willow's looked like.

"The list is pretty long, isn't it?" Willow said.

Summer looked up, and their eyes met. "It is," she said.

Willow nodded. The Willow of the past would have searched for excuses or pointed out everything she had done right. She would say, "You never missed a meal," or "I was a single mother and I did the best I could."

But today, she said none of those things.

"I'm sorry, Summer. I'm sorry for leaving you at the grocery store when you were little. I'm sorry for drinking away your youth. I'm sorry for beating you with a shoe. I'm sorry for being less than you deserve, back then and now, during the past few weeks. I'm sorry for showing up unannounced and acting like I don't agree with your choices. The truth is, I am proud of you. I admire what you've done with your life. I envy the relationship you have with Derek, and the way your children look at you. You never looked at me like that."

Where did all this introspection come from? Winter wondered. Summer swatted her away.

"I appreciate your apology," Summer said.

To Summer's surprise, Willow went on: "I want you to know I'm working on it. I want to be better. I'm not sure if we can ever get to the point where you consider me a source of support rather than a source of irritation."

Summer surprised herself by snorting out a laugh. "You have been irritating lately."

Willow's smile didn't quite reach her eyes, and Summer immediately felt guilty. "Sorry. I was just kidding. I want us to get along better, too. I really appreciate you coming this morning."

"So you accept my apology?"

Summer nodded. "I do. And I forgive you. Do you accept mine?"

"I do," Willow said.

Once Summer and Willow got their official apologies out of the way, Willow seemed to relax in her chair. Her features softened and she took a few sips of her coffee.

"So now what?" she said. "Can I still come over and see my grandchildren once in a while?"

"I suppose," Summer said. "They seem to like you an awful lot." After a long pause, she asked, "What's next for you?"

Willow shrugged. "I'm not sure yet. I need to get my own place. And I have a few more amends to make."

"Yeah?" Summer said. "To whom?"

"Well, your father for one," Willow said.

Summer wondered how that would go. She wondered if they'd become friends again. If and when they did, Summer may be ready to meet him and his son. Yes, she thought, Willow had plenty of amends to make. But now that she thought about it, she realized she did, too.

CHAPTER THIRTY-ONE

For the first time in as long as she could remember, Summer felt totally at peace during Happy Hour at Rowdy's. The lights twinkled, the music played and Summer sipped her wine, content.

Josie put an arm around Summer's shoulders. "I'm so proud of you," she said. "You did the right thing by reconciling with your mom."

Summer smiled. "Thanks," she said. "We have a ways to go, but I think we're working towards something better."

The college kids at the bar cheered at something they saw on the TVs, and Josie grinned. "See? They're excited for you, too."

"As always," Summer said, "you guys were right on. I should have listened to you from the beginning. It would have saved me so much heartache."

They both nodded, looking a little too self-satisfied for Summer's taste, and she said, "Although, if I had listened to you, I would have missed out on that incredible staycation at the hospital."

They smiled, but Delaney put a hand over her heart.

"You're freakin' me out, Summer," she said. "I thought I was looking forward to motherhood, but now I'm afraid I should really be looking forward to hospitalization."

They laughed.

"The good news," Summer said, "is that you'll be moving into a beautiful new house. And you'll be completely ready for Delaney Junior whenever she arrives."

"And," Josie said, "I haven't had a chance to tell you yet, but Paul and I actually planned a trip. A romantic getaway. We're going to Utah. Zion."

"That's going to be so awesome!" Delaney said. "I am so excited for you."

"I've heard it's really romantic," Summer said.

"See?" Josie said. "I gave you advice. But I took your advice, too. And, the ribbon-cutting ceremony for the Community Center is scheduled. The date is finalized. Reporters from the newspaper will be there. It's two weeks from today!"

As she listened to Josie talk about the plans for the ceremony, Summer felt more grateful than ever for her best friends.

She returned home that evening to five kids in bed and a husband waiting up for her. Derek sat on the couch, and he smiled up at her as she walked through the front door.

"You're home early," he said.

"I wanted to talk to you," Summer said.

Derek cringed. "You know I hate when you say that."

Summer laughed. "I know. But it's nothing bad. I swear."

He patted the couch cushion next to him. She came around and sat down. "I wanted to apologize," she said. "I know I've been unbearable lately. And I'm sorry. Really sorry. You were as stressed out as I was, and I went and had a mental breakdown. Which I'm sure only added to your stress."

Derek smiled and took her hand. "I understand," he said. "And I forgive you."

The next day, Summer watched her children play in the living room, their grandmother sitting on the couch orchestrating a game of hide and seek. Derek stood next to her in the kitchen, his arm around her.

"I'm so glad you're back," he said to Summer.

"Me, too," she said.

Just then, her phone dinged, alerting her to a text message.

Delaney: *Okay, nursery is ready. It's gender-neutral. Do you like it?*

Summer smiled at the photo Delaney had attached. The nursery was decorated in shades of tan and green. Although she had a feeling Delaney's child was a girl, she wouldn't know for a few weeks, yet.

Josie responded to Delaney's text: *Looks perfect. Plan on visitors. I can probably fit in the crib, so don't worry about an air mattress for me.*

Summer found herself laughing. This is what best friends are for, she thought. Even Winter got a little misty-eyed.

With Derek's arm around her and her kids playing happily with her mother in the living room, Summer sighed.

"I can't think of anywhere I'd rather be," she said.

"Not even the beach?" Derek said.

"Not even the beach."

"I'm glad you came to your senses."

"Me, too."

THE END

TURN **the page for a sneak peek of the first book in the Garden Club Series,** *Jasmine's Pact.*

PREVIEW: JASMINE'S PACT

BOOK 1 IN THE GARDEN CLUB SERIES

Chapter One

Jasmine Carr recognized Parker Abbott's voice before he finished saying her name. The *Daily Trumpet's* newsroom buzzed with activity, but when Parker spoke, the hive of ringing phones, fingers flying over keyboards, and reporters coming and going came to a stop so abrupt Jasmine could practically see desks sliding across the floor.

"Jasmine," Parker said when she answered her phone. "Happy birthday."

Her body recognized his voice, too, surprising her by going all tingly at the memory of his hands on her skin. She stood up, unable to contain the energy that image conjured up.

"Happy birthday, Parker," she said. "It's been a while."

He laughed, and a hot blue flame flared up in her belly at the sound. He said, "It's been fourteen years. You know what today is, right?"

She nodded, then licked her lips, cleared her throat, and said, "It's my thirtieth birthday."

"Right," he said. "And my thirty-first. Which means we have business to discuss. I believe you have a promise to make good on."

It's not that she'd forgotten their agreement. In fact, she'd realized recently that she'd unconsciously put her Real Life on hold, thinking she'd decide what she really wanted to do when she turned thirty. But with everything that had happened during the past decade, the pact she'd made with Parker had slipped to the back of her mind. A swarm of bees took up residence in her stomach. Again, she nodded, and again, she had to remind herself that he couldn't see her nodding.

"I guess I do," she said.

"I just booked my plane ticket. I'll be out there in a week."

So many questions ran through her mind. Where did he live? What had he been up to? Did he have a job? Was he still unreasonably sexy? When the two of them were together, would their chemistry still create entirely new elements?

An impatient voice cut into her thoughts, destroying the images of Parker's mouth devouring hers.

Jasmine's editor, Mikey Stockman, stood next to her desk, tapping his fat fingers on his thigh. "Jasmine."

She jumped and brought her imagination's film reel to a stop. "Look, Parker, I've got to go. I'll see you in a week."

"Hey, Mikey," she said. "What do you need?"

"What I need is for my features reporter to stop getting all twitterpated on the phone."

Could he tell?

"I'm not twitterpated," Jasmine said, barely managing not to stutter on the lie.

"Yeah, you are. See? There's a pen out of place." Jasmine hurried to put the rogue pen back in her banana slug coffee mug. Mikey went on, "Next time you're going to have phone sex, do it on your lunch break. Look, I've gotta talk to you. I know you've got that Cookies for Heroes thing to go to, but make some time for me when you get back, okay? And bring me a cookie."

"You're not a—"

"I know I'm not a hero, Jasmine. Just bring me a damn cookie."

Her face still radiating an embarrassed heat related to Mikey's phone sex comment, Jasmine picked up her purse and turned around to leave. As she got to the door, Mikey said, "And Jasmine?"

One hand on the door handle, she turned to look at him.

"Go relieve some of that ... tension before you come back."

Jasmine pushed open the door to the parking lot and squinted into the bright late-morning fog. *Okay, so I am a little weak in the knees,* she thought.

"What's wrong with *you*?"

Liza Carmack, reminiscent of smoky clubs and expensive brandy with her long fingernails and scratchy voice, stood in a swirling cloud of cigarette smoke on the patio.

"Why does everyone think something's wrong with me?" Jasmine said. She put up a hand to shade her eyes, but it didn't help. "It's just bright out here. Is it still summer? I am so ready for fall. This fog is killing me."

Liza, her long red hair tumbling down her back, lifted a shoulder (and her cigarette hand, faux pink diamond sparkling) in a lazy shrug. Of course, she ignored Jasmine's weather talk and said, "You just look a little—well, a little twitterpated."

When Jasmine flinched, Liza was quick to add, "It's not a bad thing, honey. I'm just so used to seeing you calm." She laughed, the sound raspy. "Imperturbable. I've seen a lot in my years, dear. You're twitterpated."

Jasmine pressed her lips together and shook her head. "I'll see you in a bit."

"Bring me a cookie," Liza called after her. Jasmine, who was now digging through her purse, looking for her sunglasses, gave her a dismissive wave. She heard Liza's laugh, rough and loud like it belonged at one end of a long wooden bar, and she couldn't help but smile. She realized her sunglasses were still perched on her head and she huffed out another sigh as she got into the car.

As Jasmine drove through Seabreeze, she thought about what Liza had said. "Imperturbable."

It wasn't that Jasmine was imperturbable, not really. The truth: she was shy. When she was a child, her parents had always said —"Only teasing, of course, honey"—that she should have been born a gopher so she could pop underground whenever she felt too exposed. Which was pretty much all the time. Needless to say, her sisters had called her a gopher for years, which only exacerbated things. Not only would she become paralyzed by shyness, but she also constantly worried they'd call out, "Gopher!" at the most inopportune times, like when she was walking across the cafeteria with a tray of food.

Mikey Stockman calling her twitterpated and using the term phone sex in the same breath was akin to being called a gopher. It made her long for some deep and twisting, very private, possibly endless underground tunnel. After buckling her purse into the passenger seat, setting up her phone for easy viewing and call access in the front cup holder, and then triple-checking behind the car, Jasmine backed out of her parking spot.

As she drove, she ran through the details of the Fourth Annual Cookies for Heroes event. Every year, elementary students brought baked goods to school and served them with milk to local police officers and firefighters. Without warning, Jasmine's train of thought jumped onto a different track. She drummed her fingers on the steering wheel.

Parker Abbott. He sounded exactly the same, so much so that her memories of him were starting to wake from a deep sleep, stretching and yawning and about ready to dance. Out of reflex, Jasmine checked her phone to see if he'd called again. She looked at her call log. Denver area code. What was in Denver? A zoo. A whiskey tour. Would Parker be into those kinds of things? She didn't even know him now.

She'd last seen him when he was seventeen, a strapping, muscular surfer with black hair and amber eyes and a smile as wide as the horizon. She shivered at the memory of Parker with the top half of his wet suit stripped down, ocean water glistening on his torso, his cold hands on her hot skin.

She wasn't sure she could concentrate on Cookies for Heroes. At the first stop light she came to, she scrubbed her hands over her face. It was the same story every year, really. She'd get some nice quotes from heroes and some cute quotes from kids. She'd head back to the newsroom and whip the story out.

Then, she could think about Parker Abbott and his sexy voice. She could think about Parker Abbott and the promise she'd made him fourteen years ago.

"I made these cookies with my mom," said Alex MacIlvoy, a first grader with thick glasses and a bit of an underbite. "I put too much salt in, but that's okay. Mom said we can just wing it. Just don't tell the heroes. Want to taste one?"

"I never turn down a cookie," Jasmine told him. She took a bite. "This is good," she said. "Really good. Chocolate chips with butterscotch?"

"Yeah," Alex said. "And I was just kidding about too much salt. Wanted to see if you'd taste it."

Charmed, Jasmine laughed. "You know, I'm glad I decided to stop and talk to you before I left. I saved the best for last."

She leaned in to whisper to him: "Do you think you could sneak me a couple of those cookies? My boss asked me to bring one back. And one of the other reporters, too."

Alex smiled. "I'll hook you up. Newspaper people are heroes, too."

Jasmine shrugged. "That's nice of you to say. But I think we're talking about people who put their lives on the line, here. Police, fire-fighters, soldiers."

Alex handed her three cookies. "One for you, too," he said.

Usually, Jasmine's mind turned over the parts and pieces of her story on the way back to the newsroom, formulating the lead, inserting the strongest quotes and compiling all the bits and pieces of information so that when she sat at her desk, her fingers beat out a quick, steady rhythm on the keyboard, the story writing itself.

Today, though, she couldn't concentrate on cookies or heroes or even Alex MacIlvoy's adorable smiling face. Even though Mikey Stockman had asked her to meet with him when she got back, she took the longest route possible, following the winding coast like a tour of her past with Parker.

There was the pizza place where they shared their first kiss over pepperoni and sodas. Just a ways further down was the spot where they sat on the cliffs one New Year's Day and watched the waves while writing out their goals for the year. How funny, Jasmine thought, to remember what they'd hoped for back then. She wanted to run her first half marathon, and he wanted to surf in the Light-house Point surf competition. What would her goals be, now? She wasn't sure. She'd run a handful of marathons in the past few years, and she'd won a couple of awards at work. She'd have to think about that. And what about Parker's goals?

She turned left to head back into the heart of town, and passed the coffee shop where she always stopped to pick up tea and coffee Friday mornings during their junior year of high school. And the burrito shop with the greasy, salty corn chips they so loved. They'd gorge on those chips, with salsa and guacamole, until they were so stuffed they had to take their burritos to go.

She'd been devastated when Parker's family moved halfway around the world. At first, every landmark produced a fresh round of tears. Over time, the tears turned to fond memories. The truth was, though, she couldn't even remember the last time she'd thought of Parker, until he called today.

By the time she got back to the *Daily Trumpet*, she felt scattered and, she hated to admit, quite a bit twitterpated at the thought of seeing him again.

Well, not just seeing him, said her inner voice. *But also feeling his body against yours.*

"You brought us cookies," Liza said when Jasmine walked into the newsroom. Jasmine, hoping to avoid any further conversations about her lack of imperturbability, tossed the bag onto Liza's desk.

"Share with Mikey," she said.

"I will, later," Liza said. "If I haven't eaten them by the time his visitor leaves."

"Who's his visitor?"

"No idea," Liza said. "Some puppy, still wet behind the ears. New photog. Good looking, too."

Just then, Mikey's voice reverberated throughout the newsroom. "Jasmine Carr. So glad you made it. Take the long way back?" She felt a blush creeping up her neck but didn't have time to stop it before Mikey boomed, "Come on in, there's someone I want you to meet."

Jasmine shrugged at Liza, who arched a seagull-shaped eyebrow in response. As Jasmine walked across the newsroom, she glanced around to see if anyone was watching her. She knew it was unreasonable.

The only other reporters in the newsroom at the moment—Perry Marks, city reporter and Jessie Pinkerton, education reporter—were laser-focused on their own work. Perry yelled into his phone, hitting his desktop repeatedly with his pointer finger, and Jessie alternately leaned over a stack of papers on her desk and typed maniacally. Still, Jasmine straightened her shirt as she passed them, all the while wondering why she'd worn a button-down shirt today. She hated button-down shirts. The buttons always went sideways and the hem never stayed tucked in evenly. On one side of the desk, Mikey leaned back in his chair, hands clasped behind his head and one leg crossed over the other. On the other side of the desk …

Whoa.

Jasmine might be shy, but she was still human. The visitor was young, as Liza had said, but he probably had a few years on Jasmine. His close cropped, curly hair was the color of sand when the sun hit it first thing in the morning. And his eyes—a green like the ice plant that covered the hillside going down to the beach. He wore an expensive-looking pair of jeans, scuffed cowboy boots, and a white collared shirt. His face looked like some master sculptor had created it as a tribute to masculine perfection. And the way he looked at her, like he was at once searching for clues and coming to a conclusion, made Jasmine want to pull her sweater more tightly around her body, for privacy. Only, she wasn't wearing a sweater.

She felt her throat working as her brain tried to reconnect and come up with something appropriate to say.

Mikey cleared his throat, and Jasmine jumped. She wondered if he'd call her out on being twitterpated again. "Jasmine Carr, meet Hudson Stover, photojournalist," he said.

Jasmine extended a hand, and Mikey added, "Your new partner."

"My partner?" Jasmine said, in a squeak. She chastised herself then, because repeating someone's statement as a question was one of her biggest pet peeves.

"Yes," Mikey said.

It wasn't until this Hudson character sat back in his chair and crossed his arms as if to say, "Let the show begin," that Jasmine realized she'd really liked the feel of his hand in hers. Something about it had given her a little jolt. Now her stomach was fluttering.

Jasmine shifted her weight from one foot to the other and put a hand on her hip to quell the nervous energy, but found herself making a closer and unabashed inspection of Hudson Stover, photojournalist. Although his clothes screamed city mouse, his hands were calloused, and (*my, my*) he had big muscles. Although his legs stretched from here to Texas, his shoulders were broad and sinewy. He was no stranger to hard work, then. Jasmine licked her lips. She swallowed and jumped when Mikey spoke again.

"We're going to be switching things up a little," he said.

Doom took hold as a tiny flicker in Jasmine's stomach, and began to expand, to morph into a full-sized flame. She hated change. The only thing she hated worse than change was the feeling that she had no control. And at this moment, Mikey was feeding her a change-and-no-control sandwich.

"As you know," Mikey said, "Liza's taking a few weeks off to visit her daughter and the new baby. And we need to cover her beat while she's gone. Since you have kind of a non-essential beat, I thought we'd bring you in on Liza's."

Jasmine gritted her teeth. Features were essential. Without features, you'd have a newspaper full of gloom and doom. Surely he didn't expect Jasmine to cover Liza's entire job. The woman was a pro, with more than thirty years on the police beat and a contacts list to match. As for Jasmine's own beat—features and health—and the constant pressure from Mikey and his bosses to produce a front-page-worthy feature story every day, it would be impossible to cover crime and courts at the same time. She would fail at both. Readers would notice, Mikey would fire her, and she'd have to face all her sources whenever she ran into them in Seabreeze.

When Jasmine opened her mouth to interrupt, Mikey stopped her by raising a hand. "Now, I know I can't expect you to cover your own entire beat and hers, too, which is why we're breaking things up. Together, you and Hudson will cover crime. And I'm thinking of putting the new reporter on courts."

"The new reporter?" Jasmine almost kicked herself for her second infraction. What was going on here? The world was spinning out of control.

Mikey put his hands together as if he were praying. "Yes, Jasmine. A new reporter. She's coming in next week. I have a feeling the two of you will get along just fine. Anyway, I want you and Hudson to work together so you can show him the ropes, the best watering holes, all that good stuff. That is, if you think you can do it without getting twitterpated."

Without meaning to, Jasmine glanced at Hudson to gauge his reaction. Something flashed in his eyes, but she couldn't quite define it.

She could, however, define the urge that rose up in her own body. She tried to push it back down, but the visual of her straddling Hudson in that chair took over. Jasmine closed her eyes, just briefly, to clear the vision. She'd been neglecting that urge for years and there was no reason to give in to it now.

Then she opened her eyes and Hudson smiled at her, a megawatt grin that showed all of his perfectly straight, blazing white teeth. His eyes sparkled and she couldn't help but smile back. The urge returned.

With a loud grunt, Mikey heaved himself out of his chair and stood up. He gestured to the door. "That's all I've got for you today, Jasmine. I'm going to take Hudson down to human resources to get his paperwork done. You guys can connect tomorrow."

As Mikey and Hudson walked through the newsroom on their way out, she heard Mikey say to Hudson, "You'll like that Jasmine, I just know it. Look, she brought me a cookie because she thinks I'm a hero. Want to split it?"

Chapter Two

Jasmine Carr met Parker Abbott by accident. Parker called it Fate, but Jasmine didn't believe in Fate. People chose their paths, and Life resulted from the complicated intertwining of these choices. Sure, coincidence existed, but it held no particular meaning or importance.

It was sophomore year. A late spring rainstorm moved in one Saturday and sat right over Seabreeze. It saturated the grass and filled the streets. It caused mudslides and road closures. School was closed that Monday and Jasmine and her sisters celebrated with pedicures and popcorn, "Sixteen Candles" and "The Breakfast Club" in the background.

That Tuesday morning, Parker missed the bus. He would later swear the bus came early that day, pulling away from the curb with a splash just as he exited his front door. Although he came out one minute later than usual, that should have put him at the bus stop in time for the bus's arrival. Fate made the bus early.

"But school buses never come early," Jasmine would say, every time the conversation arose.

Over the course of the next couple of months, Parker told everyone the story of how he and Jasmine met. Parker's parents were already at work, and it was Parker's responsibility to make sure his little brother, Ryder, was dressed and ready each morning. Ryder, a top student in the freshman class, was supposed to turn in his science fair project that morning. When he brought it out to the bus stop, the rain caused the ink on his display board to run, creating a rainbow of words that melted together. He'd printed everything out on the ink jet, and insisted on going back inside to print it all again. Today was the deadline to turn in the project, and he couldn't take it in looking like this. It would only take a few minutes, Ryder said, and his chances of winning any kind of prize would be nil if he didn't fix the poster.

Besides, they had seven minutes until the bus was due to arrive. Plenty of time, Ryder said.

In an effort to hurry the repair project along, Parker went inside with Ryder, and began gluing the freshly printed graphs and bullet-point lists and hypotheses to the display board as Ryder printed them out.

This time, they got smart and wrapped a plastic garbage bag around the display board to protect Ryder's masterpiece. When they walked out their front door to catch the bus, the bus was pulling away from the curb.

The rain was still pouring down, or as Parker's parents would say, "It's raining so hard the animals are starting to pair up." And now they had to walk to school.

The Abbott boys trudged along the sidewalk, their shoes making *squelch* sounds and the hems of their pants becoming soggy. They used Ryder's display board as an umbrella, but the wind blew the rain hard onto their backs. Parker muttered to himself about Ryder making them late, and Ryder muttered to himself about Parker not having a work ethic. In fact, he said to himself loudly enough for Parker to hear, Parker hadn't even completed a science fair project.

No, Parker hadn't completed a science fair project, he muttered in response, but at least he'd be on time for school, if it wasn't for Ryder. Parker despised being late. Loathed it. Although their father, a sergeant in the Army, hammered punctuality into his sons' heads, Ryder never seemed to pick up on it and they'd spent countless hours of their lives being lectured on timeliness.

At that moment, during this muttered argument, a car pulled up next to them at the curb. Parker gritted his teeth and rolled his eyes. Could it get any worse? Were they now going to be trailed by some senior bullies who would splash them repeatedly as they walked along? He'd heard of it happening.

Then the car stopped. Parker hunched his shoulders and walked faster. Ryder did the same.

Of course, the situation looked quite a bit different from Jasmine's point of view. Warm and dry and toasty in her mother's van, she turned down the Dave Matthews Band when she noticed two boys walking in the pouring rain, using a huge piece of plastic-covered cardboard as an umbrella.

"I feel so bad for those boys," she said aloud to her mom and her two sisters, Sequoia and Holly. Her mom slowed down.

"Why don't they have an umbrella?" Sequoia, the oldest and master of all things practical, said. "That was really stupid. It's been raining for like, three days. It's not like they didn't have any warning."

Jasmine, always willing to hear the entire story before making judgments, said, "Maybe something happened. Maybe they lost their umbrella. Maybe it broke. Should we offer them a ride, Mom?"

"Jasmine, they could be, like, serial killers or something," Holly, the youngest sister, said. "I can't believe you'd offer two strangers a ride."

Jasmine exchanged a look with her mom, and Sequoia laughed. "Ridiculous, Holly. They're kids. Look at their shoes. Those are expensive. And that one kid is wearing a leather jacket. I'm sure he's not a serial killer. Serial killers wear trench coats."

It seemed like sound reasoning, Jasmine thought. Mom must have thought so too, because she pulled up to the curb and stopped next to the boys.

The boys walked faster, and Mom let the van roll forward to keep up with them.

"Well, go on, Jasmine," Mom said. "This was your idea. Offer them a ride."

Jasmine's first thought was that her mom was probably trying to get her to practice talking to strangers. She always joked that while all the other parents were giving their kids the "Don't Talk to Strangers" lessons, she was begging Jasmine to talk to someone, *anyone*!

Jasmine took a deep breath and rolled down her window. She found that she couldn't speak. Sequoia nudged her and she cleared her throat. The older boy, taller by about six inches, scowled as he turned toward the van.

"Well, he doesn't look very friendly," Holly said.

Jasmine, put off by the scowl, began to roll up the window, but Sequoia reached across her and pressed the button down. "Want a ride?"

The younger boy grinned and nodded. The older one continued to scowl.

Sequoia laughed, and Jasmine, not to be deterred from completing her own act of kindness for the day, opened the door and stepped into the rain.

Initially, Parker would tell Jasmine later, he experienced profound relief. The van wasn't full of older kids planning a splash fest as they drove to school. He felt his shoulders relaxing, but his apprehension didn't dissipate completely until Jasmine got out of the car and smiled at him.

"I'm Jasmine," she said, extending a hand.

She's an angel, said a voice inside Parker's head.

He tried to speak, but had to clear the scratchiness from his throat. "I'm Parker."

His uneasiness made Jasmine feel much more relaxed.

"And I'm Ryder." His little brother, all enthusiasm, greeted Jasmine and shook her hand with far too little abandon.

"We saw you walking," Jasmine said, "And it's so wet and cold, and so, we, um, wanted to offer you a ride to school. Seabreeze High, right?"

Parker grunted and Ryder said, "Yep! Freshman, of course."

"Oh, my sister's a freshman," Jasmine said, pointing to the van. "Holly."

The three of them stood there for a moment, the rain catching in Jasmine's eyelashes and dripping off the piece of cardboard the boys still held over their heads. Jasmine looked from Ryder's face to Parker's, and then, when thunder rumbled, she remembered the reason they were there.

"Oh! I'm so sorry. So, do you want a ride?"

Ryder nodded and immediately headed toward the van. Parker remained where he stood, looking at Jasmine with something in his expression that caught her off guard. It was a hint of a smile, but something else, too.

"We're gonna be late," Sequoia called through the rain.

Jasmine quirked an eyebrow at Parker and he followed her to the van.

That day at lunch, Parker approached Jasmine. She sat with her friends on the concrete steps in front of the gym, and was stunned into silence as he walked towards her, his gaze locked on hers.

There was something so … intense about him.

"Jasmine," he said.

Not for the first time in her life, Jasmine was at a loss for words. The way he said her name made it sound like it was some kind of dessert melting in his mouth. She felt her own mouth drop open before Hannah Kirk elbowed her and she snapped it shut again.

"Parker," she said.

Without waiting for an invitation, he sat down next to her. Hannah left the scene with a less-than-casual, "I'll see you later, Jas."

"Look," he said. "I just wanted to thank you for stopping for Ryder and me this morning. I was kind of—well, I didn't get a chance to thank you."

"You're welcome," she said. "You did bolt when we got here. I thought it's just because you didn't want to be seen with the Carr girls, getting out of a minivan."

He chuckled, his expression still serious, then stood up and kicked at the concrete stair with the toe of his Converse. "Believe me, it's a step up."

After that, he walked away, and Jasmine spent the next two periods—geometry and photography—thinking about him, wondering what he looked like when he smiled.

The school year lasted only a few more weeks, during which they passed each other in the halls several times. Parker would usually studiously ignore Jasmine, but one day he made eye contact and gave her the smallest possible nod. It was an acknowledgement, at least, and it left her loopy for the rest of the day. She couldn't even finish her math test, and Mrs. Piper had to call on her three times just for Jasmine to stumble through her answer to the bell question in photography. Something about f-stops.

Then, on the first day of the new school year, which dawned cool and sunny, Jasmine walked into her biology class and found that Mr. Z. (short for Zillman) had assigned seats. She sat down at hers, and took out the textbook from her Spanish class. If she could finish the homework assignment—conjugating -ar verbs—before she got home, she'd have more time to watch "Law and Order" with Holly and Sequoia. Although Holly never finished her assignments early, and Jasmine and Sequoia always ended up waiting for her, anyway.

Some sixth sense put Jasmine's body on alert, and its accuracy was confirmed when she heard someone say, "I think this is the beginning of a beautiful friendship."

Parker.

He slid onto the stool next to hers. And finally, she saw his smile.

"Are you my lab partner?" Jasmine said. Hope rose in her chest.

"I am," he said. "Congratulations."

The tingling she'd felt in her fingertips turned into a foreign warm feeling that spread through her torso and down into her stomach, and she felt a goofy smile spreading across her face. These new sensations made her a tiny bit bolder than usual.

"I'd congratulate you, too, if I weren't a total freak about guts and stuff," she said. "I might let you down when we dissect earthworms."

The bell rang and Jasmine shut her Spanish book. She dropped it into her backpack, not even a little disappointed that she hadn't finished her homework. In fact, she wasn't disappointed that she hadn't even started her homework.

"I'm pretty sure earthworms don't have any guts," Parker said. "And besides, you couldn't let me down. You've rescued me once and I'm sure you'll do it again."

Jasmine giggled, then clapped a hand over her mouth, embarrassed. Mr. Z. rapped on his desk with a ruler to signal the start of class. Jasmine faced forward and Mr. Z. Began droning on about "policies and procedures," and "classroom safety."

Parker slid a sheet of paper across the table, wedging it under Jasmine's elbow. She lifted her elbow and slid it over to her side. When she read what it said, a new flurry of energy made its way through her body.

Would you like to have dinner with me?

Parker had drawn three little check boxes underneath, labeled, *Yes, this weekend, No, never,* and *Hmm. I don't know. Maybe next weekend.*

Jasmine, her face almost unbearably hot with pleasure or embarrassment or both, pressed her lips together to keep from laughing, and used the lab pencil to check the first box.

Friday night, Parker knocked on Jasmine's front door at precisely six o'clock. Jasmine, dressed and primped with the help of her two sisters—Sequoia made sure her outfit was practical, yet sexy, and Holly applied her makeup "so you don't look like a deranged clown"—answered it and yelped with surprise.

Parker stood on the doorstep, looking bashful. His dad stood behind him.

"You must be Jasmine," his dad said. "I'm David Abbott, Parker's dad."

Parker's dad walked Jasmine and Parker out to the car, where he insisted Parker drive them to dinner.

"I have my learner's permit," Parker said, looking at Jasmine in the rearview mirror.

"Eyes on the road, Son," Mr. Abbott said.

"I turn sixteen a week from Monday, and I'm taking my driver's test then. So Dad's making me practice today, I guess." He shrugged a shoulder.

"Hold still, Son," Mr. Abbott said. "Nice and steady."

Jasmine smiled when Parker winked at her in the rearview mirror.

"Concentrate, Parker," Mr. Abbott said. "Drive now, chat later."

They made the rest of the drive in relative silence, with only occasional interruptions from Mr. Abbott: "Look over your shoulder before you signal, Son. And never drive behind a Volvo or in front of a Honda."

Finally, they arrived at the restaurant, Linda's. Parker's dad took the car to run errands.

The restaurant's bright colors and cheerful decorations amplified Jasmine's festive mood, and the almost-too-loud mariachi music made her want to get up and dance. The server brought them a bowl of corn chips, and Parker grabbed one and popped it into his mouth before she'd even finished setting it down.

"I love the chips," he said.

"Me, too," Jasmine said. "They're perfect."

Parker considered it a sign that they both loved the chips and guacamole—with a dash of salt and a sprinkle of lime juice—and Jasmine laughed him off.

"Fate is overrated," she told him. "You make your own luck. You choose your own way."

"Sage advice coming from a fifteen-year-old," he said.

"Fourteen. I'll be fifteen a week from Monday," she said.

"Wait. So we, like, share a birthday?" he said.

She nodded. "I didn't say anything in the car because I didn't want to make a big deal of it. Since you were talking about your license and everything. And concentrating."

"And because you're shy," he said.

"I am not."

"You're so shy. And it's totally cool. Anyway, the two of us sharing a birthday is another sign," he said, nodding as though this single fact proved his hypothesis. "We were meant to meet."

Parker asked Jasmine what she planned to order, and when it was the same as what he always ordered (chicken and cheese enchiladas), he gave her a meaningful look. She found it so endearing when he ordered for her that she walked him through her usual orders at the hot spots she frequented: orange chicken at the Chinese place, a bacon ranch chicken sandwich with curly fries at the Burger Stop. They spent the next hour discussing favorite movies and favorite books, least favorite actors and most-watched cartoons.

"I seriously cannot believe I've met someone else who loves 'Home Alone' as much as I do!" Parker said at one point, and Jasmine said, "Same with 'Ice, Ice, Baby.'"

The similarities were so plentiful that the two of them were in stitches by the time the server brought their bill.

"How have we never met before this?" Jasmine said as they sat outside on the patio, waiting for Mr. Abbott to pick them up.

It was a rhetorical question, and Parker didn't answer it then, because he knew the answer would seal their relationship's fate as a tragedy.

ACKNOWLEDGMENTS

Friendships—with my own mom and with all of my mom friends (and non-mom friends, too!)—make motherhood so much more fun. A big thank you to all my friends for standing shoulder to shoulder with me on this march we call motherhood! Thank you to my husband and my little people.

And another big thank you to the eagle-eyed people who read and helped with this story: Mom and Desirae, and to Donna Rich, proofreader extraordinaire. And of course to Design for Writers, who designed the covers for all three books in this series.

ABOUT THE AUTHOR

Hilary Dartt loves great adventures, whether she's writing, reading, or living them. The author of nine women's fiction novels, Hilary lives in Arizona's high desert with her husband, their three children, her Weimaraner and running partner, Leia, a failed barn cat, and a flock of chickens. She loves camping, exploring in the Jeep, and dance parties with her kids. Learn more at www.hilarydartt.com.

www.ingramcontent.com/pod-product-compliance
Lightning Source LLC
Chambersburg PA
CBHW050338190726
48284CB00007BB/2060